A LOST ARGUMENT

A LOST ARGUMENT

A Latter-Day Novel

Therese Doucet

ભ STRANGE VIOLIN EDITIONS ৪০
WASHINGTON, DC

FIRST EDITION, AUGUST 2011

Strange Violin Editions, Washington, D.C.
http://www.strangeviolineditions.com

Strange Violin Editions ISBN: 978-0-9837484-1-0
eBook ISBN: 978-0-983-74840-3

Printed in the United States of America

PROLOGUE

MAYBE I'M STRANGE AND perverse, but I've always thought there was something sexy about a compelling argument. Especially one that threatens to persuade you of something you would never have imagined yourself believing. Especially when that something you never imagined you could believe threatens to tear through the fabric of basic assumptions that wraps around your life and holds it together, to unravel and unwind it.

In romance novels, of which I'll admit to having read a few, purloined from relatives and flipped through during lazy vacations, this is precisely the function of romance: to undo a person, overwhelm and conquer her, to overcome her resistance and leave her hair in disarray, her clothes torn and disheveled. So it's no wonder such an argument can be sexy. And all the more so when it's two potential romantic partners arguing, and the outcome of the argument could determine whether they become lovers.

This is the story of just such an argument. Some might call it a true story, but that all depends on how you define truth, and that's partly what the argument will be about. In any case, it took place almost twenty years ago. It was an argument our heroine, whose name is Marguerite Farnsworth, feared she had won, and only came to believe much later she had lost. I'm not sure I agree with her, because in the strange, topsy-turvy world of arguments, it's not always easy to distinguish between losing and winning. But I'll tell the story, and you can judge for yourself.

PART I

THE ARGUMENT

CHAPTER 1

COMING HOME

WHEN MARGUERITE STEPPED OFF the plane at the Tucson airport, the air filled her lungs like a vaporous tar. If you'd grown up in the desert, you couldn't forget what the heat was like, but even so, it knocked the breath out of her. The landscape looked grayer, beiger, and dustier than she remembered it. But that was in the heat of the day, driving home from the airport along barren highways and streets lined with ugly strip malls and floating bits of trash. At home in the evening, sitting in her parents' kitchen, she watched out the glass sliding door through the back patio, where fuchsia and green bougainvillea climbed up the iron bars of the gate and one of Tucson's storied sunsets gashed brilliant orange sear-marks at the side of the sky. Only in sight of this violent spill of color did she feel she had arrived home at last.

Provo, where she'd spent the past year, had been full of green lawns, surrounded by high mountains with snowy peaks, and there was serious precipitation there. It snowed enough that her more enterprising fellow students in the freshman dorms had spent the winter sledding on stolen cafeteria trays. Granted, there hadn't been much else to do. There was a bar or two, but it was almost a dry town, given that all 30,000 students at Brigham Young University had signed pledges not to drink alcohol while in school. Marguerite and her roommates were also broke, so their main forms of entertainment were church functions, playing Uno, and going to the dollar theater on campus, which screened depressing foreign-language art films with subtitles. Censors cut out all the swear words and nude scenes.

Marguerite had intended to stay in Provo over the summer. She began her freshman year as a music student with concentrations in piano and in composition and theory. But her first year in the music department hadn't gone well, despite the long hours she practiced every day and the hard work she put into her class assignments. She did poorly on her exams, so at the end of the semester she went in to have a chat with the head of the Comparative Literature department about changing majors and signed up for summer courses in German and history. She found a basement apartment to share with another music student, a rosy-cheeked redhead named Miriam who sang opera. They lived in a little blue stuccoed house in South Provo with a big garden. Miriam's grandmother lived upstairs amid towering piles of Depression-era clutter, and seemed to disapprove of everything they did from her perch on an old armchair one floor above them.

It should have been a pleasant enough spring and summer in the little blue house, taking the bus to campus every morning, going to classes, studying and practicing the piano, basking in the long sunny days and giggling with Miriam in the evenings about boys they liked and their many failed cooking experiments. But something about the way the light shimmered over the lawns in the mornings, the quiet houses looking guiltless and self-sufficient as she walked past them on the way to school, the echoing of scattered piano chords through the empty hallways of the fine arts building when she went to practice in the afternoons, even Miriam's implacable, rosy-cheeked cheeriness, all made her feel depressed after a few weeks. She was homesick, she realized as she lay stretched out on her bed one Sunday afternoon after church. Homesick and miserable.

She called home and spoke to her mom and dad.

"Of course you can still come home, sweetheart," said her mom. "That's what we wanted you to do in the first place. It's still early enough in the semester they'll probably refund most of your tuition. You can fly from Salt Lake. We'll get you your tickets, don't worry about it."

"You're sure? I feel bad, wasting all that money."

"We want you to be happy. That's the most important thing."

Her dad, who wasn't much of a phone conversationalist, made a noise of agreement on the other line.

"And if you want to take summer classes," her mom continued, "you can always take them here at the U of A. Their summer term starts later than BYU's, so you've still got plenty of time to sign up. I'm sure we can get Dad to pay for it."

Her dad mumbled his assent again.

"I could get a job."

"Sweetie, don't worry about it," said her mom. "You can if you want, but we'll pay for your tuition. It'll just be nice to have you home for the summer."

And so Marguerite found herself withdrawing from her classes, packing up her things, putting her few immovable possessions into storage in a back closet in the little blue house, and getting on a plane to Tucson.

THE DAY after she got back, she browsed through the University of Arizona's summer course catalog and settled on an intensive German course that was supposed to be two years worth of college German packed into a single summer. She was confident the course wouldn't be too hard for her. She'd already had several years of French and had always been at the top of her class in it. Teachers had suggested she had a gift for languages.

It was late May, and she had two weeks to kill before the start of the course. Her younger brother Max and sister Cate were gone most of the time, out with their friends, and her mother always seemed to be off running errands or doing volunteer work for the church, while her father, a cardiologist, worked incessantly. As a result, Marguerite had the house nearly to herself. She spent the days on the sofa in the living room with her feet up, writing long letters to her friends from the freshman dorms, reading, and occasionally getting up off the couch to go out to meet friends from high school. She read all of *Anna Karenina*, and started on *The Magic Mountain*. Marguerite liked to immerse herself in a story and was disappointed when it ended too quickly, so she gravitated toward thick, substantial novels by classic authors.

Of the friends she saw, she spent the most time with Mark Tierney, who had been her best friend senior year. Mark wasn't a Mormon, but he was easy to talk with. He had never been romantically attracted to her so far as she could detect, yet didn't seem to mind spending hours helping her sort out her muddled thoughts, asking probing questions and giving her sound, frank advice.

The first time she saw him after getting back into town, he picked her up at her house in the early evening and they drove over to the elementary school, whose grounds sat empty and unused much of the summer. They parked in the lot and walked across the schoolyard over the brown, dried up remnants of winter grass to the swings, where they sat down and talked, dragging their feet along the dusty indentations in the dirt below them and swaying in their seats. Mark, who had stayed in Tucson to go to school at the U of A, wanted to hear about her year in Utah and how she'd liked it. She told him about doing poorly in her music classes and the decision to change her major.

"Wow, that's big," Mark said. "Are you sure? You always wanted to be a composer."

"I know, but I have to face the fact that I'm not as talented as I thought I was. If I could do better in some other field, like comp lit, it seems like it makes more sense to switch."

"What makes you think you'd do better in comp lit? Do you think you'd be happier succeeding at something that's your second choice than doing a little less well in your first choice?"

"To tell you the truth," Marguerite said, "I was getting bored with my music classes anyway. So much of it turns out to be just drilling, practicing things over and over again. And then in my theory class for a final project, we had to write a hymn and play and sing it for the class. Most people took their texts from other Mormon hymns and put new melodies and harmonies to them, but I wrote a poem and used that as my text. No one thought much of my melody or harmony, but I got all these compliments on the poem. So I thought, maybe I'm just better with words than music."

"You wrote a hymn? That's funny."

"What's so funny about it?"

"I don't know. It just sounds so religious, kind of medieval almost."

"Well, I *am* religious. That was the whole point of me going to BYU. That, and my scholarship."

"So you're still believing, then? It seemed like you were loosening up senior year. I remember you having a lot of doubts. Do you think being at BYU's made you more religious?"

"I don't know that it's made me more religious—it's just, being around so many people who believe the same things makes it easier. In a way it's like peer pressure."

"I can definitely see that. So do you think you're happier there, without so many doubts?"

"I still have doubts. They're just easier to deal with, maybe. But no, I wouldn't exactly say I'm happier. People are so *nice* there. It's almost weird ..."

"Sounds awful."

Marguerite laughed and edged back with her feet to launch her swing into a low arc over the dark playground. "No, but seriously. The strange thing was, I felt really lonely a lot of the time, even though everyone was so nice. Like I didn't fit in, somehow."

"Because you're so not nice," said Mark, leaning back and launching his swing into the air as well. "I can see how you'd stick out like a sore thumb."

"Ha. No, it wasn't like I stuck out. It was more like I was invisible. Like there was this ideal pattern of a Mormon girl that was pretty much the exact opposite of me, and if you weren't like that pattern, you didn't count, you almost didn't exist. There are all these girls there with beautiful long, blond curly hair, and they wear lacy white blouses with long chambray skirts and bows in their hair. And they're all majoring in elementary education. And then there's me, straight dark hair and no boobs, running around reading thick Russian novels and wanting to be a composer. It was like, no one was interested in me—none of the guys at least."

"Huh. That *is* funny. So you didn't date anyone while you were there?"

"Not really. There were a few girls' choice dances I went to with all my dorm friends, and we asked guys to them, and they said yes, but only because they had to. I realize I'm no Claudia Schiffer or anything, but at least when I was in Tucson, and when I went on that summer program in Paris after graduation, guys would flirt with me. But at BYU—nothing. It was like I didn't exist."

"That really sucks, Marguerite. I'm sorry to hear that."

"Oh well. But it was probably better that way. At least it kept me out of temptation."

"Temptation?" Mark was grinning. Marguerite laughed, kicking against the ground to slow her swing.

"Yeah," she said. "I'm always freaked out when guys do like me. You know that."

"Yeah. I remember you were really rattled over that guy in Paris when you came back. But nothing ever happened with him, right?"

"Of course not." Marguerite sighed. "But it was for the best. I mean, he was 23, he was six years older than me. And he wasn't Mormon and didn't live anywhere near me in the States."

"And then there was that whole weird thing between you and Sam, senior year."

"Oh, jeez, don't remind me. That had me *really* freaked out. I was so sure we were going to wind up naked when he went back to my house with me after that party. And then we didn't even kiss—three hours of lying there together on my bed, and we didn't even get to make out. After all that flirting in civics class—I thought for sure I was going to hell. He spent the whole semester driving me crazy, and then it was him being all reasonable in the end. What is it about me that makes guys back off like that?"

Mark laughed. "But is it the guys who back off? Or is it you?"

Marguerite paused to think, her swing slowing nearly to a stop with her legs dangling below. "I don't know," she said at last. "Maybe it is me. But it feels like it's them, and then I feel all hurt and rejected. And now I've had my feelings hurt so many times, I'm always afraid of letting myself like anyone. I really wish I didn't want anything besides friendship with guys. I always feel so selfish and guilty if I want more, like I'm doing something wrong."

"Aw, Marguerite. You shouldn't feel that way. Everybody gets hurt sometimes. It happens. But the solution isn't to give up on relationships completely. That's not even realistic. And it's not selfish to want to be in a relationship. It's normal."

"I know, I know. It's just, friendships are so *clean*. They're so much safer. Like, the way we're friends, I wouldn't trade that for anything. I always feel like I can trust you and can tell you everything. You're a great friend, Mark—I don't tell you that often enough."

Mark, shifting in his seat and looking slightly uncomfortable at this burst of sincerity, said, "Er, thanks. You're a good friend, too. And by the way, thanks for all those letters you wrote last year. I liked getting them."

"You're welcome. I had fun writing them. You're good to write to, maybe because you're a good listener. You have no idea how rare that is—it's like you're genuinely interested in other people and you're truly curious about what they have to say. That's a real gift. I wish I were more like you that way. I'm so selfish most of the time. I always want to talk about myself, and I forget to be curious and just listen to people."

Mark only shrugged and smiled. "I do like to listen to people. I feel like I learn a lot from them."

"But you haven't told me anything about your trip yet. I want to hear all about it. Which countries are you guys going to? What kinds of things are you going to see? It's so exciting that you're going to Europe. I'm so jealous."

Mark had planned a summer backpacking trip with two of his friends. "I'm hoping we can spend a lot of time in Spain," he said, "I've heard Barcelona is awesome—it's supposed to be really young and hip, and the art and food are supposed to be amazing. Paris, of course, just because you can't go to Europe and not see Paris. I'm not that interested in London, but we might go to Dublin. Italy, Greece, maybe. Other than that, we'll see. The idea was that we'd sort of ramble and take our time, not just hurry through ..."

"That sounds incredible. I want tons of postcards. But what's your focus going to be? Food? Art? Touring old castles? Picking up on Spanish chicks?"

And with that, Marguerite managed to steer the conversation into safer territory the rest of the evening.

THAT NIGHT, Marguerite dreamed of walking through shifting sands. It was a dream she had from time to time, sometimes anxious like a nightmare, sometimes calmer, but the setting was always the same. She was alone, climbing over sandy dunes, trying to get somewhere, she didn't know where—trying to get to higher ground. Sometimes the wind blew sand in her face, sometimes it was urgent she find what she was looking for, but always her feet sank into the steep sides of the dunes, and she slid backward as she tried to move forward.

Once, the dream had ended happily. She found herself trying to climb up a particularly steep and hardened wall of sand. She reached for crumbling footholds and handholds and thought she was going to make it to the top. But the higher she got, the looser the sand became and the steeper her ascent felt, until it was more like a sheer cliff-face she was climbing than a dune. She was terrified of falling. At last she steeled up her courage and said to herself in the dream, *After all, it's only sand. If I fall, I fall.* And with a final burst of effort, she pulled herself up over the top as the sand poured down all around her and her footholds crumbled away.

She was able to stand up on a patch of solid ground, and a vast, beautiful vista opened out before her. She could see for miles and miles around, over a fertile green landscape spread out below, stretching off to blue mountains at an immense distance.

But that night, it was the usual dream with no vista, just the same shifting sands and blinding wind.

CHAPTER 2

IN WHICH MARGUERITE IS TYPECAST

THE GERMAN CLASS STARTED the second week of June. There were twenty-five students in the class, and Marguerite was the only freshman. Their professor was a thin, energetic German man in his late forties or early fifties with long gray hair that stuck out wildly from his head in all directions and a layer of gray stubble sprouting from his chin. His name was Bernhard Liebmann. On the first day, he asked the students to go around the room and say their name and major, and assigned each of them a German name to use with each other in class. When he came to "Farnsworth, Marguerite," he rubbed his stubbly chin, and his bright, mouse-like eyes flashed as she explained she was there as an at-large student, just for the summer.

"A-ha, so we have a Marguerite, as in *Faust*. You will be Margaret, of course. Or perhaps Gretchen?"

Marguerite wrinkled her nose.

"What's wrong? Not a fan of Goethe?" asked Professor Liebmann, his eyes twinkling.

"Oh, no, I like Goethe," Marguerite tried to explain, feeling pinned down by the stares of twenty-five pairs of eyes on her. "Um ... I'm just not a fan of his idea of the Eternal Feminine."

Professor Liebmann burst into loud laughter. "Wonderful," he said. A few other students tittered nervously, and Marguerite wanted to bury her face under her notebook. This was exactly the sort of remark that rendered you invisible at BYU. Professor Liebmann went on to the next student.

In spite of her faux pas, as she deemed it, the other students in the class seemed friendly enough during the break. Marguerite got to know her neighbors immediately behind and in front of her desk. In front was a petite woman with pale blue eyes and blond, chin-length hair standing out thickly from her head in narrow corkscrew ringlets, named Angela. Behind her sat Pam, a stocky biology student dressed boyishly in a polo shirt and long shorts with light brown hair, a snub nose, and bangs cut straight across her forehead. The three of them made small talk until Professor Liebmann walked back to the blackboard to resume the lesson. Neither Pam nor Angela mentioned Goethe, to Marguerite's relief.

Once the course had started, her days were busy. Each morning she drove her dad's battered old red stick-shift sports car to get to class by 8:00. Afterward she ate lunch by herself and went to the music building to find a free piano down among the dusty-smelling, windowless basement practice rooms, where she often played until three in the afternoon. Then she drove back home in the red car and did German homework for another two or three hours after dinner. These felt like happy, productive days to her. The class moved quickly, but she had no trouble keeping up and got a nearly perfect score on her first exam.

It was only a few weeks before Professor Liebmann, who was always brimming with fiery energy, had brought them far enough along in the language that they were able to have interesting conversations during the group exercises. The professor liked for them to do as much group work as possible. They spoke halting German with each other, using awkward phrases peppered with English words and laughter. One day Marguerite sat in a circle with Pam, Angela, another girl named Jenny, and an older student named Dan. Their assignment was to ask each other personal questions. Professor Liebmann's philosophy was that language learning was more fun if you talked about things that were highly personal or controversial, or better yet both, like religion and politics and sex.

They learned Dan had worked as a bartender for ten years before going to college. He looked like a bartender, Marguerite thought, like someone you'd see playing a bartender in a movie. He was short and barrel-chested with neatly clipped brown hair, very tan skin, and a seemingly permanent five o'clock shadow.

Jenny was sweet, pretty, and blond, with short, moussed hair, freckles, and braces that somehow only made her look cuter. She'd been a sorority girl until she met her husband and married him. She seemed young to be married, at least by non-Mormon standards. It wasn't unusual for Mormon girls to marry at nineteen or twenty, and some of the ones Marguerite had gone to high school with had already found husbands. But for a normal girl it was odd. Jenny couldn't have been more than twenty-two or twenty-three.

They went around the small circle again, this time asking about religion. Pam was agnostic, Angela was Episcopalian, and Jenny described herself simply as Christian. Dan was raised Catholic but wasn't practicing. That Marguerite was Mormon came as no surprise. It was easy enough to guess from when she'd told the class the first day that she went to BYU.

Jenny wanted to know what Mormons believed. Weren't there a lot of things they weren't allowed to do?

Marguerite was used to such questions, which came up often when she met someone new who wasn't Mormon. It came up when you were offered a drink and had to turn it down, or when someone asked what you were doing on Sunday ("going to Church" was the answer, followed by, "Oh, what church do you go to?"). So she ran through the basics as well as she could in German, resorting often to English words. It was too complicated even to begin trying to explain the plot of the Book of Mormon in German, so she went straight to the rules about what you couldn't do, which was usually what people were more interested in. She listed them off on her fingers.

"No alcohol, no drugs, no smoking, no coffee or tea, no caffeine. No swearing. No ... um ... how do you say 'sex' in German?"

"*Sex*," answered Pam authoritatively, pronouncing it *zecks*. "Of course I looked it up on the first day of class," she said, as the others laughed.

"*Na, gut. Kein Sex vor der Ehe. Kein Sex ausserhalb der Ehe.*" No sex before marriage. No sex outside of marriage.

"Wow. Is that difficult?" Angela wanted to know.

Marguerite laughed. "Which part?"

"All of it. The sex part. Is it hard to wait? What if you never get married?"

Marguerite sighed. "*Ja. Das ist eben das Problem.* But personally, I don't have much in the way of temptation."

"I don't believe that," said Dan the bartender, shaking his head. "Normally, if a guy finds out I'm a Mormon, he runs away."

"And with Mormon guys?"

"They don't like me."

"Aw, that's sad," said Pam. "That all seems a little strange to me."

"Well, it's not *that* weird," said Jenny, coming to Marguerite's defense. "Mormons aren't the only ones who believe in waiting. A lot of Christians believe that, too."

"Did you and your husband wait?" asked Marguerite.

Jenny blushed, looking down and laughing in an embarrassed way. "That's too personal a question."

Marguerite blushed, too, abashed and puzzled. She'd made another faux pas. But part of her found it strange Jenny wouldn't answer the question. If you weren't Mormon, what was there to be ashamed of?

WHEN THE group work was finished, they filed slowly back to their desks.

"I hope we didn't give you too hard a time back there," said Dan, walking beside her. "Sorry if we embarrassed you."

"No, you didn't. I guess it's just a bit of a sore point for me. The truth is, I get kind of depressed about it sometimes."

"What, being a virgin?" Dan said in a lowered voice, smiling gently. "You know, I wouldn't be, if I were you. Everyone thinks sex is such a big deal, before they do it. Then you do it, and you realize it's really not. It's not the end-all be-all of existence everyone makes it out to be. It's not that big of a deal. So I wouldn't worry about waiting, if I were you. You're not missing all that much."

"Really?"

"Really. Of course, that's just my opinion."

Marguerite shrugged, but smiled back at him shyly. A moment or two later, he put a hand lightly to the small of her back as he moved past her to take his seat in the next row over. To her shock, his touch thrilled her, sending heat flooding through her thighs and abdomen. It felt difficult to bend as she folded herself into the seat behind her desk. In the daze of arousal, she thought to herself, *If just one small touch on my back can do this to me, how can he be right?*

CHAPTER 3

THE FOUNDATIONS OF MORALITY

A FEW DAYS LATER, when group work began, Professor Liebmann divided the class up into teams and assigned them to play a game that involved trying to be the first to complete a series of exercises. Marguerite was sitting with Pam and Angela on either side of her, behind a tall, gregarious philosophy major named John. They dragged their desks out of the rows and turned them around to face one another. John was a senior, but looked older. He was a bit of buffoon, always grinning and laughing at everything and making jokes. He wasn't bad-looking, but a pair of thick, dark eyebrows combined with a perpetual grin gave his face a slightly wild, debauched air. Marguerite didn't mind working with him. It was nice to have someone funny in their group.

They were slow getting through the exercises—too slow to win the game, it appeared.

"Damn, I hate losing," John said. "I'm thinking we should just cheat and look at the answers."

"But ... that wouldn't be right," said Marguerite. "I'm surprised. You're a philosophy major. Aren't you concerned about the morality of it?"

"Nah. I don't believe in morals at all."

"What? How can you not believe in morals?" Angela and Pam both wanted to know.

"Ehhh ... there's just no objective basis for it. It's a contradiction in terms."

"No objective basis?" said Marguerite. "What about ... Kant's categorical imperative, for one thing?"

17

"How do you know about the categorical imperative?" asked John, looking amused. "I thought you were a music major."

"Comp lit. Anyway, I took a philosophy of art class last year, and the teacher gave us a run-down of the categorical imperative before we read the excerpt from the *Critique of Judgment*."

"Well, as far as the categorical imperative goes, that just doesn't work."

"Why not?"

"Guys," said Pam, "this is fascinating, but we're getting behind. We need to focus, here."

"We'll talk more about this later," John said to Marguerite, as they turned back to the game.

They lost, badly.

WHEN THEY had dragged the desks back into rows and Professor Liebmann stood once again at the blackboard lecturing, Marguerite found her mind falling into a familiar, feverish state. She was prone to fits of creativity where ideas and thoughts crowded into her mind, provoking her to write bad poetry, jot down disconnected metaphors in her notebook, or sketch outlines of longer pieces she knew even at the time she would never properly begin, let alone finish.

Her thoughts now were about where it would lead if there were no objective standard for morality, as John had said. She was trying hard to remember how her professor back in Utah had explained Kant's ideas. Quickly, under her fingers, a diagram took shape on the back of one of her grammar worksheets, her pen scratching across the paper. When it was done, she stared at it for a while, considering whether it made any sense, all the while listening with half an ear to Professor Liebmann's lecture.

She looked up from the diagram to the back of John's head in front of her, his reddish brown hair clipped short against his tanned neck, on the side of which a small pink mole stood out. She looked down at the diagram again and felt nervous. She looked back up at his head, and then back down, and then back up again. The longer she delayed, the more nervous she felt, until at last it seemed the only way to calm her nerves was to get it over with and hand him her diagram. She scribbled *What do you think of this?* at the bottom, carefully folded the paper in half, and tapped his shoulder with the folded edge of it.

He looked around quickly, and saw the piece of paper she held out over his shoulder. He took it and unfolded it on his desk. Marguerite had miscalculated. Far from being calmer, now she felt more nervous than before. He was sure to laugh at her the way he laughed at everything. Why, *why* had she done it?

After a few minutes, she saw him scribble something on the paper and hand it back to her, over his shoulder. She spread it out in front of her and peered at the two new lines of writing at the bottom, but they were mostly illegible. It was enough to gather he wasn't making fun of her though, and she sighed with relief.

When class got out, John stood up and walked her to the door, and they stood in the hallway for half an hour, talking about Kant and justifications for morality.

"So then, what did you mean about morality being a contradiction in terms?" she asked.

"The whole concept of morality is that you've got some kind of universal law that's valid for everyone. But there's no objective basis for it—it always ends up being subjective. There's the way you see morality and the way other people see morality, and everyone's got a different opinion. People try to pin it to reason, like Kant does, or conscience, or religion, but it always turns out to be something radically subjective. So that's why the concept itself doesn't even make sense, because there's this contradiction built into it from the beginning."

"Hm. I'll have to think more about it. It's an interesting argument. It's true there always seem to be a lot of exceptions to some of the rules, since you can picture situations where it might be better to lie or steal or whatever. And everyone always talks about conscience, so yeah, there is a subjective aspect to it. Of course, I definitely believe in morality, since I'm Mormon and all, but—"

"Wait a minute. You're *Mormon?*"

"Yeah. I thought that was obvious from when I said I went to school in Utah."

"Oh. I guess so. Huh, that's interesting. I never talked philosophy with a Mormon before."

"Well ... yeah ... I guess it makes things a bit more complicated for me, talking about things like morality. Because then we—I mean Mormons—we have the idea too that God commands certain things, and I feel like I know it's right, but I don't know how I know. It just *feels* right."

"But that's exactly the problem. You see, it's subjective."

"But it's supposed to apply to everybody. It's supposed to be a universal. Anyway, I'll have to think more about all this."

"Well, I'm glad if I gave you something to think about at least. Have a good weekend, okay?"

They said goodbye in the hallway, and Marguerite went to buy lunch. She spent much of the weekend trying to come up with ways you could have an objective standard of morality.

CHAPTER 4

MONSOON SEASON

THE FOLLOWING WEEK, ON a Thursday, there was more note-passing during class, only this time with Pam, who slid a small scrap of paper onto Marguerite's desk from one side.

Do you think John is cute? the note said. Marguerite snickered quietly, anxious not to disturb the lecture. She picked up her pen and wrote, *He's not really my type. He's funny though. Why, do you?*

I think he's hot. Why wouldn't he be your type? Pam wrote back.

Seems like an extrovert. I'm an introvert. Plus he's kinda goofy.

After five more minutes of listening to Professor Liebmann enthuse about German verb tenses, Marguerite tore off the corner of another sheet of paper and wrote, *So, do you like him?*

Pam pondered, then wrote back, *Maybe. We'll see. I don't think he likes me that way, though.*

Marguerite smiled. It felt like being back in junior high, but passing notes in class was fun. Pam was nice, she decided; she liked her. Privately, though, she thought Pam was right. She didn't seem like she'd be John's type at all. She was too tomboyish, in her shapeless polo shirts and khaki shorts. John would go for someone more flamboyantly sexy, the kind of girl who wore tight miniskirts and high heels and had long, smooth, flippy hair like in a shampoo commercial, and wore perfume, and hung out in bars.

THAT EVENING, Marguerite went to see a movie with her mom. It was a romance with Nicole Kidman playing the haughty daughter of an Irish landowner and Tom Cruise as a fiery-tempered serf. The two of them escaped to America together and pretended to be brother and sister so they could share a cheap apartment. Every night, they spied on each other while they were undressing behind their respective curtains, and eventually, after many adventures, they realized they loved each other, even though they were complete opposites.

Coming out of the theater, she ran into Pam, who was there with a date and had gone to a different movie. While Marguerite introduced her mom and Pam introduced her date, Marguerite observed with fascination as Pam's date put his arms around her and rubbed her back, his hand continually moving back and forth just out of view. The hand wandered down and came to rest on Pam's butt, and meanwhile he seemed to be trying to press her hip against the front of his pants as firmly as possible. Pam didn't seem to mind, and after a few minutes of friendly small talk, went off with him, arm in arm.

WHEN THEY got home, Marguerite had a message that Rachel, her roommate from freshman year, had called long distance from New York. Rachel was a pretty, bespectacled math major, a thoroughbred descendent of blond, rosy-cheeked Dutch settlers. Her side of the dorm room was always awash in a dense clutter of papers covered with equations and Simon & Garfunkel CDs. It was still early, even with the time difference, so Marguerite dialed her number. Rachel picked up. They talked for a few minutes about how it was being home for the summer, and then Rachel confessed the real reason for her call. She had news, big news. She was dating a guy, and had gotten her first real kiss. Marguerite wanted to know everything, but Rachel was frustratingly chary with the details. Marguerite had never had a real kiss herself, that is, an open-mouthed kiss. The closest she had come was a little peck on the lips, quick and chaste, from a Mormon boy she'd gone to senior prom with.

When the subject of kissing had been exhausted, Marguerite told Rachel about the movie she'd seen.

"I liked the film, but it kind of made me mad, too. I was all intrigued by the romance of it, but at the same time it just seems so mythical and unreal. Of course, I wish it *were* real. But these stories only make it harder to accept the unglamorous reality of normal guys."

"I know exactly what you mean," said Rachel. "So, have you met any guys there in Tucson? Is there anyone you like?"

"No, there's no one. But it's a good thing, since I'm just here for the summer anyway. And besides, I'm sick of getting stupid crushes on guys and no one ever liking me back. I hate it."

"Don't worry. Your time will come."

"But I don't even want it to."

"Why not?"

"It makes me think of this one opera—you like opera a little bit, don't you?"

"Yeah, actually I do."

"Well, you know what one this makes me think of? Did you ever see *Ariadne auf Naxos*, by Richard Strauss?"

"No, I don't know that one."

"Well, it's based on this Greek myth where a princess named Ariadne falls in love with a guy named Theseus and helps him out of a labyrinth. But to help him, she has to betray her family and people. Then she sails off with him, but first chance he gets, he dumps her on this lonely island and abandons her."

"But—not every guy has to abandon you, you know."

"No, the point is just, whenever I get these stupid, useless crushes, it seems like I'm always betraying things that really matter for the sake of something that isn't true and doesn't last. I lose sleep, I act stupid, I get jealous and obsessive, I don't get as much work done, I lose focus. And nothing ever seems to come of it but regrets."

"Hey, stop it. You're depressing me."

Marguerite laughed. "Sorry, I didn't mean to. But that's not even the end of the opera yet."

"There's more?"

"Yeah, so then Ariadne's on this island called Naxos, and in the opera there's a crazy vaudeville troop that invades the scene, and one of the women sings a song about how the best way for Ariadne to get over it is to fall in love with another god. So then Dionysius comes along and she falls in love with him."

"So?"

"So you see, it means we make men gods. At least, I do. I idealize guys and do this hero-worship thing, and it's just one after another, there's always a new god."

"Hm. Very interesting. You know what I think? I think you're making too much of it."

"I know, I know. It was just on my mind, because of the movie."

"Just read the scriptures and pray, and I promise, you'll feel a whole lot better."

"You're right. Of course you're right. I'll do that."

WHEN MARGUERITE had hung up the phone, she opened her scriptures, read a chapter, then knelt at the side of her bed and prayed, as she did every night. She crawled into bed and curled up into a ball under the covers, pulling the sheet over her ears.

The first monsoon of the season swept in as she lay there in the darkness, waiting for sleep. There was a crack of thunder, and in an instant rain was drumming on the roof and against her window. They weren't gentle rains, the monsoons, but abrupt and fulsome—as though the sky had secretly been in love with the desert all this time, but had been holding itself back from touching the parched earth, until at last it could hold back no longer and had to release its passion all at once in a warm, unstoppable flood.

CHAPTER 5

THE SLOUCHING BEAST WAKES UP

A WEEK LATER, ON a Thursday in the second week of July, the class took its midterm exam. Marguerite, Pam, Angela, and John all finished early.

"We're going over to Mike's Place to celebrate," John said to Marguerite as they walked out of the classroom. "Why don't you come with us?"

"Who's Mike?"

"Oh, you've never been there?" said Angela. "It's just a bar near here. Nothing special, kind of a dive, actually. But it'll be fun. You should come—everybody's supposed to meet up there after the test."

"But I don't really drink."

"Aw, come on," said John, "you can just get soda or juice or something, and hang out and talk with us. That won't violate your belief system, will it?"

Marguerite laughed. "No. Okay, then, I'll come."

It was hard to resist John, especially when he was in a good mood like today. She'd had another philosophical conversation with him a few days earlier, and she had to admit he was charming, in spite of—or perhaps because of—being an amoralist. The amoralists in the books she read were always charming, too, she reflected. They were often the characters she liked best to read about, like Anatole, who seduced poor naive Natasha in *War and Peace*.

THEY SAT outside at picnic tables on the bar's large shaded back patio. When the pitchers of beer arrived along with Marguerite's soda and grilled cheese sandwich, they talked about the exam. They were relieved at how easy it had been, and were all fairly convinced they'd done well.

John lit a cigarette and took a drag on it, blowing the smoke off to one side so it wouldn't go in their faces. He offered cigarettes to the others, who declined, except for Angela, who explained sheepishly, "I don't normally smoke, but I'll just take one, as a reward for finishing the exam."

"So—John, can I ask, how did you get interested in philosophy?" asked Marguerite. "Was it something you always wanted to do?"

"Nah. I came to it in kind of a roundabout way. I wasn't sure what I wanted to do after I graduated high school, so I was working and going to community college for a while back in New Hampshire, where I grew up. I was taking business classes, and I was miserable. I hated it. I wanted to do something more meaningful and challenging. So then I decided to make a total change and get out of that small town in New Hampshire. I applied to the U of A and got in, and one of the first classes I took was in philosophy. I really liked it, so I signed up for a philosophy major, and I was much, much happier doing that."

"What do you think you'll do with it when you graduate?"

"I'm applying to a few graduate programs. So I'll get my Ph.D. and then probably teach."

Marguerite nodded. "That's cool. You'd be good at teaching. But it's funny, I thought you had to be kind of introverted to do philosophy. You're so outgoing, I can't picture you sitting around thinking all day."

"Oh, I'm an introvert. I definitely think I'm more of an introvert. I mean, yeah, I like to go out drinking with my friends sometimes, but believe me, I spend most of my time holed up in my room listening to music and studying or writing, making notes in my journals, or having existential crises." He grinned.

"You really think you're an introvert?"

"Yeah, of course I do. Why?"

"Nothing. I guess I just didn't have you pegged that way."

"Well, I'm full of surprises. I'm deep and many-layered."

"Oh, I see."

He went off to talk with some of the other German class students who had arrived in the meantime. Eventually he came back, sat down across from Marguerite, and asked if she'd made any progress on finding an objective basis for morality. When she replied in the negative, he asked, "Why are you so worried about that anyway? Are you afraid you might do something immoral?"

"Yeah, I guess you could say that. I mean, I worry about being a good person. I worry a lot about it, actually."

"Why wouldn't you be a good person? You don't exactly strike me as the world's biggest sinner."

Marguerite laughed. "I don't know. It just seems like I'm always struggling and having doubts. I mean, I love my church, don't get me wrong. But sometimes it feels hard to always be so different. I don't mind following all the rules. It's more that sometimes it just feels ... lonely, I guess."

"But aren't you around other Mormons all the time in Utah?"

"Yeah, but I don't feel like I fit in there, either. I think maybe I think too much."

"So you're lonely, huh? You know what I think? We need to convert you away from your Mormonism. It's not making you happy. So we need to corrupt you a little. I think you'd be a lot happier if you cut loose and committed a few sins." He wiggled his eyebrows suggestively.

Marguerite rolled her eyes. "Oh, great, now I'm getting corrupted. Just what I needed."

John laughed and then looked up as two guys he knew came up and greeted him. He excused himself, rose to his feet, and threw his arms around each of them in turn, clapping them on the back. After they'd talked for a few minutes, standing a short distance away, he led them over to the table where Marguerite sat.

"Guys, there's someone I'd like you to meet. This is my brother Greg"—he pointed at a slightly shorter, darker-haired version of himself. "He goes to school here, too. And this is my buddy Damon. He's a philosophy major." Damon was shorter than the two brothers, and thinner, with a narrow, fox-like face. "And this is Marguerite. She's Mormon, but she likes to talk philosophy. So I was just saying, we need to help her get free of her belief in God, because I think she'd have a lot more fun if she weren't religious."

"Oh ho," said Damon, looking her up and down appraisingly, "you've come to the right place. I'm always happy to try to talk someone out of religion." If you were casting roles for *Faust*, he would have made an excellent Mephistopheles.

A little flustered by the attention, Marguerite said, "Well, I doubt you'll convince me, but I'm not afraid of any arguments. The truth is the truth, and it should hold up no matter what anyone says."

"Ah, well. That all depends on how you define truth. But come here, come sit by me, and let's talk." Damon patted the bench next to him.

Marguerite complied and scooted further down the bench to sit closer to him.

"What makes you believe in God, first of all? What reasons do you have for believing?"

"Well—" she blew air out of her mouth. "Where to start. There are so many reasons. The scriptures, of course, they say He exists and loves us. Then there's so much beauty in the world, and so much goodness in people. There's the fact that I was raised around a lot of people who believe, and it's hard to imagine they could all be wrong."

As she listed off reasons, he countered them. The scripture were flawed historical documents—why trust them anyway? Why should any human being be trusted solely on the basis of the authority he claimed to have from God? What about all the evil and ugliness in the world? All these things she called evidence were ambiguous and could be interpreted multiple ways. How could she be sure it was God and not something else, or pure coincidence behind them?

But Marguerite had an ace up her sleeve, and now she brought it out: There was also such a thing as personal revelation through spiritual experience. Mormons, Marguerite included, believed if you prayed, God would let you know through spiritual feelings the Church was true and He was real.

"Interesting," said Damon, "but if that's so effective, then what are you doing sitting here talking to me? If God came down and told you He exists, then why should you have any doubts about it?"

Marguerite hesitated. "I suppose it's not as clear as God coming down and telling you what's what—I mean, it's never been that clear for me. Joseph Smith, the founder of Mormonism, *did* have a vision where God came down and said, 'This is my church,' but for me and most of the people I've talked to about it, it's more like a feeling you get when you pray—a feeling of peace and calm and rightness."

"Aha."

"So I guess you'll say that's just another ambiguous piece of evidence like all the rest, because it's just a feeling."

"That's pretty much what I was going to say." He grinned. "This is going to be easier than I thought. You're doing all the work for me." His face sobered. "But you know, this is serious stuff. This is your *life* here we're talking. We only live once, and it's tragic, don't you think, to waste it on something that's not for real and give up your happiness because someone guilted you into believing in an imaginary God who's going to punish you in the afterlife if you don't obey. Aren't you worried about that?"

Marguerite shrugged and tried to think of way to answer him. While she was still considering it, Damon asked what kinds of things Mormons believed anyway—what sort of commitments and sacrifices did her belief system entail? Marguerite listed off the usual roster of don'ts, but when she got to the part about staying a virgin till you were married, Damon, who was already starting on his third beer, howled in protest.

"No, that's not for real. You're shitting me. Excuse my language. So, you're telling me you're still a virgin? A girl as cute as you?"

Marguerite squirmed in embarrassment.

"So, if you can't have sex, how far can you go? Is oral sex okay? Can you get naked with your boyfriend? Can he feel you up?"

"I don't have a boyfriend. And I guess the answer would pretty much be no." She was still in shock at having heard the phrase "oral sex."

"Oh, that is *tragic*. So all you can do is kiss, basically. God, that must be incredibly frustrating."

"Well ... I don't know ... I've never had a real boyfriend exactly, not what most people would consider a boyfriend. The truth is, I've never even French-kissed. Although that's allowed, I think."

Damon looked thunderstruck. With an expression of mingled pity, anger, and disgust, he said, "Now that's just obscene. We really have to do something about this. I mean, doesn't this upset you? Don't you want to be with someone?"

Marguerite wouldn't meet his eyes. "Well, yes, I mean—yes. But it's not *so* bad. At least I never have to worry about getting pregnant or getting some awful disease. And in a way I kind of like it—the purity of it. It's nice to feel naive and innocent, relatively speaking. And ... I like the idea that I'm saving myself for my future husband, for someone who'll love me enough to want to be with me for the rest of my life, and for eternity."

Damon leaned back and rubbed his chin with the fingers of one hand. Then he said slowly, "But what if you never get married? Or worse—what if you get married and it turns out you're sexually incompatible? I mean, if you can't even fool around before you marry him, how do you know you'll like how he does it to you?"

Marguerite struggled not to show how uncomfortable this phrasing made her. "I always thought that was sort of a myth—sexual compatibility, I mean. Everyone always says you can work on those things. If you have your whole life ahead of you to work on it together, surely you can get good at it at some point?"

"I hate to break it to you, but that's not how it works. In any relationship, it's an ironclad rule that the sex is best at the beginning, and it's all downhill from there. Because in the beginning you're all excited, and it's new and it's hot and you don't know what to expect. If it's lousy to start with, you're in for a very long marriage full of bad sex, or more likely, no sex at all, because you'd probably just give up on it at some point. So you better be pretty sure it's going to be hot with a guy if you're planning to stay with him for life. And how can you even get a sense of that if you have no experience beforehand?"

Marguerite at last managed to look up and meet his eyes. "Luckily, I have a good imagination."

"Oh, I'll bet you do." He laughed. "Jesus." He and John exchanged looks, and he laughed again and shook his head.

"But come on now—look at me." He was straddling the bench now to face her, and she swung one leg over the other side of the bench so she faced him, too. "Look," he continued, "I just want to tell you—and I don't mean to offend you, I'm telling you this as a friend—there's so much you learn about another person from having sex with them. There's so much you learn about yourself. And you're sacrificing that indefinitely, for something you don't even know is true. That's a huge risk you're taking. Maybe a much bigger risk than you realize. Sex is a part of you that you can't deny. You can't deny yourself sex without lying to yourself and hurting yourself. Don't look away. I know you're shy, but look at me—don't look away."

Marguerite looked up and let him hold her gaze with his.

"You have beautiful eyes, by the way." He paused, and then said, "Now, just let me ask you a few questions."

Marguerite nodded, mesmerized. He spoke in a slow, deliberate crescendo.

"Don't you want to feel passion? Don't you want to be able to just let yourself go and be completely free with someone? Don't you want to have *every inch* of your body touched and worshiped? Don't you want to feel someone *inside* you?"

She held herself perfectly still, intensely conscious of the shallow breaths going in and out of her lungs and the rising and falling of her rib cage. But inside her a kind of terror had arisen, as though some great, slouching beast that had been asleep for centuries down in the unlit depths of her soul was waking and stirring at last—a slavering, mindless beast that could, if it chose, gnaw away at all that was good in her and consume her from the inside out. She could feel her face burning. She turned her head away from him, breaking eye contact, and turned her body away, too, swung her leg over the bench so that now she faced away from the table. She folded her arms across her chest and after a long silence said, "You're not playing fair."

"All's fair in love and war, sweetheart."

"Are you okay?" asked John. "Are we upsetting you too much? Damon can be kind of a dog sometimes. Don't mind him. I'm afraid we're going to scare you off at this rate, and you're going to run off screaming into the parking lot."

"No, I'm fine, really. Like I said, I'm not afraid of arguments. Well, all right, maybe I am a little afraid now. But I'd feel like a coward if I left right in the middle of an argument." Saying this, she thought of the young man in the book she was reading, *The Magic Mountain*, who came to visit a Swiss mountain sanatorium for three weeks; his first day there, an odd Italian gentlemen warned him to leave before it was too late, but the young man thought leaving would be cowardly. He wound up staying for seven years. So she added, "Although—maybe I'm just too prideful, thinking I'm strong enough and smart enough to resist any and all temptations and arguments."

"It's not prideful," John said. "There's no sin in talking things through and trying to get clearer about your reasons for believing, and whether they're valid or not."

"Hopefully you're right. And besides, I'm having fun in a way."

"Good. That's the point."

CHAPTER 6

THE ULTIMATE MYSTICISM

As THE CONVERSATION AT the bar went on into the afternoon, John took over the effort to convert Marguerite away from religion. His arguments were gentler and less graphic than Damon's, but no less difficult to dismiss. After they'd spoken for a while, she asked:

"So, have you ever read the Bible?"

"I have, yes," he said.

"The whole thing?"

"Cover to cover. Well, I skimmed parts of the Old Testament, but I studied the New Testament pretty closely. Of course, I studied it as literature, not as scripture."

"And what did you think?"

"Sure, I liked it. There were some interesting things in there, definitely. I'm just ... not a fan of mysticism, generally."

"Mysticism?" Marguerite asked, "What do you mean by mysticism?"

"It just means everything's shrouded in mystery. It's easy to hide weaknesses and flaws in your metaphysics and epistemology that way and dupe people into believing—you just have to tell them it's all a big mystery. 'God works in mysterious ways.' Christianity is the ultimate mysticism."

"But—I don't know," Marguerite said. "Maybe it's not such a bad thing. Some things *are* mysterious, after all."

"Like what?"

She looked down and picked at the remnants of the grilled cheese sandwich congealing on her plate. "Like—well, love, for example. Now there's a mystery. What is love?"

"Oh," he said, pshawing with a wave of his hand, "love. That's just something made up by troubadours in the fourteenth century."

She looked up from her plate. "Ah. I know what you mean. I agree with you on that, actually. I completely agree. It's just an illusion, nothing but fairy tales. And troubadours—that's exactly right."

But the main thing he worried about, he told her, was that her religion made her unhappy because it kept her from being free. "How can you be happy if you're so ... what's the word I'm looking for ... constrained? If you're not free?"

"But don't you see, she said, "it's just what makes me free. It's supposed to free me from sin, if I follow it fully."

"But what's sin, anyway? Why would you want to be free from it?"

"Yeah," said Damon, who had been sitting next to John listening to them, "define sin."

"Well," she began slowly, "I don't know how other versions of Christianity define it. But my own personal definition, from what I've read, is that sin is that which brings death—spiritual death. Did you know, in Mormonism, there's no hell, really? There's just an inability to progress. Damnation, in Mormonism, is to remain stagnant and unable to keep learning and moving forward, unable to grow closer to God in love and understanding. Which is what I think of as spiritual death. And I believe it doesn't wait for the death of your body. You can be damned while you're still alive physically, because your spirit is sick and stuck and cut off from God, and from light and knowledge and progress."

"Huh. Wow," said John, "that's the most interesting thing you've said so far. You almost make it sound like a religion I could get behind, if the only hell is not being able to progress."

"If you liked the Bible, you'd love the Book of Mormon."

"Hmph." He looked skeptical, and Marguerite felt embarrassed, as though she'd been caught proselytizing on the sly. "But back to sinning," he went on, taking a sip of beer from the plastic cup in his hand. "It seems like most of the things you think of as sin would actually help you progress and learn, not stop you from progressing. I mean, I agree with Damon about sex being a good thing." He grinned. "A very good thing. So who decides what's a sin and what's not? If you're just listening to what some authority tells you, you're not really free to choose for yourself how to progress on your own terms."

"Well, the Bible says whoever sins is the servant of sin, and the wages of sin is death. I think the idea is, when you give in to your body's appetites, then you're a slave to them. Like if you start smoking, for example, then you might get addicted and not be able to stop. Or, say, with sex. It's your momentary desires that are calling the shots. So you might do things that hurt you and other people, things you don't even really want to do, for the sake of some fleeting, short-term pleasure that comes to an end, and gets you nowhere."

"I think I see where you're going with this," John said.

"Yeah, so that's 'death'—just to be bullied by your fleeting desires, to have no control over them, so you're not free and can't progress because they hold you back. On the other hand, if you choose to serve God instead, you're not a slave. It's more like a family relationship, father and child. If God gives you rules, they're for your own good, and it's your own free choice to follow them, not something outside of you that determines it."

"Okay, that's interesting. But my question is, how do you know 'God' really has your best interests at heart? And even if you know that, how would you know what 'God' really wants you to do? And what if I freely choose to follow my desires instead? That seems less like something 'outside of me' than God. By your logic, I'd still be free then, and not a slave to them."

Marguerite didn't know how to answer him. During the lull in the conversation, as she was reflecting on what he'd said, there was a small commotion at the next table over. One of the graduate students in the class had invited her husband to stop by and join them at the bar, and he had just arrived, bringing their small baby girl with him. A chorus of ohs and ahs broke out at the sight of the baby, and John excused himself to go over and get a closer look. Damon followed him.

There was such a press of admirers around the baby at first that Marguerite, Angela, Pam, and Greg stayed where they were, waiting for the crowd to thin out and watching the pink-clad, pink-faced child get handed around from person to person. When the baby was handed to John, she promptly fell asleep in his arms. He didn't seem to mind, but went on cheerfully chatting with the parents and the others sitting around them, cradling her all the while. Her eyelids fluttered open from time to time, but she never cried as she had when each of the others had held her.

"Well," said Greg to Marguerite, "now they're gone, I guess it's my turn to try to talk you out of religion. I may not be a philosophy major, but I'd be happy to give it a shot."

"All right, give it your best shot," said Marguerite gamely. "What's your major, then?"

"Psychology. Although I haven't taken tons of classes in it yet, so I don't know that much. Don't expect me to be an expert or anything."

"Okay. So what's your argument against religion?" She found herself liking Greg almost at once. He was quieter than John, his manner more subdued, but he was just as friendly and engaging, and even more handsome.

"Well, my thing is just that believing in God seems no different from having an imaginary friend. It's true the world can be a lonely place, and it's understandable people want something to believe in. They want to believe there's someone or something out there who cares about them. But I don't think it helps to just make something up and devote yourself to some imaginary being. It's more healthy to reach out to other people, and find people you can trust and believe in, real people who care about you."

"But what if there's no one like that? What if God really is the only thing you have? People always let you down eventually, in some way or another. The good thing about belief in God is that you do always have an ideal to believe in, something to take comfort from when people let you down."

"Well, I guess that's the question, then—is it better to be happier with a delusion, or sadder and lonelier with the truth?"

Marguerite didn't answer. After a while, Greg said, "You know, it was pretty funny watching you talking with the other guys. You're very open. But still, I get the sense you're kind of shy and not used to so much attention."

Marguerite smiled. "So, what, now you're using your special psychologist powers to guess my feelings?"

He laughed. "No, it's not that. I guess I just sympathize. I mean, I'm kind of a shy, lonely guy myself. I know how it feels."

"You—shy and lonely? I wonder if you can really be related to John. He seems like the least shy person I've ever met."

"Sometimes I wonder if we're related, too. Like maybe our mom had an affair with the postman or something. But you'd be surprised."

"So, are you guys pretty close?"

"Well, we live together, so I guess we're as close as two brothers who live together typically are."

"That's interesting. Is he a good person to live with?"

"Ah, well, we both have our faults. I guess we put up with each other pretty well."

"Hm. But in any case, you were right. I'm not used to so much attention, especially not from guys. It makes me feel self-conscious. I don't know what to think when someone says I'm pretty or something like that. You try to be objective about these things. I look in the mirror, and all I see are flaws. But you never really know how other people see you. If they don't think you're attractive, they can't exactly be honest about it. And if they say they do, you can't know if they're being sincere or have some other motive for saying it."

"Well, *I* think you're pretty. Honestly. Speaking objectively."

Marguerite knit her brows and frowned. "I wasn't fishing for compliments," she said. She looked over at John, who was still holding the baby and listening quietly to the other people talking at the next table over. He had a beatific expression on his face, and she saw him glance down every now at then at the lightly snoring bundle in his arms with a tender smile.

"It's funny how everyone's maternal or paternal instincts kicked in the second they saw that baby," she said. "I swear, John has been holding that kid for an hour. And it's funny, too, that I'm practically the only one who didn't hold the baby, considering I'm the Mormon girl who's supposed to be getting married and making mini-Mormons. But probably that's just because I know I'll have plenty of time for holding babies if I ever do get married."

"What do you mean, 'if'? Of course you'll get married."

"No, seriously, I'm worried I might never find someone. I'm a difficult case. But what about you? Do you think you want to get married someday? Not to me, obviously, but in general?"

Greg laughed, but then said earnestly, "Yeah, I'd definitely like to get married and have a family at some point."

"Well, that should be easy for you at least. You and John both. You're so ... likeable, both of you. I don't know what it is, but half the girls in our class seem to have a crush on your brother. He seems like a good guy, though, and so do you."

He chuckled. "Yeah, I have no idea why, but people do seem to like us, for some odd reason."

The afternoon was wearing on, but no one was leaving and there was still a general atmosphere of celebration. Enough pitchers of beer had been drunk that people were getting tipsy and friendly. Marguerite spoke to classmates she had hardly talked to all semester, and though she hadn't had any beer, she felt inebriated, as though she were absorbing some of the intoxication around her by osmosis.

John gave the baby back to its parents at last, and he and Damon wandered back over to sit with them.

"John," said Angela, "it was really cute watching you with that baby. Who knew you could be so sweet and fatherly?"

"Ah, I couldn't help it. There she was, all tiny, looking up at me with those big blue eyes."

"So all a girl has to do is bat her eyelashes, and she has you wrapped around her little finger—is that what you're saying?" asked Angela.

"Yeah, I'm a sucker for that, I gotta admit. But you should have seen Damon holding her. He was just as smitten."

Damon responded by declaring, "I want to be a father. Wouldn't that just be so cool, to be a *father*? Philosophically, I mean, it would be cool. It's the only form of immortality I believe in, fatherhood. Passing along a little of myself to the future."

He and John began to talk about things various philosophers had said on the subject of fatherhood and immortality.

"But you don't believe in any kind of immortality besides that?" asked Marguerite.

"Nah. I'm gonna be worm food," said John. "*Worm food.* Worms are going to be crawling all over me in my grave and eating out my eyeballs, and it'll be *disgusting* ..."

Angela squealed with delighted revulsion. "John, that is so gross."

"But fatherhood—yeah, it's kind of a way to pass a little of your spirit on, like Damon was saying."

"*Spirit?*" Damon interrupted, practically roaring. "Did I just hear the word *spirit* cross your lips?"

And now the two of them flew into a loud philosophical brawl, with names of German and French philosophers flying furiously back and forth like blows of fists while the girls looked on in amusement, understanding nothing except that their role was to provide an audience for the fight.

"You're almost as bad as Marguerite," Damon said to John, as their contretemps was winding down. "Why don't the two of you go off to church and say some prayers together? That'll give you your *spirit.*"

"Hey, at least Marguerite has a coherent belief system. Unlike you, you nihilist."

"You Hegelian."

The girls were nearly doubled over with laughter now. Between giggles, Marguerite said, "John, I can't believe it—you actually defended me just now."

"Ah, well, don't get too excited. Just because your belief system is coherent doesn't mean it's not totally wrong."

"Gee, thanks."

"So how are you doing anyway? Are we making any progress here? Still a Christian?"

"I'm afraid so."

"Damn. You know, I always seem to end up dating Christian girls. It's awful. It never works out, because our belief systems are just too different. The last two girls I dated were both Christian. The other night I was out with some of my buddies at a bar, and I met this really cute girl and started talking to her. And what do you know, of course it turns out she's Christian. I wanted to get her number and call her, but then I was like: 'John. What are you doing?' So from now on, if a hot, nice Christian girl comes along, we just can't be anything but friends."

"Well, I can't say I feel too sorry for you," said Marguerite, laughing again. "If that's the type of girl you're attracted to, maybe God is trying to tell you something. But anyway, friendship isn't so bad, is it?"

"It's true. Actually, friendship is infinitely better than dating. You don't have all the drama and jealousy like in a relationship. And even if you're not dating that long—I don't know. You go out with someone, you connect, you sleep with them, and then you might never even talk to them again. It's depressing. It's so transitory. At least with friendship it lasts over time, and you can actually get to know the person."

"I completely agree. I'd take a long-term friendship over a short-term fling any day. Not that I'd have a short-term fling anyway, but you know what I mean."

"Well, flings do have their place. But yeah, I know what you mean."

They sat and talked and drank together for several more hours. When it was nearing five o'clock, Marguerite looked down at her watch.

"Do you realize we've been here for six hours? I think it's time to go home, for me at least. I haven't even practiced the piano yet today."

"No, you can't leave," said John. "We're just getting warmed up."

"Yeah, stay a while longer," said Angela. "This has been so much fun."

But Marguerite insisted. Angela hugged her goodbye and then invited everyone to a baseball game the following evening.

"My mom's boyfriend plays for the Tucson Toros. I can get us all discounted tickets, although they're pretty cheap to begin with. You should come, Marguerite."

"I don't know—I don't know a thing about baseball."

"You don't have to," said John. "Just come. We'll all go, and we'll hang out and talk. It'll be fun."

"All right, I'll come. I'll see you guys tomorrow night, then."

Before she left, Damon made a point of hugging her goodbye too, sending her into a paroxysm of shyness.

"I hope I didn't upset you or offend you too much," he said. "I think you're a really sweet girl. We were only trying to help, you know. We meant well." And he added in a low voice in her ear, "Just promise me you'll think about the things we talked about, okay?"

"I don't think I'll be able to help it," she said, trembling inwardly. She waved goodbye to them all again and left.

CHAPTER 7

A CRISIS OF FAITH

THERE WAS NO CLASS Friday, the day after the exam, so Marguerite slept late. For all that she'd complained about not having time to practice the piano, in the end she'd been too distracted to get anything done after leaving the bar in the early evening. Before going to bed, near midnight, she had knelt to pray.

"Dear Heavenly Father," she whispered, "please help me be strong and stand as a witness of Thy truth. Please, please give me wisdom and understanding and help me find answers to all these questions and doubts I'm filled with. Please don't let me fall in love with John or Damon or Greg, and please don't let any of them care about me that way, either. Please help me resist temptation and just be a good friend to all these nice people I've met. Thank You for letting me be friends with Angela and Pam and John and the rest of them. In the name of Jesus Christ, amen."

As it got closer to the time to leave for the baseball game the next day, she found herself pacing around the house with a clawing feeling in her stomach. She hardly understood why she was so anxious. She was afraid of seeing the boys again, she thought. Maybe they had only been so friendly toward her because they were drunk, and when she showed up again, as Mormon and timid and homely as ever, they'd be cold and disdainful. But what a dumb thing to be worried about, when it was really her morality and soul she should be afraid for.

She called a Mormon friend from the freshman dorms, a girl named Ellen she'd been exchanging letters with regularly over the summer. Ellen was studying to be a nurse. She was a practical-minded girl with a good sense of humor, staunch in her

41

commitment to Mormonism and a reliable source of uplifting advice. Marguerite tried to tell her about the day before and the state of confusion she'd been left in emotionally and religiously, but stumbled over her words. It was hard to convey that it had been what she'd felt as much as what she'd heard that had upset her and made her feel estranged from herself. She couldn't exactly tell Ellen how turned on she'd been when Damon spoke to her, or about the slouching, slow-moving beast that had woken in her depths. Still, she was comforting to talk to.

"You know what the scriptures tell us," Ellen said. "We have to put on the whole armor of God." Ellen didn't see how any good could come of getting involved with boys who were so against Marguerite's religion. And as a general rule, you couldn't take it too seriously when boys told you that you were pretty or had beautiful eyes.

WHEN MARGUERITE got to the baseball park, she saw immediately all her worry had been for nothing. Damon and Greg weren't there, only John, Angela, Pam, and a handful of other students from their class, two guys named Shawn and Oscar and a couple of girls. Angela hugged her when she arrived.

"I'm so glad you could come," she said. "That was really fun yesterday, wasn't it?"

Marguerite agreed. "I think it was about the craziest six hours of my life so far, though."

"I have to admit," said John, "I thought it was pretty funny. You should have seen your face when Damon was talking to you."

"You guys must have thought I was a pretty hopeless case," said Marguerite.

"Nah, I wouldn't go that far. I don't think you're a hopeless case. I just think you're ... confused." His tone was affectionate, and Marguerite couldn't help but smile. "But you gave me some things to think about."

"I gave *you* things to think about?" She shook her head.

It was a while before the game got going, and when it did, their little group didn't make much of a pretense of watching it, although from time to time Angela and one or two of the boys jumped up and cheered at something that happened on the field.

Marguerite spent most of the time talking with Angela and John. It seemed Pam had given up on John as a romantic prospect and had moved on to greener pastures. She was off flirting with Oscar and Shawn. Angela, on the other hand, had clearly succumbed to the same force of infatuation against which Marguerite was struggling.

When she and Marguerite had spoken on the phone to make plans for the evening, Angela had asked Marguerite what she thought of John.

"I'm not completely sure yet," Marguerite said, "but it's hard to help liking him, isn't it?"

"Yeah, I think I'm starting to like him a lot," Angela said. She didn't sound happy about it.

"What's wrong with that?" Marguerite asked. "I'm sure he likes you, too."

"No, I mean, I wish he'd ask me out. I'm kind of wondering if maybe I should ask him out."

"Sure, why not? We're liberated women, right? And he was kind of flirting with you, I think."

"I don't know," said Angela with a sigh. "I'm just not sure he's interested in me that way. And he spent so much time talking with you, when you guys got on that religion kick."

"So? He said he wouldn't want to date a religious girl anyway."

"He did? Huh. And you wouldn't mind if I asked him out?"

Marguerite made a derisive noise. "Pff. Of course not."

"Well, maybe I'll hold off for a little bit. See how he acts tomorrow night."

"Good idea."

"I mean, what if he said no? I'd be so embarrassed, and then we'd still have the class together, and it'd be awkward for the rest of the summer."

"I'm sure he'd be nice about it," Marguerite said. "But it couldn't hurt to wait a little and see."

Observing them together now, it seemed to Marguerite John treated Angela like a little sister, and treated Marguerite much the same. John and Angela were good company, though. As always, John was full of jokes and stories. He told them about growing up in New Hampshire with its snowy winters. In school everybody skied, and the guys who wore lycra ski pants would come down the hills bent over in pain because their balls got so cold. He did comical impressions of people, drank beer after beer, and capered around like a puppy. Angela's dimples came out, and she told stories, too, although many of hers were sad. She'd had a difficult life so far, short as it was. Her mom and dad had split up when she was in high school, and it had been a wrenching, messy business. Then there'd been a series of mean and worthless boyfriends, and a long struggle with anorexia.

By the end of the evening, Marguerite was slightly infatuated with both of them—with Angela for being such a sweet person in spite of all the difficulties she'd gone through, and with John for his cheerfulness and charm, which didn't seem to be strategically directed or even something of which he was conscious, but were radiated indiscriminately on everyone who came near him.

Marguerite believed her own life to have been an unusually difficult one, if in a way that was different and less easy to pinpoint than Angela's. But her ordeals weren't the sort that lent themselves to storytelling, and she was secretive and ashamed about them: fits of despair she'd learned to fear from the age of twelve, a terror that in one of these black moods she might someday do harm to herself, and a feeling of being irrevocably bent and different because of them, barred from ever living an ordinary life as an ordinary person. These were things of which she'd never been able to speak with anyone, not even Mark Tierney, who was now traveling around Europe with a backpack and a Eurail Pass, staying in a different youth hostel every night. She could hardly even talk to God about it without blaming Him in her heart. She was better off putting such things out of her mind and listening to the others talk. Around friends like these, it was easy to do, and she was as happy as she'd been in a long time.

MARGUERITE SPENT several hours the following day making notes to herself on arguments and scriptural responses to counter points John and the others had made against her religion during the talk at the bar. She scrutinized her feelings intermittently, too, for warning signs of a more serious crush. To her relief, each time she checked, her infatuation with John hadn't yet reached the danger point and still amounted to little more than strong liking and admiration.

In church on Sunday, one of the speakers gave a long address on the scriptural passage Ellen had quoted to her on the phone, about "putting on the whole armor of God." Heavenly Father was going out of His way to hammer this point home, Marguerite thought. But what was the chink in her armor? Would a friendship with John be the point of weakness through which sin would enter her life? But it couldn't be. Surely God wanted her to take pleasure in such rare acquaintances as this, and learn from them. In any case, the scriptures said, *Unto the pure, all things are pure.* The chink must not be in the friendship but in herself, in her lack of knowledge, in her own weak will. She needed to remedy these weaknesses as best she could, through prayer and study. Surely that was the message God meant to send her.

But the more she studied and prayed and thought and wrote notes to herself, the less certain everything she believed in became. Her doubts began to feel like the shifting sands in her old dream, or like quicksand. The harder she tried to wriggle her way out of them, the deeper she sank. Along with her doubts came fear and unhappiness. Faith seemed like a shining silvery mirage she chased after like a dying man in a desert, stumbling and parched. To lose sight of that far-off, faint glimmer of otherworldly beauty would be worse than dying of hunger and thirst and sunstroke.

If she was brutally honest with herself, she couldn't say it was anything more than a mirage. She didn't know whether God existed. She didn't know whether the scriptures were true. But to concede this was to stand on the edge of a black, yawning, bottomless chasm, to stand so close to the edge there was an equal chance of falling or drawing back. If she fell, all would be lost. If she fell, she would be utterly alone in the universe, alone with nothing but her worthless, starved, battered and ugly soul. There would be nothing to grab hold of, nothing around which to orient herself, no gravity, no up or down or right or wrong, there would be nothing but nothingness and vertigo and the whistling of the air rushing past her.

Her doubts reached a fever pitch Monday evening as she sat on her bed with her German homework shoved off to one side and her head in her hands. Just when she began to think the uncertainty might drive her mad, she found a new thought to comfort her.

Love. It was love she was chasing in that distant, glimmering, ever-retreating image that led her always deeper into the desert inside her. God was love, and this godly, unknowable, beautifying love—not the trivial love made up by troubadours in the fourteenth century—was what she sought. She couldn't give up on looking for God without giving up on love. There was no certainty in her beliefs, but there was certainty in her love, in the longing she felt for these mirages and what they promised.

Of course she didn't, couldn't know whether they were anything more than illusions. She could only have faith in them. That was what having faith meant, after all: not knowing for sure.

THE NEXT morning in the shower, Marguerite found herself having an imaginary conversation with John. "I'm going through a sort of dialectic," she told him. "Like my philosophy of art teacher explained Hegel to us. There are the three stages, thesis, antithesis, and synthesis. Although maybe I'm getting Hegel all wrong—you'd know better. But as I understood it, you have an argument, then a counterargument, and finally a whole new level of understanding as you resolve the conflict between them.

"The thesis was 'I know.' The antithesis was 'I don't really know for sure.' And the synthesis is, 'I have faith'—that's my new understanding.

"Do you know, it makes me think of the three kinds of love in Greek thought. C.S. Lewis talks about them in a book I read. Eros, philia, and agape—romantic love, friendship, and godly love or charity. I wonder which one I'm doing with you. Probably some combination of all three. Maybe the three kinds of love form their own dialectic. You begin with eros—blunt attraction, and that's your thesis, a false certainty, an illusion of oneness. Then comes friendship, where you begin to challenge and argue with and learn from each other, and you have to be separate for that, so you lose your certainty and your illusion of oneness, that temporary dissolution of ego boundaries. And this brings debate and growth and change. But ultimately you strive towards agape, a true oneness because it means loving the other as oneself, empathy and compassion. It's a bond stronger and less changeable than mere attraction or even friendship."

And so she went on in her head like this for a good twenty minutes, using up all the hot water and almost forgetting to put conditioner in her hair.

IN CLASS, during the break, she told John she'd had an imaginary conversation with him in the shower that morning.

"You were talking to me while you were naked?" he said. "That's kind of a turn-on. I'm trying not to picture it too vividly."

"No, no, it wasn't like that. I was telling you all about my Hegelian dialectical progress."

"Ah, you're ruining the image. Who talks to people in the shower, anyway? You're a strange girl."

THAT EVENING, Marguerite met Angela, Pam, and John to study together at an all-night diner. Toward the end, when they'd been at it for three hours, there was a lull in the conversation, and Marguerite told John about the crisis of faith she'd had over the weekend, and how miserable it had made her while it lasted.

"It's funny to hear you talk about wrestling with your faith," John said. "I always thought it was a lot easier to have faith than not to have it."

"It doesn't seem easy to me at all. It seems like I'm in a constant fight with myself to hold onto it—it's so hard sometimes, like it's a burden I always have to carry. But then the thought of losing it is even harder to bear. It's hard either way. Sometimes, though, I really would love not to have faith. Sometimes I think I would throw my faith into a trash can in two seconds if I could only conceive of being happy without it."

"You think you couldn't be happy without faith? Aw, Marguerite, I'm sure that's not true. I mean, a lot of people are agnostics or atheists and still live happy lives. Look at me. Okay, maybe I'm not the best example. But there are plenty of people who are happy without faith."

"Yeah, look at me," said Pam. "I'm agnostic and I'm not miserable. At least, I don't think I am."

"Maybe it works for some people," said Marguerite, "but then maybe there are other people like me who need to believe in order to be happy. Or maybe it's the kind of thing where if you've never had it as part of your life, you don't know what you're missing. But once you've experienced it, the thought of losing it makes you miserable. Like when you've fallen in love with someone."

"You're in love with God?" asked Angela doubtfully. "That sounds like being a nun."

"Maybe that's it," said Marguerite. "I'm in love with the idea of God, you could say. I love having ideals to believe in. There's a part of me that seems to need that to be happy."

"But you can still have ideals without religion," said John. "You don't have to give that up just because you stop believing in God."

"I don't know. I don't think so. I love the ideals that come from *my* religion. I don't know that it'd be possible not to throw the baby out with the bathwater. It's so bleak and painful even to think about. I don't know about other people, but I'd be lost and miserable."

John was staring at her, his dark brows raised and knitted with concern. "Look," he said, "that's not what I wanted at all. I just started that whole conversation thinking it'd be helpful for you. But if I'm going to mess with your belief system and it's going to make you unhappy, forget about it. I just want you to be happy."

Marguerite felt as though the ground had dropped out from under her.

It was time to go home, so they stuffed their worksheets and notebooks back into their bags, settled their bill with the waitress, and left.

When Marguerite got home, everyone else was in bed already. She paced back and forth in the living room with her thoughts in a ferment.

There was charity for you. That John would rather she be happy than prove himself right in their ongoing argument. *There* was agape. She blinked hot tears from her eyes. This was exactly the sort of love she'd been seeking in her mirage-like visions. Could he be right then, that what she loved in her faith could also be found outside it? Was he going to win the argument that way—by giving it up?

But there was something else, some nagging unspoken truth that unsettled her. Did she really have to admit it, even if only to herself? It was too humiliating. But she forced herself to say it in her mind in the bluntest way she could. *I want to give up my faith so I can have sex with John.*

She almost burst out laughing. It was absurd on so many levels, but it was true. There were more of this at the heart of all her doubting and spiritual writhing around than any disinterested love of truth for its own sake. It was all the more absurd given that John had never given the slightest indication of wanting to sleep with her. And why should he want to? She was plain, nose and eyes too big for the rest of her face, crooked teeth, a mushroom-like complexion prone to blemishes, stringy hair. She tried hard to be a nice person and beautiful on the inside, but she knew well enough that sort of thing didn't make men want to go to bed with you.

Once she'd admitted to herself what the real problem was, Marguerite had an easier time solving it. Even if in some wildly hypothetical realm John were interested, it would hardly make sense to trade the religion she loved, her eternal salvation, and the integrity of her soul and conscience for a few minutes of pleasure.

Still, there could be no harm in admiring him, so she indulged herself in that. Before she went to bed, she prayed God would bless John and thanked Him for letting her be friends with him.

CHAPTER 8

LION AND RAM

THE NEXT DAY IN class, John was clowning around, goofing off, and making jokes as usual, but instead of laughing as she normally would have, Marguerite frowned disapprovingly. She frowned when he flirted with Angela, and she wrinkled her nose disdainfully when he pulled out a cigarette to smoke during the break. Marguerite, Angela, and Pam were standing with him in the meager shade of one of the short, spindly trees set into square planters in the brick courtyard at intervals, while the brutal mid-July sun beat down on their heads. They were talking about what they'd done over the weekend after the baseball game, and John admitted after some prodding and teasing and elbow-nudging from Pam that he'd gone out to a bar and met a thirty-year-old woman. He was supposed to go on a date with her at some point. Marguerite and Angela exchanged glances. The relief was plain on Angela's face that she hadn't asked John out.

Marguerite frowned even more, then, and asked spitefully whether this woman wasn't a bit *old* for him, and wasn't that kind of sleazy anyway?

As soon as she said it, she knew she'd gone too far. He frowned back at her, looking annoyed and hurt.

Their break over, they trooped back into the classroom. It was time for group work. Professor Liebmann assigned them to work together in pairs to discuss each others' zodiac signs and read each others' horoscopes in German.

"You want to work together?" asked John. Marguerite said yes, glad for the chance to show she was contrite for her earlier spitefulness. She was still smarting and embarrassed over the epiphany she'd had the night before about wanting to sleep with

50

him. But she'd only meant to inure herself against his charms and gird up her loins against temptation, not to hurt or insult him.

When they had read each others' horoscopes out loud to each other—Marguerite was a Leo and John an Aries—John lapsed back into English.

"It's no surprise we don't get along, since you're a lion and I'm a ram. I'm obstinate, and you're stubborn, too, and we both always have to be right. And as a Leo you're proud, jealous, possessive, egotistical ...'"

"Jealous?" Marguerite asked, horrified at her own transparency. But then again, she was a forthright, attention-hungry Leo, and it was only to be expected she'd be an open book. As a Leo you wore your heart on your sleeve. She shook her head sadly and sighed. "It's true, I'm afraid. I'm a total Leo. But it makes me sad. I'd like for us to get along."

John's expression softened. "I'd like for us to get along, too."

"I'm sorry if I was rude and judgmental earlier."

"Apology accepted."

"Anyway, it's sad to think of not being friends just because of some dumb zodiac-type difference in our personalities. And besides, we Leos aren't all bad. We're doggedly loyal and we're generous and warm-hearted, even if we are prone to drama."

"All right, all right, maybe you're not so bad after all," he conceded. They smiled at each other, and Marguerite felt her equilibrium restored.

AFTER CLASS John asked if the girls wanted to meet up for another study session later on.

"Ooh, I can't, I'm busy tonight," said Pam.

"Oh really?" said John. "You got a hot date? Who's the lucky guy?"

Pam blushed. "Yeah, a friend is taking me to the Guns N' Roses concert up in Phoenix."

"So you're a fan, huh?" John asked her.

"Yeah. You like that stuff, too?"

"Some of it's okay. Well, I like pretty much anything, but mostly I just listen to classical."

"Really?" Marguerite broke in. "*You* like classical?"

"Sure," he said, turning to face her. "You know, I told you I always hole up in my room for hours studying and listening to music. Classical's the only thing I can listen to while I'm studying, so it's almost the only thing I listen to. It's been that way for years."

"Seriously. You listen to classical music," Marguerite repeated.

"Yeah. Why, is that so surprising?"

"What kind of classical music? What composers do you like?"

"Oh, I don't know, the usual ones, I guess. Bach, Beethoven, Brahms—you know, the classics."

"You are too much."

"What? It's not that big of a deal."

Marguerite shook her head. John liking classical music was the last straw. She could feel herself tipping into the danger zone.

They agreed to meet in the library to study at 6:00, without Pam this time. As Marguerite walked to her car and drove home, she thought to herself, *Too much. He really is too much.* He was too much of everything. Too tall, too golden, too funny, too bright, too frightening, too intensely and healthily and wholly himself. And she'd thought him a buffoon. As her old red car sped over the sun-baked asphalt streets, she thought to herself he was like a building with a false facade, built to look ordinary or even small and dingy from the outside. But through clever tricks of engineering, or even some kind of magic, the building was vast and maze-like on the interior. He was larger on the inside than he looked on the outside, large and complex enough that she was afraid of getting lost in him.

The metaphor pleased her, so when she got home, she took out a pen and a fresh sheet of paper, and tried to turn it into a poem. At length, scratching out and rewriting some of the lines many times over, she wrote:

Labyrinthine Friendship

In a wilderness place there crouches
An old shelter, half dug out of the ground,
And one expects within the door
Only a warm impoverished smell,
Small cramped dark space, nothing more.

Enter, then, and find
A benevolent, unyielding world
Of corridors, sunlit gardens, shadows,
Downwards and upwards stairs, and always
The mystery of what lies further on,
The danger of what lies deeper and beyond.
No wonder I halt in confusion here,
Remembering the outer world as a dream.
Faith, fear, all but hunger forgotten,
I long to retrace my steps, but having stepped in,
I can't so easily step out again.

SHE MET John and Angela again in the evening outside the library. They found a small group study room with a blackboard where they could close the door and talk without disturbing anyone. Although they began by taking out their German books and flashcards, the conversation quickly wandered away from grammar, and they chatted more than they worked.

Marguerite tried hard not to seem jealous of Angela, or for that matter, to be jealous. John, as usual, had been right—she was terribly jealous, not just of the 30-year-old women, but of the way Angela giggled at his jokes and flirted with him. Marguerite liked Angela and wanted her to be happy, and she felt the same about John. If the two of them, John and Angela, might be happy together, that was certainly a good thing, viewed objectively. Besides which, God would surely prefer it if she was kind and generous-hearted rather than spiteful and jealous. *I will make weak things become strong unto them*—that was what the scriptures said; surely God would help her overcome the fault of jealousy in herself.

Angela made a reference in passing to one of the sad stories she had told at the baseball game. By way of self-mortification, Marguerite said, "You know, Angela, I really admire you."

"Me? Why?"

"Because even though you've had to go through all kinds of hard things in your life, you've kept on going. And not just that, you've managed to stay such a sweet, nice person through it all. You should win a prize or something."

Angela laughed. "Aw, thanks, you're sweet. Too bad they don't give out prizes for niceness."

"They should. I'd totally vote for you."

Later they talked about what books they'd each read most recently. Angela had read a historical romance, and John was reading about primate research in psychology. Marguerite was still working away at *The Magic Mountain*, but talked about *Anna Karenina*. She'd liked the writing and the characters, but found it dispiriting to read about adultery.

"Yeah, well, Tolstoy's kind of old-fashioned," John said. "A little adultery never hurt anyone."

What a terrible thing to say, thought Marguerite. Aloud, she said, "I can't even tell if you're being facetious or not. Is that another one of your jokes? Adultery has destroyed half the marriages in America. To me that seems like hurt enough."

"Yeah, well, but were they marriages worth saving?"

"Sure they were," said Marguerite, with conviction. "If people would only use a little restraint, for goodness sake."

"Hey, I'm not saying *I'd* go out and commit adultery," John said. "I'm very restrained." He looked back and forth between Marguerite and Angela, as if to ask, *Aren't I?*

Marguerite looked back at him, considering it. Of course, you could never tell if a person was restrained or not unless you happened to know what he wanted to do that he was restraining himself from doing. But she supposed she could take his word for it. If a person thought of himself as restrained, in all likelihood he was. She wondered if he was restraining himself with Angela, who would certainly be at his disposal if he gave any sign of wanting it. And with Marguerite—was he restrained with her, too? Could he tell she'd passed the tipping point?

At any rate, she couldn't picture him using the sort of tactics on anyone that his friend Damon had used on her during their epic conversation at the bar the previous week. Unlike Damon, John fought fair. He wasn't the sort to try to talk a girl out of believing in God by telling her she had beautiful eyes (which had been so dangerously effective in Marguerite's case).

So she nodded at him.

Toward the end, when they'd been there for three hours

without getting much studying done, the conversation came back to Marguerite's thinking about faith.

"I had a new thought," she told them. "Maybe it's not faith that's hard for me, but my belief system that's hard to swallow. Maybe faith is sort of the sugar that makes the medicine go down, if you see what I mean."

"Ah," said John. "Interesting. I could see that. But then the question is, how do you justify your faith in that belief system? Why have faith in that belief system, and not a different one?"

"I was thinking about that. There's a scripture in the Book of Mormon that makes an argument about why to have faith and how to justify it."

"An argument? In the Mormon scriptures? This should be interesting. What does it say?"

"Well, I don't have it memorized exactly. But hold on, I think I've got my Book of Mormon with me." And she bent down to rummage through the disorderly contents of her overfull backpack, in which there was also her copy of Thomas Mann and a number of piano books, besides her German things.

"You carry a Book of Mormon around with you?" asked Angela.

"Well, sometimes, or the Bible. You never know when you might need them. Ah, here it is." She opened the leather-bound book and flipped through the gilt-edged pages until she found the passage she'd been thinking of. She read it aloud to them.

"'Behold, if ye will awake and arouse your faculties, even to an experiment on my words, and exercise a particle of faith, yea, even if ye can no more than desire to believe, let this desire work in you, even until ye believe in a manner that ye can give place for a portion of my words.

"'Now, we will compare the word unto a seed ... if ye give place that a seed may be planted in your heart, behold, if it be a true seed, or a good seed, if ye do not cast it out by your unbelief, that ye will resist the Spirit of the Lord, behold, it will begin to swell within your breasts; and when you feel these swelling motions, ye will begin to say within yourselves—it must needs be that this is a good seed, or that the word is good, for it beginneth to enlarge my soul; yea, it beginneth to enlighten my understanding, yea, it beginneth to be delicious to me.'"

Marguerite looked up from the book. "It goes on like that for a while, but mainly it says your faith grows as the seed sprouts and starts to grow. The more the seed grows, the more you realize it's a good seed, and when you get to the point of being sure, your faith is replaced with knowledge and goes dormant."

"Huh," said John. "I don't know if I'd call that an argument exactly."

"Well, it's arguing that if you do the experiment of having faith, you'll gradually get knowledge. Do you think that's plausible?"

"I don't know. I'd have to think it through. Hey, do you know what we could do? We could outline it and go through it up on the board." He got up out of his chair and went to the blackboard that hung on one wall. "How does it go again?"

"What's that you're doing?" asked Angela, looking up from her German worksheet.

"We want to map out the argument to make it easier to see the logical structure of it."

Marguerite began reading the passage over again. As she read, John wrote out quickly on the board:

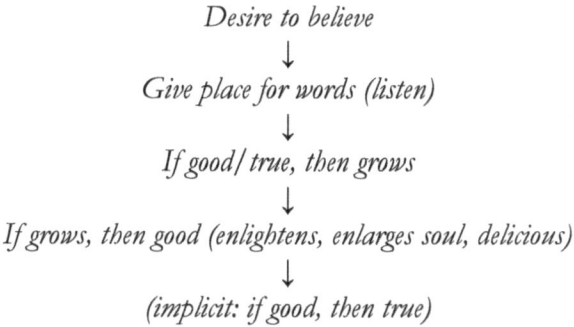

Desire to believe
↓
Give place for words (listen)
↓
If good/true, then grows
↓
If grows, then good (enlightens, enlarges soul, delicious)
↓
(implicit: if good, then true)

When he was done, he stepped back to admire his handiwork. "Does that look about right to you?" he asked.

"Yeah," said Marguerite happily, "That's it, I think. So does it work? It looks good to me. Is there anything wrong with it?"

"It's kind of circular. If it's good then it grows, and if it grows then it's good. And it conflates the good and the true. Nah, I don't think it works at all. Plenty of things are true without being good, and plenty of statements sound good and might make you feel happy, without being true. See what I mean?"

Marguerite despondently agreed. "But do you know—" she began, and then broke off.

"Know what?"

"Nothing—it'll sound weird and fanatical if I say this."

"No, go ahead. What were you going to say?"

"Yeah, now you've got us curious," said Angela.

"I was just going to say... I've seen real power in faith. Things that *could* be coincidence but were so unlikely it's hard not to draw a connection."

"Like what?" asked Angela.

"I was thinking of one story in particular that happened in my dorm last year. It's kind of a long one, though."

"Go ahead."

"There were these two girls on my floor who were roommates, Juliette and Esther. Juliette and I were friends, and one night she came to me crying. She was freaked out because her roommate Esther had just had sex with her fiancé—Esther's fiancé wasn't a BYU student or active in the Church, and apparently he had talked her into it.

"Of course, that won't sound like a big thing to you guys, but at BYU, it was a very big thing. If Esther got found out, she would have been kicked out of school. When you go to school there you sign an agreement saying you'll live by the rules of the Church. And not only that, you're also supposed to report it if you know other people are breaking the rules. The person who breaks a rule can go to their bishop and confess, and they might be able to work through it and not get kicked out. But Esther wasn't planning on going to the bishop. Juliette wasn't about to turn Esther in, but she was disgusted at what she'd done and hated feeling like she was responsible for knowing about it."

"Wow, I didn't realize that kind of thing was such a big deal at BYU. That's crazy," said Angela. "So what happened?"

"Well, I didn't know what advice to give her. We decided we'd both fast and pray that Esther would change her mind and go to the bishop. The amazing thing was, it worked. Every church lesson that Sunday was on chastity. And then there was a huge fireside—at BYU, that's like a devotional speech, given by one of the main church authorities, with all 18 stakes, meaning 30,000 students. The topic of the fireside was published in advance, but at the last minute the speaker decided to change it and talk about chastity instead. The next day, Esther went and talked to the bishop.

"Of course, at the end of the year, she transferred to another school anyway. But it was just amazing the way it all happened. It was hard to believe that was just by chance."

"Wow," said John. "That doesn't convince me at all, but it's a really interesting story. So all she had to do was confess, and she didn't get kicked out?"

"Not exactly. She had to repent. It's a whole process in Mormonism, and how it works depends on how serious the sin is. But for her it meant going to the bishop and getting advice and counsel, and then typically you'd have to pray and ask God for forgiveness, and sincerely regret having committed the sin, and promise not to do it again."

"I remember you saying Mormons weren't allowed to have sex before marriage, but I didn't get how serious it was. That she'd get kicked out of school for it, and it'd be such a drama," said John.

"Yeah, well. Mormons do take this whole chastity thing really seriously."

"But ... that means I could never be Mormon." John sounded strangely forlorn, as though it were some club he might have been interested in joining, but hadn't realized how exclusive it was.

"You could," Marguerite said, trying to sound positive. "You might have to, um, repent a little."

John still looked sad and seemed lost in thought.

"Whoa, look at the time," said Angela. "It's 9:30 already. I've got to get home."

Their study session broke up. Outside, Angela left them first. Marguerite had parked far away, so John offered her a ride to her car. When they were alone in the car together and John had begun driving, he still seemed meditative and melancholy. She tried to cheer him up.

"Thanks for going through that argument with me up on the board the way you did, and helping me think it through," she said. "It was cool how you outlined it, and it all got clearer. You know, sometimes I feel like you're an intensive course all by yourself, and I'm learning as much from you as from the German class."

John smiled. Marguerite went on.

"I actually wrote a poem about you today."

"You did, huh?" John's grin was back now; her words were having their intended effect. "I didn't know you wrote poetry."

"Not so often. Every now and then when the inspiration strikes."

"So I inspired you, did I? What did your poem say about me?"

"Just that you're surprising. Like a building that's bigger inside than it looks from the outside. It's like you've got a large soul. You're a great soul, I think," she finished shyly. She wondered if she was going too far, afraid of sounding sentimental. But her leonine frankness, as usual, had already gotten the better of her, and it was too late to take it back.

He didn't laugh at her or seem to take offense, but only said in the same melancholy, half-joking, half-reproachful tone as before, "But ... I can't go to heaven, can I? Because I don't believe in God."

Marguerite was thoughtful. "I don't know. I think God judges everyone according to their desires. There's a scripture that says that. What do you think you'd desire—I mean, eternally? If you weren't going to be worm food, with worms crawling all over you in your grave and eating out your eyeballs. If you were going to stick around forever, what would you want?"

John thought for a while, then said quietly, "I think I'd just want to go on learning. And helping other people learn."

They had reached Marguerite's car by now, but were still sitting in John's car in the parking lot with the engine and lights off. Marguerite said, "Do you know we—Mormons, I mean—we don't exactly believe in heaven anyway. Not the kind of heaven where it's pearly gates and angels with wings and halos sitting around playing harps. That would be so boring, I've always thought. And who would want to go there, anyway?"

"So what do you believe in, if there's no heaven?"

"There are three kingdoms. The celestial, terrestrial, and telestial. The telestial is the lowest. That's for really bad people, the murderers and rapists and thieves and liars. Their punishment is having to continue existing alongside each other, without any of the good people, cut off from God, and not being able to progress beyond where they are. Kind of like in Sartre's *No Exit*."

"Wow, so Joseph Smith was kind of a closet existentialist?"

Marguerite laughed. "I guess so. Then there's the terrestrial kingdom, and that's for the people who were good and well-meaning, but never accepted the Gospel. Again, their main problem is that they can't really progress beyond where they are, and they're not together with God. The celestial kingdom is the best one."

"The cool place to be."

"Yeah. That's where you get to go if you accepted the Gospel and lived it faithfully. And you have to be married in a Mormon temple to get to the highest level of it, where you're in the presence of God and you have a chance at eternal progression. People can ultimately become gods and goddesses and create their own worlds and their own spirit children."

"That's nuts—I thought I'd heard something like that before, but I didn't know it was for real, that you really believed that. And you have to be *married* to get to the highest kingdom?"

"Not just married. Married to another Mormon, in a special temple ceremony only Mormons can be in."

"Jeez. So if you never get married, you're screwed?"

"Not quite. You can still hang out in the celestial kingdom. You just can't get to the highest level, which is called exaltation—the one where you become a god with your own world and all that."

John shook his head, but then admitted he could see the appeal of it. "Making your own world, being a god and all, that would be cool, obviously. It just doesn't seem fair to me that you have to be married, or even that you have to be Mormon to get there."

"You'd be good at the godhood thing, though. I'd go visit your world anytime," said Marguerite, smiling.

John looked out the window and gave a short, quiet laugh. Then he looked back over at her and said, "Well, I guess we'd better call it a night, huh?"

CHAPTER 9

KORIHOR COMES FOR DINNER

THE GROUP STUDY SESSIONS in the evenings continued, with John, Marguerite, and Angela as fixed constants and others joining them irregularly. They also went back to Mike's Place on Friday after class, and every Friday after that. They called it their *Stammtisch*, which Professor Liebmann had explained was a German tradition where you met up regularly with a circle of friends at a given bar to drink and talk.

Saturday morning, Marguerite called Angela and Pam and invited them to Sunday dinner at her house. She wanted to reciprocate for Angela planning the baseball game, and had fixed on this as the main form of entertainment she was able to provide. The girls accepted. Marguerite put off calling John, whose phone number she'd gotten from Angela. She waited until the afternoon to try him, thinking maybe he'd been out drinking the night before and would be sleeping in, hung over. When she finally called, he didn't pick up. She left a message on his answering machine and resigned herself to not hearing back from him. In her experience, boys rarely called back. But he returned her call two hours later and sounded genuinely pleased to be invited.

She must be a curiosity to him, she supposed, the way the Amish were to many people. Here he was, invited to dinner with a real live Mormon family; he'd be able to observe their peculiar customs up close. But no matter if his interest was principally anthropological, the important thing was that he was coming, and it gave her something to look forward to the rest of the day and during the long, dull three hours of church Sunday morning.

There was a wrinkle in her plans when, a couple of hours before everyone was due to arrive, Marguerite's mother told her she'd clean forgotten about signing up to feed the Mormon missionaries that night as well. The families in the ward were supposed to take turns feeding them dinner. It was expensive to serve a mission, and it helped save on living expenses when local families pitched in. There were four of them coming.

"Oh, no," breathed Marguerite, horrified.

"Oh, come on," said her mom. Mrs. Farnsworth (who generally thought of herself as Sister Farnsworth, as the women addressed each other at church) was a petite, round lady with a pretty face, a page-boy haircut, and a cheerful disposition. "The more the merrier," she said. "Your friends won't mind, will they? It's not like the missionaries are going to try to convert them."

"Won't they? Isn't that what they're there for?"

"No, of course not. They're just coming for dinner. It'll be fine, you'll see."

Marguerite doubted that. "My German class friends are totally going to think I invited them just to try to convert them. Maybe I should call them and tell them not to come."

"Well, do what you want. I'm making plenty of food, so it won't matter either way as far as that goes. But I think it'd be rude to cancel on them at the last minute. I'm sure it'll all be fine. Just relax."

Marguerite went off to her room to fret and think. In the end, she couldn't bear to uninvite them. She'd just have to use a certain amount of finesse to keep a safe distance between John and the missionaries, she decided.

The doorbell rang a little after 5:30, and Marguerite ran to see who it could be. The guests weren't supposed to arrive until half past six.

"You're early," she said in surprise when she opened the door to find John in front of her. She was still in her church clothes, a long skirt and short-sleeved cotton blouse. John was in jeans and a button-down shirt and stood there rubbing the back of his neck, looking embarrassed.

"Yeah. I was so afraid of being late I got here ten minutes ago," he admitted. "I was just going to drive around for a while, but that started to seem silly. So I decided I'd just come ring the doorbell."

Relief washed over her.

"I'm so glad you're here." She told him about the missionaries and how she'd been panicking over them coming.

John was unruffled. "That's fine. Don't worry about it. It could be interesting to meet them anyway."

To pass the time until the others got there, she took him on a tour of the house, which was an ordinary Tucson bungalow built in the seventies, with most of the floors in shag carpeting. When they came to Marguerite's bedroom, she hesitated at the door before opening it and letting him follow her in. Her parents had let her decorate and pick out furnishings for the room when she was in her early teens. It was painted light lavender, with one wall of cream paneling. There was cream-colored furniture and a lace-trimmed lilac-print bedspread. It was girly-looking, the sort of room that might have set Faust off singing an aria. (Marguerite had read *Faust* the year before while sitting on a bench on the highest level of the atrium in the fine arts building during a choral concert that was going on one level below. The sound of the choir had reverberated from the ceiling and walls all around her, and she'd cried for poor Margaret, seduced and abandoned by Faust.)

John didn't burst into an aria, but instead looked around the room and noticed the stack of books on her bedside table. He picked up the top one.

"*The Magic Mountain.* Is that any good?"

"Yeah, I'm liking it. You might like it too. There are a lot of philosophical parts. Come to think of it, I read something interesting in there the other day I wanted to show you—something about how we should view death." She took the thick paperback from him and flipped through the pages. When she found the passage, she read it aloud to him.

"'The only healthy and noble and indeed ... *religious* way in which to regard death is to perceive and feel it as a constituent part of life, as life's holy prerequisite, and *not* to separate it intellectually, to set it up in opposition to life, or, worse, to play it off against life in some disgusting fashion—for that is indeed the antithesis of a healthy, noble, reasonable, and religious view. The ancients decorated their sarcophagi with symbols of life and procreation, some of them even obscene. For the ancients, in fact, the sacred and the obscene were very often one and the same. Those people knew how to honor death. Death is to be honored as the cradle of life, the womb of renewal. Once separated from life, it becomes grotesque, a wraith—or even worse. For as an independent spiritual power, death is a very depraved force, whose wicked attractions are very strong and without doubt can cause the most abominable confusions of the human mind.'"

John sat down next to her on the bed when she began to read and nodded several times when she was finished.

"I just thought it was interesting," she explained, "because of how we were talking about death the other day, and you were saying you'd be worm food. Of course, your views aren't religious. But I was wondering which way of thinking is more 'healthy' in this sense—the idea that there's life after death, or the idea that death is the end and there's nothing after it. Which view separates death more from life?"

"Well," John said, "if you believe in life after death, it's like you don't believe in death at all. So that definitely seems to separate death more from life. It's like being in denial about it."

"But we believe in *spiritual* death ..."

"Yeah, that's the thing. Religions always tend to think in these kinds of dualistic terms. Life versus death, good versus evil, light versus dark, heaven and hell. But that just doesn't work. It's like seeing the world all in black and white. Life isn't really like that. It's in color, or at least, there are lots of shades of gray. And people aren't all good or evil, either. The way I see it, most people are basically decent, but everyone has their dark side."

Marguerite was quiet for a moment, thinking about her own dark side that no one knew about, the black holes in her past that had threatened to pull her in and crush her, hurting everyone around her. The idea of death as a depraved force of attraction was more familiar to her than she wanted to admit.

"What about you?" she asked him. "Do you have a dark side?"

"Oh yeah. I definitely do. Everyone does."

"But it's funny you say that about dualism. There's a Mormon scripture that says, *There must needs be an opposition in all things.* And I think with good reason; there are a lot of dualisms, a lot of dichotomies built right into nature. Male and female. Night and day. Up and down. It's only natural to think in those terms, isn't it?"

"It's not natural. Nature abhors a dichotomy. When you look closer, you see things are never that neat and binary. We all have 'masculine' and 'feminine' qualities in us in varying degrees. Even me, you could say I have some feminine qualities. I'm secure enough in my masculinity to admit that. Not that I'm gay or anything—believe me, I'm as heterosexual as they come. So to speak." He sniggered at his own joke, which Marguerite didn't get. "I'm just trying to say, it's not that simple—that's an overly simplistic way of seeing the world. If there's night and day, there's also dawn and twilight, eclipses, periods that are in between, complicating factors. And up and down are relative. It all depends on where you start from. And things in nature don't just come in opposed pairs, they come in ones and threes and fives and sevens ..."

"Okay, okay," Marguerite laughed, feeling she'd been bested. "I get it already." She set the Mann book back down on the bedside table and picked up the book that had been underneath it, her Book of Mormon. "There was something else I wanted to show you that I thought you might find interesting. It's a passage in the Book of Mormon. There's a guy who has arguments a lot like yours sometimes—kind of a philosopher. His name is Korihor. I was just thinking about it because we had a lesson on him today in church."

"Oh yeah? Korihor, okay, let's hear it."

She found the passage, but it was too long to read aloud, so she handed it to him to read silently. They were still sitting side by side on the edge of Marguerite's bed with its lace-trimmed cream and lilac–print bedspread. In the story, which she had read and heard so many times she knew it by heart, Korihor preached to a group of righteous people in the Book of Mormon. He was an atheist and proclaimed there was no God and no Christ. He said things like, *Oh ye that are bound down under a foolish and a vain hope, why do ye yoke yourselves with such foolish things? Why do ye look for a Christ? For no man can know of anything which is to come. Behold, these things which ye call prophecies, which ye say are handed down by holy prophets, behold, they are foolish traditions of your fathers. How do ye know of their surety? Behold, ye cannot know of things which ye do not see; therefore ye cannot know that there shall be a Christ. Ye look forward and say that ye see a remission of your sins.*

But behold, it is the effect of a frenzied mind; and this derangement of your minds comes because of the traditions of your fathers, which lead you away into a belief of things which are not so.

Korihor used such arguments to convince people they could do whatever they wanted and everything was permitted within the bounds of worldly prudence. Everyone "fared in this life according to the management of the creature, prospered according to his genius, and conquered according to his strength." When you were dead that was it. No divine judgments in the hereafter.

People believed his arguments and started committing "whoredoms," which basically meant a free love-fest ensued. Korihor's libertine doctrines were so popular he got arrested and sent to the top religious and political leader, Alma. In the chapter that describes their meeting, Alma and Korihor have a strange philosophical argument where Alma tries to get Korihor to admit he really does believe in God but has been lying to everyone just to trick them and make trouble. Korihor insists he genuinely doesn't believe and only will if Alma shows him a sign. So Alma does. He asks God to strike Korihor dumb, and God apparently thinks it's a good idea, because He complies.

Korihor, now aphasic, confesses in writing that Alma was right all along. He knew God existed, but allowed himself to be deceived by the devil disguised as an angel of light. In the end he gets kicked out of Alma's palace and becomes a beggar. All the people who believed his phony atheism realize the error of their ways and repent of their whoredoms. Korihor wanders off to an area populated by less nice people than Alma's, where he gets run over and trampled to death.

Every time Marguerite read the first part of the story, she was struck anew by the bleak persuasiveness of Korihor's arguments, which didn't need the devil disguised as an angel of light to stand on their own. They were strong enough to remain disturbing even with that absurd ending tacked on. Korihor was winning the argument with Alma before brute miraculous force intervened.

As Marguerite recalled the arguments now, she felt her old fear of the abyss return. Through them she glimpsed a world where what you could manage on your own was all you had, where there was no merciful higher law, no beautiful soul within you to make you still valuable even if you lacked outward beauty, genius, or strength. In that world, there was no Eternal Father looking out for you. Everything was permitted; there was no protection for weak and fragile people like herself. It was a gray, heartless, desolate world, of which she wanted no part.

John's arguments led straight into this heartless world; they were Korihor's. Yet John himself didn't seem bleak or heartless or desolate. The world in him she had envisioned through the lens of her poem was benevolent if unyielding and sunlit though also shadowed and labyrinthine, with its intimations of depth and danger. In giving John the story of Korihor, what she wanted was for him to explain to her how this could be, to tell her what his and Korihor's world looked like from the inside.

John was still sitting quietly next to her on the side of the bed, reading with the book spread open between his hands in his lap. The book looked small and flimsy in his large hands. He hadn't yet finished the chapter about Korihor when the doorbell rang. It was 6:30, and the other dinner guests were arriving all at once: Angela, Pam, and the four missionaries. Marguerite rushed to the door to meet the girls and pull them inside to make her hasty explanations and apologies as to why the missionaries happened to be there too.

In the end, there were twelve of them at the table, which meant both the spare table leaves had to be pulled out. Marguerite sat with John, Angela, and Pam at one end, with her brother Max and sister Cate next to them, then the four missionaries, and her parents at the far end.

The missionaries wore dark suits and ties with white shirts, and all had short, neat, corporate-looking haircuts. They were introduced as Elders Jensen, Whitaker, Andersen, and Lopez. As soon as everyone was seated, John turned to Marguerite and whispered, "Hey, aren't they a little young to be called elders? How old are they, twenty, maybe? I feel funny calling someone an elder who's younger than me."

Marguerite giggled.

Mrs. Farnsworth, at the head of the table, cleared her throat. "We should say a blessing on the food." Marguerite saw 15-year-old Cate, who was sitting next to her on the right, roll her eyes. Across from Marguerite, Max, who was a high school senior, heaved a stoical sigh. "Brad, why don't you say it?" Mrs. Farnsworth asked her husband.

Dr. Farnsworth wasn't the most articulate prayer-giver, but was often asked to say prayers because of the speed and efficiency with which he did it. He folded his arms, closed his eyes, and bowed his head. The rest of the Mormons at the table did the same. Angela clasped her hands in front of her, and John and Pam remained as they were, looking confused and uneasy.

John leaned over quickly and whispered in Marguerite's ear, "Is it rude if I don't do the prayer part?"

Marguerite had just enough time to shake her head and whisper, "No, you're fine," before Dr. Farnsworth began the prayer.

"Dear Heavenly Father," he said in swift monotone, "we thank Thee for this food that we are about to eat, please bless it so that it will nourish and strengthen our bodies, we're thankful the elders and Marguerite's friends could be here to share it with us, too, in the name of Jesus Christ, Amen."

"Amen," the missionaries and Marguerite's family repeated.

"Amen," Angela chimed in, a second or two late.

"So, Elder Jensen," said Mrs. Farnsworth brightly, when everyone had settled themselves and started in on the food, "where are you from? I was wondering if you might be related to the Jensens in the Tucson Stake."

Elder Jensen was by far the most handsome of the missionaries, with limpid brown eyes framed by long dark lashes and a boyish face with a cleft chin. He yawned, revealing a set of perfect white teeth.

"Excuse me," he said, covering his mouth. "I'm from Littleton, Colorado. And I think we probably are distantly related, although I'm not positive. We'd have to compare our genealogical records, I guess."

Elder Whitaker yawned loudly, too. "Sorry, it must be catching," he said. Elder Anderson was rubbing his eyes with pale, freckled hands, and Elder Lopez, who was small and dark-skinned, was staring straight ahead as if in a trance.

"You guys look pretty tired," said Dr. Farnsworth.

"Yeah," said Elder Whitaker, "it's been a long week." He raised his bony, tanned arms above his head in another yawn, and the edges of his temple garments peeked through the armholes of his short-sleeved white button-down shirt. "Gosh, now I can't stop. And I'm not even in a food coma yet."

"Don't worry, you will be," said Cate, "if my mom has anything to do with it."

The elders laughed and all four of them turned their eyes worshipfully on Cate, who was looking inordinately pretty with her honey-colored hair pulled up in a messy topknot, wearing a tight-fitting pink v-neck tee shirt that showed a hint of cleavage.

"Has the mission president been working you too hard?" Mrs. Farnsworth asked.

"Oh, no worse than usual," said Elder Jensen, reluctantly turning his eyes from Cate to the other end of the table. "It's just, you know, a *lot* of knocking on doors."

"A lot of shaking hands, a lot of biking in the heat, a lot of talking ..." Elder Whitaker added.

"Sunup to sundown," said Elder Jensen. "That's the way it goes."

"Although we do get a lot of referrals from the members here," Elder Whitaker said. "And thank goodness for p-day and basketball." Elder Whitaker was tall and looked like someone you'd want on your basketball team.

"What's 'p-day'?" John asked in Marguerite's ear.

She whispered back, "It's their preparation day, the one day of the week they get off."

Dr. Farnsworth had served a mission in Argentina in the sixties and still spoke fluent Spanish. Upon learning that Elder Lopez was from the state of Monterrey in Mexico, the doctor tried to draw him into a conversation in Spanish, but Elder Lopez demurred. In a heavy accent and a voice that was barely audible, he explained that his English was not very good, but he was determined to speak as little Spanish as possible in hopes of improving it.

"So, Max, do you play basketball?" Elder Whitaker asked, leaning around Elder Jensen. "You look like you could give us a run for our money."

This was true enough, but Max had no interest in sports, Marguerite knew. His dream, as far as she could gather, was to learn to play drums in a Straight Edge punk band, write novels in the style of Jack Kerouac, and paint pictures in the style of Edvard Munch's *The Scream*.

"Nope, sorry," Max said.

"Do you follow the Wildcats?" Mrs. Farnsworth asked Elder Whitaker. "We usually get season tickets. Just Brad and I—the kids aren't that interested."

"Sure," said Elder Whitaker, "I used to, that is. They're a good team. Of course, we can't watch games on TV, so I pretty much missed the whole last season."

"Oh, that's right, of course, I forgot," said Mrs. Farnsworth.

Elder Whitaker sighed. Elder Anderson, who was from farm country in Idaho and had been up at Ricks College, a Mormon-owned community college in Rexburg, for a year before leaving on his mission, asked Mrs. Farnsworth's opinion of the BYU Cougars' prospects for the coming season, and before long he, Elder Whitaker, and Marguerite's parents were absorbed in a long, intense conversation about college basketball teams. Meanwhile, at the other end of the table, the conversation turned to German class gossip and quickly became lively. John cracked jokes continuously, keeping Marguerite, Pam, Angela, and even Cate and Max in peals of laughter.

When the meal was finished, the missionaries broke into another round of yawning and eye-rubbing and soon made for the front door. Mrs. Farnsworth trailed after them with promises of U of A basketball paraphernalia, asking what sweatshirt sizes they all wore. There were few things Mrs. Farnsworth enjoyed more than buying things for people, and Marguerite was tempted to warn them they were in for a deluge of everything from logoed socks to red-and-blue Christmas ornaments.

Instead, she and John and the other two girls waved goodbye, then helped bring all the empty dishes into the kitchen. John turned the water on in the sink and started rinsing dishes to put in the dishwasher, but Mrs. Farnsworth bustled in and shooed him away. Marguerite led them outside through the back patio to sit on lawn chairs on the deck beside the pool and watch the sunset. It was a good one, with all the brilliant shades of orange, red, pink, yellow, lavender, and indigo you could ask for.

"So how do I get a date with one of those missionaries?" asked Pam. "They were pretty cute, especially that Jensen one. Could you maybe set me up with one of them? We could do a double date or something. It seemed like there were enough to go around."

Marguerite laughed. "You have a one-track mind, Pam. *No,* they're not allowed to date at all. They have to be completely celibate for two years. They're not even allowed to use the telephone to call girls. They're only supposed to write to their families once a week, on their p-day. They do get to write letters to their girlfriends back home, too, but they're not supposed to write too much or too often."

"Oh, that explains it," said John.

"Explains what?"

"I was wondering why your parents weren't pushing you to talk to them more. I would've thought they'd want their daughter dating someone like that. So, what was with them leaving so early? I was kind of disappointed I didn't get the chance to talk more with them."

"I don't know, I think it's part of their mission rules. They're not supposed to hang out socially after meals with members, or something like that. They have a lot of rules. They're very focused and dedicated. Anyway, I was actually relieved you didn't get into a discussion with them."

"Why? Oh, come on, I would've been good. And it would have been interesting for me."

Marguerite made a doubtful-sounding noise.

When the sunset had faded, they went back inside, and the four of them squeezed onto a couch in the living room to look at Marguerite's photo albums from high school and her first year of college.

It was so pleasant for Marguerite, sitting crowded cozily on the couch, chatting with these friends who were so lively and funny and kind and finding herself the center of attention for once, that she wished the evening would never end. It was all because of John, she thought. Wherever he was, there was excitement, laughter, and tension.

He was the last to leave, and as he stood at the door she asked him to wait a moment. She dashed to a bookshelf where several extra copies of the Book of Mormon stood, awaiting evangelical opportunities to be given away. Grabbing one, she returned to where he stood in the doorway and held the book out to him.

"Would you like a copy of the Book of Mormon?" she asked breathlessly.

He chuckled, shook his head, and said kindly but firmly, "No. I'll never read it. Give it to someone else."

Marguerite's shoulders slumped in disappointment. Only then did she realize how badly she'd wanted him to say yes. "I'm sorry," she said miserably, "I just thought it might interest you."

"Oh, all right then," he said. "Sure. I'll take a copy."

"Are you sure?" Marguerite felt worse now, realizing she'd pressured him into taking it just to avoid hurting her feelings.

"Yeah, I'm sure," he said and took the book from her hands, with its shiny gold-painted cover and the strange symbols squiggling down the front and back of it.

Marguerite put a finger to her lips and said, "Shh," as though he were supposed to keep quiet about it. Why she did this, she wasn't sure. The action somehow seemed to fit the extreme awkwardness of the moment.

"Is it supposed to be a secret?" he whispered back.

"No ... I just feel embarrassed." She was whispering too.

"Why?"

"I don't know," she admitted, her face flushing scarlet to the tips of her ears.

"Don't be embarrassed. It's okay." His tone was soothing. "There's nothing to be embarrassed about." And Marguerite felt relieved, as though she'd been granted absolution. "Good night," he said. "Sleep well. I'll see you tomorrow morning in class. And thanks again for inviting me. I really enjoyed it."

He left with the book in his hand.

When he had gone, she went to her mom and thanked her for having made such a good dinner. She asked what she'd thought of her friends.

"They were really nice. I liked your friend John especially. He reminded me of Mark Tierney, the way he's so talkative and cheerful and full of stories. And they all seemed to have a good time. You see, and you were so worried."

"I think they had a nice time, too. And so did I." She hugged her mom, gave her a kiss on the cheek, and went to get ready for bed. She lay awake for a long time before she fell asleep, thinking over the evening. Her happiness was mixed with sadness, because it was clear John would never be anything but completely opposed, diametrically opposed, to religion. And yet, she thought, with God nothing was impossible. He worked in mysterious ways, and you never knew what miracles might be wrought ...

Why did she want a miracle so badly, specifically for John? Because if, miraculously, he were not so opposed to religion and could become Mormon, and if a hundred other circumstances were different—if both of them were older, if they went to the same school, if they lived in the same town, if she weren't going back to Utah in six weeks, if she were prettier and had smooth, shiny hair like a girl in a shampoo commercial, if he could ever care for her as more than a friend—she thought he would be a good person to marry. If she could take her pick of what to do throughout eternity, or at least for the rest of her life, it would be talking and listening to him, learning from him and learning with him.

It was too bad that, barring a miracle, it could never happen, as she knew too well. But this was the second of three epiphanies she had concerning John. The first epiphany had been that she wanted to have sex with him. Now, six days later, she realized she wished she could marry him.

CHAPTER 10

AN INTERVIEW AND THREE ESSAYS

THE NEXT MORNING IN class, Professor Liebmann divided the students into pairs and assigned them to interview one another in German. ("John and Marguerite, why don't you two work together?" he'd said with a cheerful leer. Marguerite had lately begun to suspect Professor Liebmann of having a secret penchant for matchmaking.) The interviewer had to find out the interviewee's opinions on a number of controversial topics, including marriage, abortion, and sex education.

"Okay," said John, with evident relish. "I'm going to be the interviewer, and you have to answer the questions." He began to go through the list of topics. Naturally, Marguerite told him in response to his questioning, she didn't believe in abortion, but felt sex education was a good thing, particularly with a view to preventing the sort of circumstances that led to people having abortions.

It wasn't long before John moved on to the subject of marriage.

"Have you ... met the man you're going to marry?" he asked in ungrammatical German.

It wasn't one of the questions she'd been expecting. *Had* she met the man she was going to marry?

"Maybe," she said, smiling and looking into his eyes. He looked back at her for a moment without saying anything. She could almost see the gears turning in his head as he worked out what she might mean, and her stomach flip-flopped. She looked down and fidgeted nervously in her seat. Shoot, shoot, that was a big mistake. Oh, Lord, she had to get a grip. If he guessed she'd been fantasizing about marrying him, she'd never live down the embarrassment. She groaned inwardly. *I'm living in a dream world.* "Dream world" was a phrase John used often. Whenever he thought people were crazy or deluding themselves, he'd say it loudly, as though it were all one word—*Dreamworld!*—and shake his head.

After a pause, John cleared his throat and asked, "Why aren't you married already?"

Marguerite groped for an answer in her limited German, and at last said haltingly, "Because ... I'm still very young. I still have a lot of studying and ... and other things to do before I can get married."

"And ... when would you want to get married?" he asked. "I mean, how old would you be, ideally?"

She could feel her face starting to redden. Oh Lord, not good.

"I don't know ..." she said. "It depends on the man, and when he wants to. And of course, it depends on when I meet him."

"When you meet the *right* man," said John, with an odd, almost savage gleam in his eye.

"*Ja,*" she laughed. "*Herr Recht.*"

WHEN THE interview was over, Marguerite sighed and rested her cheek against one hand with her elbow propped up on her desk. It would be so nice if only John had been asking those questions because he really wanted to know the answers. If only he were living in the same dream world as she was and had experienced the same epiphany, so that he saw her now as a potential *Frau Recht.* But of course, the idea was ludicrous. To him the exchange could only have been a joke, a prime opportunity to tease her and make her blush.

Hoping to dislodge all the stupid ideas that were making such a nuisance of themselves in her brain, she sat up and gave herself three good knocks on the side of her head with the palm of her hand. John watched her do it and laughed, meeting her eyes, almost as if he knew exactly what she'd been thinking.

It was a strange day. Angela seemed out of sorts and said she wasn't feeling well. As Marguerite was in the habit of taking everything personally, she worried it was her fault for taking up too much of John's attention, when probably Angela was still as infatuated with him as ever.

Professor Liebmann handed back the results of their last exam. Marguerite got a perfect score, Angela got a 95, and John had an 86.

"Damn," he said, sucking the air in between his teeth. "I *hate* getting B's. What did you two get?" Marguerite tried to hide her exam under her notebook, but John was too quick and saw the score written at the top. "What? Damn it, I'm going to have to work harder. It's aggravating; we've been studying a lot, haven't we? I just don't seem to have an ear for German. You do, though, I can tell," he said to Marguerite. "Your pronunciation sounds a lot more like Professor Liebmann's than mine. Man, it's really frustrating not to be good at this. It's driving me crazy."

Marguerite tried to say consoling, encouraging things while she looked over her exam. At the end they'd had to write a ten-sentence essay, either on how to help homeless people, or describing their dream man or dream woman, or composing a short fairy tale. Marguerite had picked the second option and had written in her awkward German:

My dream man would be a little unusual. First he would have to show himself a true friend for a long time. It would be especially important for us to be able to talk and understand each other easily. When I say a 'true' friend, I don't mean true so much in the sense of loyal (treu), but in the sense of genuine (echt). To me that means we could both be independent. We could argue, even fight sometimes over ideas, but we would both have to love truth. We would always look for truth together—in each other or through each other or out in the world. Then it would be a true union. And the goal of the relationship would be to help our spirits grow. But it's only a dream, which I shouldn't forget.

FOR HOMEWORK, Professor Liebmann asked them to write a short fairy tale, a *Märchen*, and turn it in the next day. When Marguerite got home, she wrote:

Once upon a time, a quite ordinary girl was walking through the woods. She happened to be a princess, although you couldn't tell just from looking at her. She wasn't beautiful or ugly, just normal-looking. In any case, that day she happened to meet a prince. "Guten Tag!" said the prince, who looked exactly like a prince. They began a pleasant conversation. But soon the princess found him boring, because her intellect was of a philosophical nature. Then a thief came along and robbed the prince. The princess began a conversation with the thief. She found him more intelligent than the prince and fell in love with him, so they got married and had a lot of children.

ON TUESDAY, when class let out for the break, Marguerite made a beeline for the bathroom. When she came back, John was standing under one of the spindly trees in the courtyard by himself, smoking a cigarette. She headed over to talk to him. He greeted her and asked how her day was going, then said, "Hey, you know, I almost called you last night to see if you wanted to study together or go see a movie or something."

"You almost did? Why didn't you?"

"I ended up going out drinking with Damon instead. You remember him?"

"Of course. How could I not remember Damon?"

They moved on to talking about other things, and before long the break was up, but Marguerite's mind was racing. So he'd thought about her, and he'd thought about getting together, just the two of them. It might not be a marriage proposal, or even a sign that he wanted to sleep with her, but it was a start.

Then she thought, *Dreamworld! You're dreaming, Marguerite, wake up.* Almost was the operative word here. He almost had, but then hadn't. Going drinking with Damon had been more appealing. It was practically an insult when you thought about it: she'd been his second choice. But still it was a flattering sort of insult, which was confusing.

Why would you tell someone you'd *almost* called them? She tried to puzzle out what motives a person could have for saying such a thing. Perhaps he hadn't been sure she'd want to see him one on one like that, without the usual crowd of friends around them. Maybe he was testing the waters, to see what she thought of the idea. But the concept of John being shy or unsure of himself in any situation was hard to wrap her mind around. Particularly with her, when she was clearly so attached to him, leaning toward him during all the hours they spent together each day like a sunflower following the sun.

In any case, it didn't matter, since he couldn't possibly be interested in anything but friendship. Probably he'd only wanted to study with her because she'd done so well on her test.

A FEW hours after Marguerite had settled this in her mind, she found herself thoroughly confused again. After class she and John and the others went to the library for a short group study session. When they finished and were walking down a corridor on their way out, John put his arm around her. They walked along for several steps like that, and then he turned it into a hug, giving her a squeeze and releasing her.

She tensed at his touch. People rarely touched her that way, especially not guys, and she didn't know how to react. She felt as though she couldn't breathe at first, but at the same time intensely happy. And when he let her go, she felt bewildered.

"John," she sputtered, turning to look at him, "that was ... kind of affectionate."

He grinned, looking away and laughing, as though he'd won some kind of victory.

What was that? A friendly hug, she told herself. It was just a friendly hug; friends hugged each other. But she felt weak, frightened, and muddled, as though she were stumbling pell mell, blindly, toward another abyss.

PROFESSOR LIEBMANN assigned them yet another essay for Wednesday and again gave them a list of three topics to choose from. When Marguerite settled herself in at the kitchen table to write that evening, she picked "Heiraten zwischen Religion" as her subject—marriage between different religions. She wrote:

The problem of marriage between different religions is important to me. I love my faith, but I've noticed no boys in my church are interested in me. I'm still young, but I'm getting older, and sometimes I'm afraid I'll never marry. So the question becomes, would I accept a compromise if a man who believed something different from what I believe loved me, and if I loved him too? This is difficult. You might say if two people love each other, they can accept each other's differences and can learn a lot in the process. The disadvantage is, if they have children, they don't know which church they should go to. That can work like a wedge in the marriage, and can destroy it or tear it apart. I believe there has to be more than just love to keep a marriage from coming apart. It might be a shared love for God, or for truth, but whatever you call it, it's still something like religion. You have to have something like that in common to build a happy marriage.

———

On Wednesday, she turned her essay in. There was no study group planned for that evening, and she and the others went their separate ways after class without lingering to talk. Later that afternoon, Marguerite paced around the living room for half an hour. Finally, she went into the kitchen, picked up the phone, and dialed John's number. When he answered, her heart thudded loudly in her chest. She asked if he'd like to study together that evening.

"Oh—tonight?" he said. "I've already got plans for tonight, so I can't. I'm sorry. But we could get together and study tomorrow. Do you want to do that? I could come over to your house. Should we say around four?"

Marguerite said this plan suited her fine.

"But … don't tell the others, okay?" John said. "Because, you know, then they'll want to study with us and we won't get anything done."

Marguerite was fine with that, too.

CHAPTER 11

THE THIRD EPIPHANY

MARGUERITE SPENT THE NEXT morning in a state of nervous excitement. In class and during the break, John made no mention or acknowledgement of their plans for the afternoon, and by the time class let out, Marguerite was starting to wonder if she hadn't just dreamed the whole thing. She sidled up to him as they were walking out, and asked, "John, are you still—?" He nodded before she could get the question out and winked at her conspiratorially.

Relieved, she waved goodbye and went home to wait.

He was early again. When the doorbell rang, she ran to open the door, and there he stood, filling the space with his tall frame, hands in his pockets, smiling down at her.

He followed her in and they sat at the old pale green formica kitchen counter, where Marguerite usually did her homework perched on one of the tall bar seats with her legs curled up under her. They made small talk for a while, then gradually settled down to work in their usual ratio of one part studying to three parts conversation.

John remarked on what an easy time Marguerite seemed to have with learning German. She told him she probably had an advantage from having already studied French in high school and college. She launched into a long story about the six weeks she'd spent in Paris the summer before in a language program for American students. She thought the trip would be terribly romantic, but instead she was homesick and got hopelessly lost every time she tried to go anywhere on the Métro. It was hot, the city stank, and she met no one apart from foreign tourists like herself and scary, swarthy men, who flocked like great dark birds around the courtyards of the Cité

Universitaire where she lived, staring with glittering black eyes at her and the other American girls as they passed by.

One day a kind young Algerian man began a polite conversation with her in the cafeteria and convinced her to go to Sacré-Coeur with him, only to insist on holding her hand and putting his arm around her on the Métro. When she pointed out that at seventeen she was a full ten years younger than him, he said, *"Mais l'âge n'a rien à voir avec l'amour,"* and was put out and mystified when she finally managed to ditch him.

John laughed loudly and appeared to enjoy the story immensely.

From language-learning abilities the topic of conversation moved on to intelligence generally—the different types of it, and how it manifested itself. John admitted to a fair amount of confidence in his own high intelligence. But he looked at Marguerite thoughtfully for a long moment and at last said, "You know, though, I think you might be smarter than me." As soon as he'd said it, he smacked himself in the forehead. "Damn, why'd I say that?"

Marguerite laughed, but looked back at him for several long moments herself, considering whether it could be true. She'd be disappointed if it were. She wanted him to be superior to her, to be able to look up to him. But she was afraid on some level he might be right. Certainly when it came to learning German there was no contest. At last she decided he wouldn't be able to frighten her the way he did sometimes if they weren't close to being equals, and perhaps she was very much in his shadow when it came to certain other areas of knowledge.

She opened her mouth to say this, but he stopped her.

"Don't," he said. "You're too honest sometimes. I never know what's going to come out of your mouth."

Marguerite stared at him, not knowing whether to laugh or feel hurt. Finally she laughed, said, "okay," and turned back to her German homework.

When they'd finished their worksheets, they moved to the living room floor to study irregular verbs, both of them leaning back against the coffee table and laying their flashcards out on the floor.

"Anyway," Marguerite said, as she doled out her cards, "being intelligent doesn't help anyone if they don't care about things that really matter. At least you care about important stuff, like truth and reason and all that. Well, that's the impression I get from you, anyway. And that's the most important thing. I really admire you for it."

"I do care about truth and reason and all that. It's probably what I care about most."

They talked about what truth could mean and what it meant to look for it, and about faith and how it might relate to truth. They talked until the shadows started getting long across the driveway and the front yard, strips of light and dark weaving through the tangle of cactuses, ocotillos, mesquites, and palo verde trees at the front of the house. Marguerite felt an awe unfolding inside her at the intimacy of this talk and their physical closeness sitting next to each other on the carpeted floor, as the late golden light of the desert evening poured in through the big living room windows. It was as though the borders that kept their two worlds separate were getting blurry around the edges and then pushing into and intersecting each other like the circles of a Venn diagram, creating a new category in the space where they overlapped. And there they sat, the two of them, in this newly created space together, searching for the same thing, truth.

The sunset began to erupt outside, glowing like currents of magma bubbling up over the rim of the mountains. John went out and stood on the front patio to smoke a cigarette, leaving the door open behind him. Marguerite went to the piano, an old black upright of her mother's that stood in the living room across from the windows. She played a Brahms intermezzo, a piece with a yearning, sad melody floating over a quietly rippling undertow of dark, low arpeggios. When she had finished, she heard the crunch of John's feet on the gravel outside, coming in from the driveway. Seized by a fit of shyness, she fled into the kitchen. She stood on the inner side of the counter near the sink, leaning over the counter onto her elbows. John found her like that as he came in from the other end of the room and stood on the opposite side of the counter with his hands on one of the chair backs. He looked at her with a slightly dazed expression for a moment or two, then pulled the chair out and sat down.

"You know," he said, "sitting out there with the sunset and the breeze, listening to you play—it was ... borderline romantic."

Marguerite blushed a deep pink. Looking away and laughing,

she said, "Give me a break." She looked back over at him, and he was grinning in a way that made her stomach flip. What would he do, she wondered, if she came up behind him where he was sitting, put her arms around him, and leaned her head against his shoulder?

Instead, she asked, "Are you thirsty?"

"Yeah, I'm really thirsty. Could I have a glass of water?"

She filled a glass for him at the sink and then poured herself a glass of milk from the refrigerator. She sat down at the end of the counter next to him. They drank quietly, looking at each other. The silence and John's eyes on her were beginning to make her feel flustered and unsteady, when they heard a car drive up. Dr. Farnsworth was home from work.

"Hi Dad," she said, as her father shuffled in, setting his briefcase down and thumbing through the mail pile. "You remember John?"

Her dad looked up from the mail, as though he had only just noticed the two of them sitting there, and nodded affably. He worked such long hours that at home he had little energy left for social conversations, though he was always kind and even-tempered.

"Studying, huh?" Dr. Farnsworth said. "You guys getting lots of work done?"

Marguerite smiled and nodded as her dad handed her a postcard from Mark Tierney that had come in with the rest of the mail that afternoon. It had a Spanish stamp and a short scrawled note on the back, and on the front was a picture of a huge, spiky-looking church in Barcelona called the Sagrada Família.

"Oh, by the way," Dr. Farnsworth asked as she turned the postcard over in her hands, "have you seen the cordless phone?"

"I saw it," said John. "It's by the TV in the other room."

Dr. Farnsworth thanked him and shuffled off in the direction John had pointed him in.

When he was gone, John looked around with an air of contentment.

"It's nice being in a house like this, a real house. I hardly ever get to do that, except when I'm home visiting my mom on vacation. Most of the time I only get to see crappy student apartments. I like your house. It's sort of … homey, and comfortable."

Marguerite looked around her, trying to fathom what he could possibly see in it that pleased him. She'd always thought her parents' taste in decorating ran to the tacky and kitschy, with her mom's collection of angel figurines spilling out of all the corners and her dad's penchant for clocks and decorative objects made of polished driftwood.

"Well, I'm glad if *you* like it," she said.

"I got kind of a kick out of being able to tell your dad where the phone was just now," John admitted.

She laughed.

"So what do you want to do now?" he asked. "I think I'm kind of studied out for the time being."

They decided to get take-out food and rent a German movie from the video store. John drove them to the restaurant. When they came back to the car with their food, Marguerite looked in her wallet and saw it was nearly empty.

"Do you want to stop by an ATM?" she asked John. "I don't have enough money left to pay for my half of the movie rental."

"Oh, don't worry about it, I'll get it."

"Gosh, no, you don't have to do that."

"Seriously, it's fine."

"But it's no problem just to get some money out of the ATM. I'll pay my half." A note of anxiety was creeping into her voice. At a level not wholly conscious, she was convinced that if she allowed him pay the extra two dollars to cover her half of the movie rental, the evening would count as a date and she'd be morally obligated to let him kiss her, or possibly worse.

"Well, you can owe me if you feel that strongly about it," he laughed, "but a couple of bucks between friends is no big deal."

We're friends? she thought. *We're friends.* She breathed a sigh of relief. Nothing to worry about then, nothing at all.

They were hungry enough they decided to sit in the car and eat their food in the video store parking lot. While they were eating, John asked her questions about Mormonism and what it was like going to church. Marguerite told him about life at BYU, about how sincere and kind and glowing everyone was there, and how when one of the apostles of the Church came to give a talk, everyone went to hear it, and the giant indoor stadium on campus was filled to bursting like it might be for a rock concert or a big basketball game.

"Apostles," mused John. "I like that word, 'apostle.' It'd be sort of cool to be called an apostle. Although I think I like the word 'disciple' even better."

Marguerite smiled. "John the Apostle—has a nice ring to it. I like the word 'disciple,' too. It's from Greek, they told us once in Sunday school. Originally it meant a learner, someone who was willing to be taught. That's what the twelve apostles are called in the Book of Mormon—they're the twelve disciples instead of the twelve apostles, and they advise the prophet."

"So do you think you'd like to be a prophet or a disciple someday?"

Marguerite laughed. "Well, it doesn't quite work that way in the Church. It's a bit chauvinistic, I guess you'd say. Women don't get to have those kinds of roles. But in theory I could be 'a woman of God.' And I guess I could give birth to a disciple or prophet. Or I could marry one."

"That's too bad. Hey, maybe you could be a theologian. That'd be cool."

"You think so? I don't know. Mormons aren't really big on theology." They were quiet for several moments, chewing their food. "But I guess I have a while before I have to think about what I'm going to do when I grow up. I don't even turn nineteen for another two weeks."

"Yeah, you are young. You seem older though." There was another silence. Finally John shook his head. "It's just too bad—that you're not free, I mean."

"What do you mean I'm not free? You mean because of the Church? But I choose to go and do all that stuff."

"But I don't think you're really choosing it. I think you've been indoctrinated from birth to believe that's what you're supposed to do, and that's the real reason you do it."

Marguerite tried to consider this fairly. "Okay, maybe on some level there's something to that. But even if that were the case, what's so wrong with going to church? How do you think that would make me not free? How is that hurting anyone?"

"What I don't like about it is that it's like you've got some big long list in your head of things you can and can't do. Every time you want to do something, you have to run through that checklist of rules in your head and see if it's allowed or not. And if it's allowed, you get to put a little checkmark next to it." John hunched down and mimicked holding a pen like a conscientious, overworked, near-sighted accountant ticking something off a list. *"Check."*

Marguerite couldn't help giggling at his impression of her and her checklist.

"And that whole checklist and belief system are imposed on you from the outside, by your religion," he concluded.

She was still laughing, even if she didn't want to agree this was really what she did. They'd finished their food, so they crumpled up their wrappers and threw them into the garbage can on the way into the video store. They went straight to the back, where the foreign and independent films were shelved. They browsed through the small selection, picking up video cases and reading the plot summaries on the backs. John wanted to rent *Tie Me Up, Tie Me Down,* or else maybe *The Cook, the Thief, His Wife, and Her Lover.* Marguerite vetoed both, especially as they weren't even in German.

"You see," he said, "If it weren't for your belief system and that checklist in your head, we could watch one of these movies."

"But they look like porn, seriously."

"What's so wrong with porn? Okay, how about this one—this shouldn't violate your belief system. *Wings of Desire.* It's supposed to be really good, a classic."

"Oh, yeah. I heard it was good. Let's get that." Marguerite put down another video she had picked up and they started to move toward the checkout counter.

"Wait a minute," said John, "aren't you going to put that other video back where it belongs?"

"Um ... gosh, should I? The store people will get to it eventually, I'm sure."

"But what if someone really wants to rent it tonight, and can't find it because you left it sitting out? According to your belief system, you have to go and put it back. Which is proof you're not really free like you think you are."

Marguerite felt herself on the horns of a dilemma. On the one hand, if she went to put the video back, it would prove she wasn't free. On the other hand, if she didn't put it back, she would indeed be violating her belief system by doing something unkind. And particularly now that he had pointed it out, she was sure to feel bad about it. She left him and went to put the video back in its place.

"See, I was right," he said, when she came back to stand in line with him.

"But I wonder—can't you be free if you serve something or someone by choice?"

"Nope. No way. Sorry."

WHEN THEY got back to Marguerite's house, they put the videotape into the player in the TV room and sat down together on the couch to watch it. They sat close together in the dark, but without quite touching. The movie was about an angel with a weather-beaten, pockmarked face who went around Berlin accompanied by other angels with weather-beaten, pockmarked faces, dressed in trench coats with their long hair in pony tails, listening to people's thoughts and trying to comfort them. They lived in a world of black and white. Then the angel fell in love with a trapeze artist in a circus and decided to fall from heaven and become human so he could be together with her in a world of colors.

Halfway through the movie, Marguerite's mom and Cate got home. They'd been at Cate's swim meet. Mrs. Farnsworth wanted to tell her about the races and how well Cate had done. She chatted about people they'd run into there, some of whom had asked her to pass on greetings to Marguerite. Marguerite paused the movie to listen, but was impatient to get back to it. She answered her mom only in brusque monosyllables, so as not to encourage her to talk more.

When Mrs. Farnsworth had finished talking and gone off to the kitchen, John turned to Marguerite. "Hey, you weren't very nice to your mom just now."

Marguerite hung her head. "I know. I'm sorry. She just drives me crazy when she does that—you know, starts telling me a long story in the middle of a movie, so then I have to pause it. She does that all the time."

"Aw, I like your mom. She's so sweet. She's just so exactly like a mom, it's great. I love moms."

A winning sentiment, to be sure. Marguerite was sorely tempted to lean over and hug him. But who knew what would happen if she did that? Who knew if he'd even let her? After all, he'd said they were friends, which probably meant she wasn't allowed to do things like crawl into the crook of his arm and nuzzle up to him in the dark, as she would have liked. So she contented herself with smiling and saying, "You're probably a good son, then." She paused and after a few moments asked, "Do you think you could see me as a mom?"

"Yeah, definitely. Of course I could."

They went back to watching the movie. They had moved a little further apart when Marguerite's mom came in and stayed like that to the end of the film.

As the credits ran, Marguerite stretched and yawned. "Wow. How did it get to be past eleven already?" she asked, genuinely mystified. They'd spent more than seven hours together, she calculated, but the time hadn't seemed anywhere near as long.

"Yeah," he said, looking at her with an expression she couldn't read, but that might have had something like regret in it. "It's *schlafen* time. I'd better get going."

Oh, no, he couldn't leave. For Marguerite the thought of saying goodbye was like being plunged into cold water. But there was nothing for it but to resign herself. She couldn't ask him to stay.

She walked him to the side door. They said goodbye without hugging or touching, and then he was gone.

After he left, Marguerite had her third and last epiphany about him, four days after her second epiphany, ten days after her first, and fourteen days from that fateful conversation with Damon in which the great, slouching beast had awoken down in the swampy, lightless depths of her soul. The epiphany was that she loved him. Whether she was *in* love with him, she couldn't say. But that she loved him, that much was certain.

CHAPTER 12

THE PROBLEM OF SOLIPSISM

THE PROBLEM OF SOLIPSISM was something John talked about often. Marguerite wasn't entirely sure what he meant by it. It had something to do with loneliness and doubt, with the fact that you were alone in the world with your own consciousness and couldn't get outside yourself to have your impressions validated by some external source. But she began to understand it better during the week that followed.

The day after they studied together, everything was just as it had been. Nothing had changed in spite of the sense she'd had of their having created a new category together as they sat on her living room floor studying irregular verbs and talking about truth. It wasn't long before she began to doubt all her impressions of the evening.

John was spending that weekend in Las Vegas with some high school buddies of his, he told her. When he was back on Monday, Marguerite wondered if he'd gotten laid, if he'd spent the whole time drinking, smoking, gambling, and hitting on girls in short tight skirts who wore high heels and perfume and had beautiful long hair like in a shampoo commercial. But she didn't ask what he'd done in Sin City. They hardly spoke to each other, and he didn't wait for her to talk after class the way he often did. She went straight to the music building to practice the piano and felt terrible.

From then on, it seemed something *had* changed, but not for the better. The problem was that her usual solipsism had been briefly interrupted by this sense of boundaries blurring into one another, and now that the boundaries were back in place, she was unhappier than she'd been before. Solipsism would be no problem if it weren't for those moments of blurred boundaries; they were the real problem.

In class that week they watched a movie in German about a girl in a small Bavarian town who did a research project for school on the resistance movement in her region during the Third Reich. But as she dug deeper, she uncovered shocking things about the degree of collaboration some of the older citizens had engaged in with the Nazis and a nearby concentration camp. The town tried to give the girl an award for her research, but she got angry because she suspected they only did it to stop her from digging any further for the truth. She kept digging and digging until she alienated almost everyone and her husband divorced her. All she cared about was finding the truth.

In one scene of the movie, the girl attended a party with all her old schoolteachers, and one of them tried to pinch her cheek affectionately. The girl didn't smile, but only looked at him quizzically, as though to ask, "What in God's name are you doing?"

John laughed. "That's a Marguerite look. That's such a Marguerite look."

When the movie was over, Marguerite asked him what he'd meant by it.

"That's exactly how you looked at me when I tried to hug you the other day."

"But I'm sure I didn't look at you like that. I liked it when you hugged me."

"I think that's how you looked."

"Well, if I did," she said in a whisper, as the lecture was starting, "it's just that I'm not so used to being touched. I guess it's true that if I don't know someone very well and they touch me, I kind of tense up at first. It just takes me a while to get used to it. But I don't mind if it's someone I know and ... and trust."

They turned their attention back to Professor Liebmann and the lecture.

That evening, after she had practiced the piano and finished her German homework, she wrote a short essay for John, in which she set forth several arguments as to why she was free, contrary to what he'd argued earlier. The gist of her main argument was that you had to serve *something* one way or another, just as everyone had to work for a living. You couldn't free yourself by choosing not to serve, any more than you could free yourself by choosing not to work and support yourself. You might choose to serve God, or serve the cause of goodness and truth, or you might choose to serve the whims and cravings of your body, the commands of pleasure and pain. But either way, freedom consisted in choosing whom or what you served, as the scriptures said, *Choose ye this day, whom ye will serve,* and *No man can serve two masters,* and *Whosoever committeth sin is the servant of sin.*

It was also bound up with what she'd read in *The Magic Mountain,* that for the sake of goodness and love, man should let death have no mastery over his thoughts. If you believed death was the end, you'd be more likely to choose to serve the dictates of pleasure and pain, because you'd have a shorter-term view of things—you never knew when your consciousness in its empty solitude might not just blip out of existence. But if you believed in the eternality of your consciousness, of your soul, you'd choose to serve God, or morality, or the cause of truth, or goodness and love, because they were the masters who would pay you better over the long term, over the course of eternity.

ON FRIDAY they went to *Stammtisch* at Mike's Place as usual. As they walked in, John declared, "I think it's time for one of my *heroic* drinking sessions," grinning in a feral way that Marguerite found disconcerting.

John had read her little essay on freedom, and after pausing to finish a conversation with another group of German class students, he sashayed over to talk to her about it. He went through it with his usual destructive thoroughness, explaining why each point or connection worked or didn't. He thought she'd taken part of one of her arguments straight from the *Critique of Pure Reason,* and Marguerite had to remind him she'd never read it. She and Kant had just coincidentally thought the same things. And so he explained to her, too, where her argument intersected with Kant's and where it diverged. Marguerite greedily drank in his explanations and attention, which she'd been desperately craving all week.

She liked that he was never pedantic when they talked philosophy. He never told her things merely for the sake of showing off his knowledge, wasn't condescending, and didn't use jargon where he could avoid it. He was passionate about the subjects they discussed, but not in the humorless way pedantic people are passionate. And instead of mocking her clumsy attempts at contradicting him and constructing counterarguments, he took them seriously, even when they were clearly full of holes and faults.

While they talked, he drank beer after beer, and after a while Marguerite began to notice that although he still sounded coherent, he was starting to lose some of his inhibitions. For one thing, he kept praising her intelligence.

"You know, Marguerite, you are really bright. I have to tell you, it's attractive."

"What are you talking about?"

"I mean it. You are."

"How many beers have you had?"

"I'm being serious. Don't try to make a joke out of it. I think you're really, really intelligent. I like that about you, a lot."

A little later, he sat down next to Angela and began flirting with her, laying the compliments on thick. Marguerite and Pam observed the exchange with wry amusement. Eventually, John took Angela's hand in his and asked if she'd like to go out on a date with him. She pulled her hand away.

"Stop messing with me," she said. "I know you don't mean it. You're just messing with my mind."

He laughed a wicked sort of laugh. "Yeah, yeah, I know. But it's fun teasing you."

"Hey," interrupted Pam, "what ever happened to that thirty-year-old woman you were supposed to go out with? Aren't you dating her?"

"Who? Oh, yeah, her. Yeah, well ... we made plans, but I just wasn't feeling it, so I never went."

"You never went?" said Angela. "You mean, you stood her up?"

"I can't believe you'd stand her up," said Marguerite. "That's so mean. It doesn't seem like you at all."

"Oh yeah, I stood her up. I mean, come on. She's a grown up person. I'm sure she'll survive."

The girls looked at each other and shook their heads sadly, in sympathy with the thirty-year-old woman they'd never met.

"So, are you dating anyone else?" asked Pam.

"No, not really, not right now. Honestly, it's been a while. If you want to know the truth, I haven't slept with someone in so long ... I keep thinking the next time I'm out at a bar, I should just go up to some girl and proposition her and take her home with me."

"Is it that easy for you?" asked Marguerite (who had yet to learn the important life-lesson that tall men generally have an easier time getting laid).

"Oh yeah. It's not that much of a challenge. Girls'll sleep with you if you just say the right things. All you have to do is make them think you care about them."

"You are *awful*," Marguerite said.

"Nah, I'm only joking. But you know, I'd ask you out, if only you weren't hampered by those warped religious views of yours."

Marguerite paled. "Please. You're not serious about anything."

"Sure I am. Why not? You're smart. You've got those intense green eyes. And I like talking to you. You make me feel smart too, because I get to explain all these different philosophers to you."

"John, I think you're drunk."

"Yeah, maybe a little. But it doesn't make that much of a difference. People use being drunk as an excuse for all kinds of things, but it doesn't change who you are. It just takes some of your inhibitions away. The things you do and say when you're drunk are things that were part of you all along, anyway. It's what was in your character already, only it finally comes out when the inhibitions are gone."

"Really, you think so? That's interesting. It's the kind of thing you don't learn when you grow up Mormon."

"I'm betting there are a lot of things you don't learn when you grow up Mormon."

"Well, you're right about that. But you're so strange, John. It's like you have this dual personality. On the one side, you're kind and sweet and ... sort of *earnest*, and I really like you. And then on the other side, you're just ... awful and ... and evil, and I wonder why I put up with you. The whole dual personality thing is kind of scary."

John threw back his head and laughed. "Oh yeah, that's completely true. It is kind of scary. But there you go."

———

LATER, JOHN and Angela got into a discussion about dating in general.

"With short-term flings," Angela was saying, "what's actually in it for the girl? We usually want more than that."

"Well, I don't know about other guys, but I think with me there's something in it for the girl."

"Oh yeah?" said Pam, raising her eyebrows. "What exactly is in it for her?"

"I don't want to get too graphic or anything, since Marguerite's listening and we have to protect her innocent ears. But let's just say I've gotten some very good, uh, *feedback*."

Angela groaned. "Oh, come on. And you don't think they could have been faking it? Men. You always just assume you can take these things at face value, because you want to believe them."

"I guess that's possible, but I don't think it's likely." He lowered his voice. "I think you can tell when the person you're with loses control. They arch their back, and they …" He paused to take a swig of beer from his cup and seemed to think the better of finishing the sentence. "Anyway, it's all about pleasing the other person …"

"And you think you're good at that."

He shrugged. His face was slightly flushed—whether from the beer or embarrassment, it was hard to tell. "Yeah, I think I'm pretty good. I think I've got skills." He looked away, squinting off into the distance of the parking lot, and said, "I think I'm a good kisser. My last girlfriend taught me how to kiss." Marguerite was watching him carefully, and when he looked back their eyes met. She turned her gaze away quickly, but to her embarrassment, she felt her face getting hot. And worse, as Pam and Angela egged him on to tell them about his skills in more detail, she felt wetness between her legs, and couldn't meet his eyes anymore.

She really needed to find out if her religion was true or not.

CHAPTER 13

THE BEST DEFENSE

How did a person find out if her religion was true or not? Marguerite spent the first weekend in August pondering it.

Her father owned a good-sized motor boat, and on his rare free weekends, liked to take it out to some of the lakes in driving distance, or down south to the Mexican coast for ocean fishing. This weekend he'd planned a water skiing expedition out to Canyon Lake for Max and a couple of Max's school friends, and Marguerite had said she'd tag along.

She'd tried water skiing before and hadn't much liked it, finding it frightening and nearly impossible to stand up on the skis in the wake of the speeding boat. But she loved sitting up front on the boat's bow, as close to the edge as she could manage without getting thrown off, clinging to the railing with her legs dangling below, and feeling the motion of the waves under her. When the wind was up and the boat bounced across the lake at full throttle, it was like riding a galloping horse, the prow leaping and plunging and the waves going *slap slap slap*, hard against the side of the boat. She would settle into a trance-like state, watching the turquoise horizon and the pale rocky hills that rose around it flecked with the grey-green of cactuses and bushes, their colors bleached out under the harsh sun, while the wind flew through her and tore at her clothes and hair.

It was a good place to think, at the bow of the speeding boat, and as they flew around the lake, she thought about religion and John. During the lulls when the boat stopped so that one of the boys or Dr. Farnsworth could swim out and wriggle into the skis, she moved to sit in the back of the boat next to the cooler, snacking on chips and sipping juice while the sun beat down on her hatless head, watching the boys yell encouragements to each other, and thinking more about religion and John.

Max was no more athletic than Marguerite was, but liked to have friends and counted on the ones he had brought being grateful for the rare opportunity to go water skiing. He accepted his inevitable falls with his usual laconic resignation while his friends hooted and clapped until it was their turn. Then the boat would roar into motion again and Marguerite would resume her station up at the front and fall back into her meditative trance.

Now there was a shout, however, and the boat stopped too abruptly. Max had taken a bad fall. His long face was white, bobbing up from the water as the engine chugged indignantly and slowly brought them back around to him.

When Dr. Farnsworth was worried, his face took on a blank expression, and it did so now as he extended his hand to Max to help him aboard. Max could put no weight on the foot and collapsed heavily onto one of the benches. Dr. Farnsworth knelt down to examine the ankle. He turned it one way and then another, pressing on spots and asking if it hurt. When he hit tender spots, Max gasped and pressed his lips together tightly. Max's friends were silent, looking on with horrified stares.

At length, Dr. Farnsworth declared it was only a sprain; the bone wasn't broken. A sigh of relief went round. Marguerite helped her father scoop ice from the cooler and seal it into a plastic bag, then found a discarded tee shirt to wrap it in so Max could hold it against his ankle.

After that, no one wanted to take another turn at water skiing, so they docked at a muddy cove to go swimming, and then cruised around the lake until it was time to go home. Marguerite sat in the front seat of her dad's pickup truck on the long drive back and watched out the window, still trying to puzzle out the question of religion and thinking about John.

She was in a bad mood when they got home, a headache throbbing between her temples, feeling she had made no progress at all in her thinking; it was like beating her head against a brick wall.

Mrs. Farnsworth made a fuss when she saw Max's ankle and scolded her husband for letting Max take too many risks.

"We'll call the home teachers," she said. "Brother Bryant and Brother Ruiz can come over and help you give him a blessing."

Dr. Farnsworth protested, "You've got to be kidding me. Come on, it's just a sprained ankle. I'm sure they have better things to do than come over here on a Saturday night."

"*Brad*, that's what they're *there* for."

"Mom, I'm fine," said Max gruffly. "Seriously, I'm not dying of cancer here."

Mrs. Farnsworth hesitated, her hand already on the phone. She looked to Marguerite, her usual ally in spiritual matters.

"It *is* getting late, Mom," Marguerite said with a sigh. "Do we really want to disturb them and take them away from their families over something minor like this?"

Mrs. Farnsworth threw her hands up in the air and huffed, "Fine, what do I know? I'm just your mother. By the way, Marguerite, one of your friends called and left a message—it's here by the phone."

The message was from Ellen, the practical-minded nursing student from her freshman dorm at BYU. Since they'd last spoken they had decided through an exchange of letters that Ellen would live with Marguerite in Provo in the fall. The unexpected kindness of a long-distance phone call touched Marguerite, and when she called back and talked to Ellen, she was even more cheered. Ellen had called to ask what she wanted for her birthday, which was coming up in a little over a week.

After they had talked for a while, Marguerite confessed some of her troubles to Ellen: she was developing a terrible crush on one of the non-Mormon boys she'd told Ellen about earlier, and it was causing her to struggle with her testimony. At length she asked Ellen how she knew the Church was true.

"Well, I don't know *all* the time," Ellen said. "Some times I know better than others. When I'm praying and reading the scriptures a lot, it helps." She went on saying the usual kinds of things Mormons said to explain how you stayed strong in your testimony. As she talked, Marguerite tried to listen to more than just her words, which were all too familiar. She tried to listen to Ellen as a whole, to her essence and soul, to understand what made Ellen such a soothing, comforting person to talk to. And as she listened, the delicacy and prettiness of Ellen's soul seemed to shine like a lantern down into the murky confusion of Marguerite's own inwardness, showing her a way out of her aporia.

By their fruits ye shall know them, the scriptures said. Marguerite thought of the Mormons she'd known at BYU, the ones who strove so earnestly to live their beliefs and to embody the ideals of goodness and love. As much as she'd felt out of place and invisible in the midst of all that blond blandness, these were good, guileless people. With them, you knew where you stood; they were trustworthy. You knew you could call on them for help if you needed it. They were cheerful, lovely people, whose faces always looked freshly scrubbed and glowing. They were the fruits of her religion, along with Ellen.

The fruits of unbelief were John and his friends. You never knew quite where you stood with them. Were you a friend? A prospective conquest? A mere acquaintance deluding yourself you mattered one way or another? The fruit of unbelief was a person who vacillated between being charming, affectionate, and sweet one day, and despicably crass and cavalier the next. A person who smoked, indulged in heroic drinking bouts, and probably slept with girls he didn't care about, probably even tallied them up with little notches on his bedpost.

By their fruits ye shall know them, the scriptures said, and Marguerite knew. Her religion was the true one.

THE BEST thing for it, Marguerite decided, was to make a concerted effort to convert John to Mormonism. In telling her he would date her if only it weren't for her warped religious views, and in bragging about his sexual prowess in front of her, he had thrown down a gauntlet and gone on the offensive. She had to defend herself, and the best defense, Marguerite figured, was a good offense.

A few days later, her opportunity came. She and John and the others were sitting around outside in the shade chatting after class. Marguerite was in a bad mood again, and John was brimming with a strange, manic energy, bubbling over with mischief and saying all kinds of provoking things. He was offensive but magnificent as he stood there in the sun with one hip thrust out like Michelangelo's

David and a cigarette between his fingers, like some young Greek god out of a myth, an Adonis or a Dionysius, a demigod of merriment and revelry. At last he made a remark Marguerite found so vile, even if he only meant it as a joke, that she couldn't bear it any longer and stood up, brushing the dust off her hands. She slung her backpack over her shoulder and yelled, hands on her hips, "John, are you a vile worm or are you a ... a demigod? Make up your mind, and then I'll associate with you."

John and the others stared. Marguerite turned to leave, but after only a few steps, she turned around again and repeated for emphasis, "Figure out who you are, and then I'll talk to you!" before flouncing off in a huff.

Later that evening, after she had finished her homework and sat down to think through her day, she knew she'd made herself ridiculous. She'd been melodramatic and mean, too. It wasn't just a single absurd remark; her bad mood had made her unkind and peevish all day. She wasn't behaving like a good fruit in the slightest, and how was she supposed to convert John if she was a hypocrite who failed to live up to her own ideals of being sweet, good, and kind? She resolved to do better and make amends the next day and prayed for Heavenly Father to help her.

The next morning, it did seem a better spirit inhabited her. She had a smile for everyone; she was sweet and good and kind. During the break, she apologized to John for having been so rude the day before. He sounded slightly traumatized.

"You called me a vile creature."

"No, a vile *worm* I think it was," corrected Angela.

Marguerite laughed. "Oh, jeez, I don't know what got into me. I'm sorry. I kind of get carried away sometimes."

"I think you just like to make dramatic exits," John said. "I've noticed it before. You always have to say goodbye to everybody three times before you leave."

Touché. But he had a right to make fun of her now, she felt, since she had acted exactly like the egocentric drama queen of a Leo he'd once accused her of being. So she only replied, "Hmph."

But after class let out, John caught up to her and asked, "What did you mean by all that anyway? All that 'figure out who you are' stuff. You think I don't know who I am?"

"Oh, no," she said sheepishly. "It's just—what I was saying the other day, you know, about how you have a dual personality. On the one side you're so great; you're kind of a god—a philosophy god. And on the other side ..." she tried to think how to put it more kindly and delicately than she had earlier.

"I'm a vile worm."

"No, I didn't mean that. Although you can be kind of awful. I guess I was just thinking about something, because I was having another existential crisis about religion the other day." She told him her train of thought about knowing them by their fruits, trying to downplay as much as possible the part about John being an example of bad, rotten fruit. "Existential crisis" was a phrase she had picked up from him. As far as she could tell, it meant when you had painful moments of doubt about your own being and the choices that made it what it was, when you weren't sure how or what or whether to be. John talked about having them often, and after hearing so much about them, Marguerite had begun to be conscious of having them, too.

John agreed that Mormons were awfully nice people, at least Marguerite was—at least, she was when she wasn't going around calling people vile worms. But he still wasn't convinced niceness was enough to prove the truth of Mormonism to anyone.

Marguerite's evangelizing moment had come.

"Listen, I'll make you a promise, and a challenge," she said. "If you read the Book of Mormon and pray sincerely to ask God if it's true, you'll know it's true."

"How will I know it's true?"

"The Holy Ghost will tell you."

"The Holy Ghost."

"Yep. The Holy Ghost. You laugh, but I'm completely serious. I've never heard of it not working for anyone. You know, the head of our philosophy department at BYU was converted that way, he told us, when he was fifteen. He told us the story when he taught my Honors writing class last year. He's an extremely intelligent, philosophical guy, just like you. If it worked for him, it could work for you."

"Aren't you afraid I might take you up on that and prove you wrong?"

"I'm not afraid. I think I'd be fine with it if you could prove me wrong, because at least then I'd know. But if *you're* too afraid to try it, I'll understand."

"Oh, I'm not afraid."

"Well, maybe you should be."

"Why should I be afraid?"

"Because if it's true, then you'll have to change."

"But I'm not going to find out it's true."

"Well, okay then. You should have nothing to worry about."

John had gotten a gleam in his eye as though he were thinking he'd finally found something he could nail her on. Marguerite had at last thrown down her own gauntlet.

They looked up and saw Damon coming towards them. He and John greeted each other with mock punches, and Damon said, "Hey, Marguerite, long time no see. How's it going? You made any progress yet on what we talked about last time?"

"Nope. No, I'm still completely sexually frustrated. Thanks for asking, though."

He and John raised their eyebrows at each other and broke into guffaws.

"Don't worry," said Damon. "I'm sure you'll get plenty once you find your Mormon man and settle down with him."

"Yeah," said Marguerite. "Everybody says Mormons hump like bunnies when they first get married." (What on earth had gotten into her today?)

"Ha. You know, I've heard that. They just hole up in a hotel room for a month and do nothing but have sex. I don't blame them, I would too."

"Hey," John said, as Angela and Pam walked up and joined them, "let's all do something tonight. You guys want to go see a movie? There's a new one playing at the Loft." The Loft was an independent, locally owned theater that screened artsy films and foreign language pictures with subtitles.

"Oh, yeah," said Angela, "I read about that, the new Merchant Ivory film. It's supposed to be good. *Howard's End.* I'd go see it."

"Howard's rear end," said Damon. "Sounds pretty gay. That'll be perfect for you, buddy. Count me out, though." They threw more mock punches at each other.

"I like going to the Loft," said Marguerite, when the boys had settled down. "I always feel deep and intellectual when I go to watch a movie there."

"Hmm, I don't know if we'll fit in, though," said John. "We'd better wear black turtlenecks, just in case."

"Oh, good idea."

"Okay then," John said. "How about this: let's all wear black and meet up at that one artsy coffee shop, you know, Bentley's, before the show. Maybe we'll catch a poetry reading while we're at it. I'll bring some Gauloises to smoke. We'll be total existentialists."

IT WAS a fun night, with a mood of expectancy and giddy risk-taking in the air. Marguerite and John were the only ones who followed through on the idea of wearing black. John in black was excitingly criminal-looking, and Marguerite felt gamine and French in the short black pleated skirt she'd bought in Paris the summer before. She thought she caught John looking down at her legs a few seconds too long while they stood in line to buy tickets, but then decided it was only her wishful thinking again. She and John sat next to each other during the film and talked in whispers through most of it. At the end, after the others had driven off, John walked Marguerite to her car, and they stood there in the parking lot next to it for a good while longer, talking and laughing, and Marguerite didn't want to leave. At last, reluctantly, she put her key in the car door to signify she'd really better go, and they said goodbye.

CHAPTER 14

LOST

On a Thursday afternoon a few days later, Marguerite started when the phone rang. She was even more surprised when she answered and heard John's voice on the other line.

The entire German class was supposed to meet for dinner that night at a restaurant called the Gasthaus, the only German restaurant in town. John wanted to know if Marguerite had directions. Marguerite hadn't thought to get them, so John hung up, called someone else to find out how to get there, and called Marguerite back.

"These directions are incomprehensible," he complained. Marguerite was thinking to herself that a set of directions had to be truly convoluted if someone as smart as John couldn't figure them out, but he cut short her reverie by saying, "Hey, why don't we go together? Then at least if we get lost, we'll be lost together."

"Oh," she said, blinking. "Oh, right, okay. Um ...do you want to drive?"

"Nah, why don't we take your car? It's cooler than mine, and I'm more on the way for you than you are for me." They agreed she would pick him up at Bentley's, the coffee house they'd been to before the movie.

As Marguerite left home in the early evening, a monsoon storm broke overhead. Thunder boomed, lightning flashed, and purple-gray swaths of rain sheeted down against the gray-green mountains encircling the valley. She hummed to herself as she drove, thinking it was excellent luck to have such bad weather. Maybe they'd get stuck somewhere along the way, wind up on the wrong side of a flooded wash. Alone in some quiet desert place, they'd have to wait out the storm in the little red car together. One thing would lead to another, and they wouldn't be able to help themselves. They'd end up making out, or maybe more.

But there she was, living in a dreamworld again. Surely he'd only called because he liked her dad's car. He couldn't really be interested in getting lost with her.

In any case, by the time she got to Bentley's to pick him up, the rain had let up, and it was only drizzling lightly. He got in and they headed east toward the highway and out of town.

Marguerite wasn't used to driving in the rain. At an intersection where the houses had grown sparser and farther apart, a van in front of them stopped suddenly, and Marguerite put her foot to the brake too late. The little red car slid forward over the slick wet asphalt and rear-ended the van.

There wasn't much damage, only one headlight out on Marguerite's car, and a dent on the van's fender. John took care of everything. While they waited for the police to arrive, he stood out in the rain talking to the driver of the van to exchange insurance information and did most of the talking when the police came, too. The rest of the time he waited in the car with her, chatting cheerfully and making her laugh.

"Oh, I don't even want to think about what my dad's going to say when he hears about this," she said, twisting her hands together worriedly.

"Nah, it'll be okay, you'll see," John said. "Your dad seemed like a pretty low-key guy when I met him. If you're really worried, though, I can take the heat. You can tell him it was my fault. Tell him I was distracting you."

Marguerite laughed. "Uh, I'm not sure if that would be the best idea."

When everything was settled at last and they were ready to drive on, he asked in an unassuming tone, "Hey, do you mind if I drive the rest of the way?" Marguerite smiled and agreed that would probably be best. They got out of the car to trade places.

"My hero," she said as he started the car. She tried to bat her eyelashes at him, without much success. He waved off all her attempts to thank him.

"Anyone would have done the same thing. Seriously, it was nothing."

It was a long drive to the restaurant, which was out beyond Gates Pass, along the same route you took to get to the Desert Museum, past the Saguaro National Monument, winding up sharp narrow ascents in places and down steep drops. As they drove and got lost and retraced their path and drove some more, a lurid sunset gleamed red through the storm clouds, turning them a fiery glittering copper around the edges. Marguerite felt herself drowning, nearly suffocating in the dense, heavy beauty of it. At the same time, a desire to touch John, to have his hands on her, came over her so strongly she had to grip the edges of her seat with both hands to keep herself from putting a hand on his arm and asking him to stop, dragging him out of the car and ...

She sat motionless in her seat, breathing shallowly, watching his profile as he drove, letting the desire wash through her unopposed. She was a conduit. If she tried to break its flow, it would only rise up stronger and twist her down into its depths, the way a flash flood would do if you got caught in a riverbed in one of these storms. If she stayed still it would run its course without hurting her, streaming down from wherever it came from and rushing off to wherever it went. Each time he spoke to her, she answered, hardly understanding him or knowing what she said, she was so intent on the currents of wanting that tumbled through her.

At last they found the restaurant. They had started out so early that even between the car accident and getting lost, they'd made it in time to have dinner with the rest of the class. They explained to the others how the accident had made them late and sat down across from each other at the end of the long banquet table. They ate schnitzel and kraut and talked mainly to each other, not mingling much with the other students, which was uncharacteristic behavior for John. She caught looks from Angela and Pam, but thankfully no one commented openly on the oddness of it. They finished eating quickly and didn't linger long. The two of them walked back out to the parking lot, and as John turned the key in the ignition, the car winked with its wounded headlight into the starlit darkness.

It was easier to talk on the way back, in the dark where she couldn't see more than the outline of his face and her senses weren't so overwhelmed by the wild damp beauty of the rained-on desert all around them. The conversation wound its way gradually through safe subjects (homework, German syntax) to riskier ones, until it came to the topic of relationships.

"Relationships are just impossible," John was saying. Marguerite agreed. Not that she'd had much experience in that area, but even theoretically, it was hard to see how they could work. If you had strong feelings for someone, you were always in a storm of emotions: fear of rejection, nervousness if the other person returned your feelings, jealousy, hope, longing, grief over every trivial obstacle or disappointment. And if your feelings weren't so strong, you might have to worry about hurting another person who felt more strongly. And that was without even mentioning the cases where strong feelings might be mutual but their expression wasn't allowed.

In theory, marriage was supposed to be a kind of solution to all these difficulties, at least as Marguerite had been taught growing up, she explained, because it elevated the relationship from being founded in unstable emotions to a firmer foundation of Christian love and ethical obligation.

"But I don't know if I can see myself getting married ever," she said to John, after a lengthy pause. A cool breath of despair washed over her as she said it.

"Why not?" he asked.

"I'm afraid I might just be too independent."

John nodded slowly, looking over at her without smiling and then turning his eyes back to the road. "That's true," he said evenly. "You are very independent."

"I think what I need is a ... a *forceful* man, who will just *make* me like him. Otherwise, there's just no chance."

John opened his mouth as though he meant to say something, but then closed it and said nothing.

She leaned her head against the window and thought what nonsense she was talking. She hardly knew what she meant by it. She couldn't call herself independent when she was prone to these infatuations in which every moment of happiness or misery depended on some man's actions and feelings for her. And it wasn't as though John had to make her care for him. If anything, he should probably try to make her stop caring so much.

Well, she thought, she was independent in the sense that at least she struggled against her infatuations and pushed boys who cared about her away. She struggled against love as though against a form of insanity and was probably right to, since insanity was the form her love invariably took.

As for what she meant by needing a "forceful" man, it was clear enough. What she wanted was to be pounced on. (In a movie she had seen called *Caberet,* this was a piece of advice Liza Minelli's character gave to a young red-headed man who was in love with an unattainable, terribly rich Jewish virgin: to pounce on her. Which he did, over the girl's protestations. She fought him at first but then gave in and fell helplessly in love with him. Marguerite wanted to be pounced on in just this way, which is to say, she wanted not to have the responsibility of choosing. She wanted to have the choice made for her by someone else, or in other words, to be the opposite of independent. These two opposing forces battled in her, the struggle for independence on the one hand and her desire to lose herself on the other, to be swept up in someone else's will and desires. Which is to say, her longing for religion took much the same form as her longing for John, as did her struggle against each of them, her most effective weapons against both being doubt and mistrust.)

The conversation moved on to religion, and from there back to marriage. It was a shame, John said, that religion, much as it seemed to give people comfort and do them good, also served so often to divide people and keep them apart.

"How do you mean?" asked Marguerite. "Give me an example."

"Like with Jews who only want to go out with other Jews, or Christians who won't marry non-Christians."

"Oh, I see. Yes, but—that's difficult. Of course, it's the same thing with Mormons. I've actually thought a little about what it might be like to ... to marry a non-Mormon." She looked over at him in the dark as she said it, wondering if she was being too transparent and he'd be able to guess which non-Mormon she'd thought of marrying.

"You have?" he asked. "So ... what did you think?"

"Well, I could see problems with it. If I did, he might smoke or drink a lot, and it could end up hurting our family—our kids, I mean. He might, you know, mess with our children's minds or something."

"But I—" He broke off. "I mean, *he* would not mess with their minds. Why on earth would you think that?"

Marguerite heard the pronoun slip with some astonishment, but pressed on.

"It's just that, as Mormons, we grow up with a strong culture of the family. Marriage is taken seriously as a binding covenant, and divorce is seen as a last resort, not the first thing you think of doing when you have a fight or a problem. So we all grow up with this family-centric culture and this shared set of values. If I married someone from outside that culture, I don't know if I could be sure he'd share that same commitment to love each other and love our kids absolutely."

He answered her in the first person singular without faltering this time. "Oh, I'm full of love," he said with a little laugh.

Marguerite was shocked into silence. Had he really just used the word love? But no, of course he'd meant love for the hypothetical children in a hypothetical marriage, not love for her. Of course not. Dreamworld.

Having resolved this in her mind, she took courage and asked, "But … don't you think it could be complicated? I mean, all the questions, like what religion our kids would be raised in, and whether they could go to church with me on Sundays? We might argue and fight over it all the time."

"Sure, it could be complicated. But people work these things out. And I might not mind if my kids went to church, as long as I didn't have to go. It's not such a bad thing for kids to go to church when they're young. As long as they get to choose for themselves whether to join or not when they're older. That's what my mom did with me and my brother."

"You really wouldn't mind?"

"Probably not, as long as nobody tries to convert me."

Marguerite hesitated, then asked cautiously, "And … what about the smoking? Second-hand smoke isn't good for kids. Lots of studies say that."

John only laughed again. "Yeah, I know, it's a disgusting habit. I know I'm going to have to quit eventually."

———

THEY PASSED the rest of the drive talking until they found themselves back at Bentley's. John turned the engine off.

"Do you think you'll be okay driving home by yourself?" he asked.

"I don't know. I—I still feel a little shaky somehow," said Marguerite. "Maybe my nerves are still a bit jangled from the accident."

"What do you want to do?"

"Maybe I could have an herbal tea or just something warm to drink. Maybe that would soothe my nerves. Is Bentley's still open?" She looked at her watch. "It's not too late, actually."

"Sure, we could go in and have a drink. That's a good idea."

When they had settled themselves at a table inside with a chamomile tea for Marguerite and a cup of coffee for John, he joked, "Damn, we probably just missed another poetry reading."

"Ha. Actually, that could be interesting for me," Marguerite said. "I like to read poetry sometimes, even if I can't write it worth a darn."

"Oh, yeah, I forgot you write poems. You know, I'd be curious to see yours some time, if you didn't mind showing them to me."

"Oh, hm. Maybe one of these days." There wasn't the slightest chance she would ever show him her poetry. It was too maudlin and sentimental, too intimate, and her judgment of it too unreliable. She would finish a poem and think it decent, only to come back to it a week later and find it horribly, unreadably embarrassing. Thematically, her poetry revolved around depression, unrequited love, and God, which was another reason not to show it to anyone, let alone John.

"Do you ever read poetry?" she asked.

"Not much. But I'm sure yours would be better than any of the stuff that gets spouted into the open mic here."

"No, honestly, it's not. Anyway, I'm not sure I'd even want to be a real poet if I could. We read this essay by Jung in my philosophy of art class last year. He talks about how artists are doomed to lead miserable lives, because they're constantly pulled in two different directions. They have the pull of ordinary human needs on the one hand, for love and closeness and affection, and on the other side they have this ruthless drive to create. It doesn't sound very fun to me, I have to say."

"But you could do it if you wanted to."

"Oh, I don't think so. Seriously, much as I like the flattery, I'm not all that smart. I'm no rocket scientist, that's for sure."

"Well, for poetry, you don't have to be a rocket scientist. I mean, it's a different type of intelligence you'd need for that."

"True. I suppose you don't have to be great at logic to be a poet. You just have to … feel … hugely. And that I can do."

"Feel hugely?"

She hesitated, then admitted, "Yeah, that's sort of a specialty of mine. But like I said, I don't know that I'd want to anyway."

He was looking at her strangely, she thought. There was a bright intensity to his gaze; a smile played around his lips, and his face looked flushed. It made her feel like she was floating dizzily an inch or two above her seat, lost to gravity, held down only by a taut, invisible line that ran from his eyes to the center of her.

They talked on for another hour, telling each other about their families and friends. John told her his father had passed away while he and his brother were still young, and after that, his mother had moved them from small-town New Jersey to smaller-town New Hampshire. He was close to his mom and admired her. She had worked hard to support them while he and his brother were growing up and had always been there for them. Marguerite imagined her as a strong, attractive woman, careworn but spirited and independent. She loved her two sons fiercely, beyond all reason, Greg the dark, quiet one and John, loud and golden. She'd taught them to laugh, to be emotional and affectionate, to take pleasure in being themselves, to want more than their little town could offer, to work hard and fight fair. (Sometimes they worked hard and fought fair, sometimes they didn't.) They'd seen her helplessly sad at times too, and had learned some of that sadness from her, taking it on themselves, wishing they could take it away from her. She dreamed of smart, loyal wives for both of them when they got older, and a big pack of grandkids for her to spoil and tickle and chase around the backyard.

Marguerite told John more about her family, how her mother had sung opera in Utah and Nevada until she'd gotten married and had kids. She still had a flamboyant streak and a flair for the dramatic. Her father on the other hand was quiet, unassuming, and hard-working, a fan of lists, analyses, and goal-setting. Her parents had a difficult time in their marriage at first, being so different from each other, but had persevered and learned to get along better over the years. Marguerite admired them for staying together and working it out. Then there were her siblings, her athletic older sister Lisa who was away in Utah studying to become an engineer and had gotten married a year earlier at twenty-one; and of course, Max and Cate, whom he'd already met. Max was quietly rebellious, with artistic leanings, she explained, while beautiful blond Cate was extroverted and stubborn. Taken together, they were a weird, delightful bunch, and Marguerite loved them to pieces.

"I love families," she said in a burst of enthusiasm as she finished telling him about them.

"Families," he repeated, smiling and looking at her with blazing eyes that burned into her dizzyingly so that she had to look away.

Marguerite asked him about his friends after that. "I picture you as having, like, a million friends," she said. "You're so good at talking to people."

"Nah, it's not really like that. I mean, it's true, I've met a lot of people out here at school. You could say I have a lot of acquaintances, I guess. Like Professor Liebmann talked about the other day, *Bekannte.*"

"Right, I remember—*Bekannte* are acquaintances, and *Freunde* are your real friends, and it's a big deal to go from *Bekannter* to *Freund.* They don't take it lightly."

"Yeah, exactly. So I wouldn't say I have a lot of friends, not *Freunde* friends. Damon is probably my best friend."

"Oh yeah?"

"But you're good at talking to people too," he said. "You're not as shy as you make yourself out to be. I've seen you in action, making the rounds at Mike's Place, chatting and flirting with everyone."

"That's because I like most people I meet, once I've met them," she explained. "It's meeting them that's the hard part. Once that part's over, I suppose I can talk with almost anyone and enjoy myself. But I don't meet many people I can really communicate with, if you know what I mean. My thoughts aren't the sort of thoughts a lot of people are interested in hearing. You're rare that way—not that I think you want to hear all my thoughts or anything, but I feel like when I tell you things, you understand and can respond, even when you don't agree. That's really ..." she trailed off, unable to say what it was. He was looking at her in that strange, intense, dizzying way again.

She looked down at her watch. "Gosh, it's late."

John, who didn't have a watch, took her wrist in his hand so he could see the time. Marguerite's breath caught in her throat.

"Yeah," he said, "I'd better get home. I still have some studying to do for the test tomorrow."

They finished their drinks, paid, and left.

"Come on, I'll walk you to your car," John said, putting an arm around her shoulders. He let his hand slide down to the small of her back as they walked, and kept it there till they got to Marguerite's car. Marguerite tried to walk smoothly and not too quickly, half-afraid that if she made any sudden moves, he might withdraw the hand from her back and stop touching her. He took the hand away when she opened the car door, but then put it under her elbow to steady her as she got in. She rolled down the window to wave goodbye, started the engine, and drove away.

He only likes me as a friend, she repeated to herself again and again on the way home, like a mantra. It didn't make any sense for him to have feelings for her that went beyond friendship. So what if he'd looked at her in a funny way. Just a trick of the light, combined with her wishful thinking. So what if they'd talked hypothetically about how they'd raise their children if they were married. Why not? Hypothetical conversations were interesting. It didn't mean anything. So what if he'd told her the week before he'd ask her out if it weren't for her warped religious views. He'd been drunk. It didn't mean anything. So what if he'd put his arm around her just now. Friends did that. It didn't mean anything. *He only likes me as a friend.*

CHAPTER 15

THE MERMAN HESITATES

WHEN MARGUERITE LOOKED IN the mirror the next morning, she saw dark circles under her eyes. She hadn't been sleeping well for the past few weeks. She stepped onto the bathroom scale to weigh herself—something she rarely bothered to do, as her metabolism allowed her to eat like a horse and never gain a pound—and realized she'd lost eight pounds since the start of the summer. No wonder her hipbones stuck out above the elastic of her underwear, and what little she'd had in the way of breasts to begin with had nearly vanished. Her face looked white and pinched.

She vowed to herself she'd skip the usual Friday *Stammtisch* after class and come straight home to sleep. But when the time came, as usual, her protests accomplished nothing.

"You're coming," said Angela. "Come on, it won't be the same without you."

"Aw, you're sweet." Marguerite hugged petite Angela around the shoulders. (*See? Friends hug*, she thought.) "But I really need to get some rest. Besides, I'll see you guys at the barbecue at your place tomorrow. That's still on, right? One o'clock?"

"Of course we're still on. I'm expecting you all to come. But that doesn't get you out of *Stammtisch*, Marguerite, sorry."

Marguerite had to laugh. And then John asked her to come, too, and she couldn't say no to him.

"But I'm not staying long," she insisted. And she didn't; she only stayed for two hours, which, in the strange, quasi-magical wormhole outside the normal space-time continuum that Mike's Place inhabited, was a very short time indeed. While they all sat drinking and talking, a pretty girl sitting at another table, a girl who wasn't from their German class, looked over and did a double take. She got up, walked over to them, and said hello to John. John stood up, and he and the girl moved a little ways away from the others and talked. John didn't introduce the girl to them, and Marguerite pretended not to notice or care, but went on chatting animatedly with Pam and Angela and Oscar.

Out of the corner of her eye, Marguerite saw Shawn from their German class leaning over and saying something to John, interrupting his chat with the girl. The girl waited for him to finish and turn back to her, but then got into a conversation with a third student from their class who said hello to her and introduced himself. After several more minutes, she got up, said goodbye to John and the others, and left. John didn't seem to hear her say goodbye or take any notice of her leaving.

When John came back, Pam asked him, "So, who was that girl you were talking to just now? A friend of yours?"

Marguerite liked Pam because she always asked the kinds of blunt questions Marguerite wanted to ask but was too shy to.

"Yeah," John said, "just a girl from one of my classes last semester."

"She said goodbye to you and left without you noticing," Marguerite couldn't resist pointing out. "You might've hurt her feelings."

"Ah, she'll get over it," John said.

Marguerite breathed a sigh of relief, then frowned. There he was, being cavalier again.

After two hours outside in the heat of the bar's back patio, her exhaustion hadn't lessened, so finally she got up to leave. There were scattered protests from the others. She couldn't leave so soon, they'd only just got there. The afternoon was still young, and after all, it was a Friday.

Marguerite cleared her throat in mock-primness. "Ahem. I'm just too nice-looking for this establishment." For emphasis, she gestured toward a couple of the picnic tables in the back, where what looked like a troop of homeless people on the lam had settled in. It was a good joke, as she was dressed more primly and properly than usual. She looked like a schoolgirl in her navy blue shorts, white short-sleeved cotton blouse with a smocked front, and her flat leather t-strap sandals, with her long hair pulled back in a white bow.

"You're just too nice-looking in general," said John, looking her up and down and letting his gaze come to rest on her face.

"Ha. I didn't mean it in that sense, obviously. Just in comparison to those ratty-looking people over there."

"Well, I did mean it in that sense. Those big, pretty green eyes of yours and your straight brown hair ..."

Marguerite could feel her face turning red. It would be easier to convince herself he didn't like her that way if only he wouldn't say such things.

"You can't honestly mean that," she said. "Look, I know for a fact my eyes are just hazel. And my hair and my looks generally are nothing to get excited about. I'm not pretty." Her year of invisibility at BYU had taught her that if nothing else. "Can't we just be honest about that?" she pleaded.

"I am being honest, and you're completely wrong."

She changed her tack to sarcasm. "Gee, John, that's almost as flattering as last week when you were telling me how smart I was."

He nodded, unrepentant. "Of course. I'm going at it from both sides. Your intelligence and your beauty. You've got brains, looks ... what else is there, really?" He looked down into his beer and sighed. "There's your belief system. It's such a shame. It makes me depressed sometimes. I go home at night and lie awake thinking about it, and it makes me feel sad."

Marguerite was becoming more distressed and agitated by the minute. *Don't do this to me*, she wanted to say, *it isn't fair.* Hadn't she watched him flirt with Angela and hold her hand right in front of her, just the week before? It was fine for him to tease the other girls that way, but not her, not when she was clearly so far gone on him, and when he must have some sense of how desperately she wanted to believe him.

"John ..." was all she managed to say.

"Maybe in a couple of years—when you've grown dissatisfied with your belief system. Then you can look me up. And then we could really get something going." He winked, cocked his thumb and forefinger at her, and nodded to himself.

"Look, I have to go." She grabbed her book bag and left, without even stopping for the usual three rounds of goodbyes to everyone.

———

WHEN MARGUERITE arrived at Angela's house for the barbecue the next day, at a quarter after 1:00, half the guests were already there. Apart from Angela, Pam, and John, there were Oscar and Shawn from the German class, both of whom had brought friends along, as well as Angela's sister and several of her and Angela's friends. In the end, there were about a dozen guests altogether, which was a good number for a party in Marguerite's view—small enough that the shy people like her didn't feel overwhelmed and lost, but big enough to generate a collective energy and buzz you couldn't get from smaller gatherings.

John, Oscar, and Oscar's friend Nick were already in the pool, so Marguerite changed into her swimsuit and came out to join them. She was in the habit of wearing an old tee shirt over her suit (a modest one-piece) to keep her shoulders from getting sunburned, and pulled it on as usual without thinking about it. She sat down on the diving board and stuck a toe in the water. John swam over and hoisted himself up to sit next to her on the edge of the pool. He looked her over and wolf-whistled.

"Se-exy."

She laughed.

"I can't believe you're wearing a tee shirt over your suit," he said. "What've you got on under there, anyway? Please tell me it's a bikini at least."

She shook her head. "Sorry to disappoint you, but what were you expecting? That I'd prance out in a g-string and some teeny tiny little top?"

"I was kind of hoping for topless. Maybe a little masking tape, just to cover the nipples."

Marguerite squeaked and folded her arms across her chest. "Ouch, that couldn't be fun to take off. Get a grip on yourself, please, I'm all traumatized now. Anyway, I don't see you wearing a Speedo. When do I get to see you in a banana hammock?"

"Ugh, now you're traumatizing me. You're going to pay for that." He reached over and shoved her off the diving board into the pool.

"Oh! That's really cold. You're evil," she yelled, when she'd surfaced and spit the water out of her mouth.

"Ha, you know you like it."

They chased each other in and out of the pool, occasionally managing to throw each other in, with Marguerite getting the worst of it, until they were both out of breath and Marguerite was light-headed from giggling so much.

"Come on," John said to her, "we're going in the hot tub. This water's too cold. I'm freezing my balls off." Marguerite climbed out and followed him and Oscar and Nick into the tub.

"Ooh, this feels good," she said, easing herself into the hot water and closing her eyes for a minute. When she opened them, John was picking something out of her hair.

"You had a leaf or something in there," he explained.

"Ah. Okay. Hey, you have a leaf in your hair, too." She plucked it out and flicked it over the side of the tub onto the ground.

John muttered something unintelligible.

"What was that?" she asked.

"Simian mating rituals. Reciprocal grooming."

"Simian who?"

"Monkeys, apes. I read about it. They pick leaves and lice and grubs out of each other's fur before they mate."

"Uh ... okay. You're very strange, you know that?"

THERE WERE hamburgers off the grill, and then a game of Marco Polo in the pool that everyone joined in.

Afterward, they toweled themselves off and everyone came inside to put on dry clothes. Marguerite sat down on Angela's living room couch just in time to see Pam emerge from the kitchen carrying a large rectangular sheet cake in her arms.

"Surprise," she shouted cheerfully. "Happy birthday."

"What? It's for me?" Marguerite asked, staring open-mouthed. "You're kidding."

"Nope. I baked it myself. Hope you like chocolate."

"Oh my gosh." Marguerite got up to take a closer look as Pam set it down on the table. "Wow. Chocolate frosting. And sprinkles, and candles, and everything. This is incredible." She was getting tears in her eyes. "I didn't even know you baked."

"Okay, so I used a mix. But I put the sprinkles on myself, and we counted out nineteen candles exactly."

Marguerite smiled tearfully. "That's the nicest thing anyone's done for me in ages."

"Ah, it was nothing."

Angela came out with a cigarette lighter and lit the candles, and everyone gathered around to sing "Happy Birthday."

"Make a wish," said Angela, giving her a squeeze around the shoulders.

Marguerite blew out all the candles with one breath. She closed her eyes and thought, *I wish John would marry me.* When she opened her eyes again, everyone was smiling at her.

"What'd you wish for?" asked Pam.

"Nothing that could ever come true," Marguerite said glumly. Then, remembering her manners, she smiled and turned to hug Pam and thank her.

"Oh, wait," said Angela. "There's a card, too. Everyone signed it."

Marguerite opened the card and read it while Angela and Pam sliced the cake and put pieces of it onto plates. She laughed over the funny, kind notes people had written. With a fleeting sense of disappointment, she saw John hadn't written a note, but had only signed his name—she recognized his near-illegible scrawl at once.

While people talked and milled around inside and ate cake, Marguerite began to feel tired.

"I'm just going to step outside for a bit of fresh air," she said in Angela's ear as she moved past her to the sliding glass door and let herself out. She sat down on one of the lounge chairs in the shade of the patio by the pool. Someone had left a CD playing in the stereo outside, an album by the Indigo Girls, one of her freshman roommate Rachel's favorite bands. Marguerite liked the Indigo Girls too, and felt happy and relaxed sitting outside by herself, listening. It was the time of day, late afternoon in Tucson, when the light got richer and more golden, slanting thickly through the air, and hadn't yet begun to redden with the setting sun. She sighed with contentment.

Behind her, the sliding glass door opened, and John came out.

"Oh, there you are," he said. "You look peaceful, sitting there. I won't bother you—I just came out to smoke a cigarette. I'll stand over here so you don't smell the smoke." He crossed the patio to stand at the other end of it and lit up his cigarette. The Indigo Girls were singing,

My nights of desire
Are calling me here back to your fold,
And I'm calling you, calling you,
From ten thousand miles away.

Marguerite felt her contentment evaporate, replaced by diffuse longing and impatience. She forced herself to look in the other direction, away from John, out into the blue sky beyond the wall around Angela's yard, while the Indigo Girls sang, *My nights of desire ... Calling you, calling you.*

After what seemed an eternity, the song ended, and she felt as though she'd bobbed up to the surface from underwater. She got up from her chair and walked over to stand near John, who finished his cigarette and flicked it away. She looked away from him, toward the swimming pool a couple of feet in front of them. And then, to her surprise, she felt herself being lifted up off her feet. John had scooped her up in his arms as if she weighed no more than a bag of groceries. She laughed, delighted and afraid, as he carried her closer to the pool and held her over the edge.

She didn't want to go back in the water, not in her dry clothes, not when she didn't have anything else to change into. So she threw her arms around his neck and clung to him tightly enough that he couldn't throw her in without being dragged in too. The moment seemed to last a curiously long time, and she rested her head against his chest, suspended there in midair. It was almost worth getting thrown in the water, she thought, to be so close to him, to breathe in the salty sunburned smell of his skin and feel the back of his neck warm against her hands. At last he set her gently back down on the ground.

She looked up at him and smiled. "I knew you wouldn't do it."

He shook his head. "No, I couldn't. You're much too ..." His voice trailed off, and he shook his head again.

THE TWO of them moved back under the patio and sat down on separate chairs.

"I can't believe the summer's almost over," said Marguerite, leaning back and putting her hands behind her head and her feet up. "It's crazy how fast it went. I'm going to be sad when I have to go back up to school in Utah. I'm really going to miss everyone. But it's been fun, hasn't it? Or interesting, at least."

"Yeah, it's been ... strange," John said. They lapsed into a long silence. Behind them, the sliding glass door opened again, and Pam's head popped out.

"Hey you guys, we're starting some board games. Want to play?"

"Sure." Marguerite rose from her chair and followed Pam into the house. John came in behind her.

They played board games for hours. Teamed with John and Oscar, Marguerite was on the winning side most of the evening. The boys gloated over their wins and toasted them with beers. Angela's mom got home from work, poured herself a glass of wine, and joined them, sitting cross-legged on the floor. The last pieces of cake were eaten. Everyone trooped outside to watch the sunset and sat around the table on the patio. Marguerite took John's wallet, which he'd set out on the table, and idly went through its contents while he looked on. She didn't find much informative or revealing in it. There were a few crumpled dollar bills, receipts for groceries and gas, and a small grainy photo of his mom with her name and a date written on the back, *Charlene Haberman, May 12, 1991*. Marguerite pulled out his driver's license and examined it.

"Bryce John Haberman," she read off it. "I didn't know John was your middle name. Bryce is kind of an unusual name. Didn't anyone ever call you that?"

"Nah, I always hated it actually. I pretended I didn't have a first name in school. Otherwise people'd tease me. You know, 'BJ.'"

"BJ? What's wrong with that?"

"Short for blow job."

"Ohh." Marguerite felt stupid.

"Hey, it'll be dark soon," he said, tapping her knee with his wallet, which he'd taken back from her. "How are you getting home? You've only got one headlight, remember?"

"Oh, yeah, that's right. Maybe I should get going soon. But I don't want to leave, I'm having too much fun."

"I'd drive you home, but I've had too much to drink. I've got to sober up a bit before I get in the car."

"You're welcome to stay the night here if you'd like," Angela said to Marguerite. Angela looked over at her mom for confirmation, who nodded back at her. "That'd be no problem."

"I don't know." Marguerite hesitated. "I have church in the morning, at 9 a.m."

"Oh, well, it's up to you."

Marguerite stayed. Later she called her parents to let them know why she wasn't coming home. The boys all left around ten, and a couple of the other girls slept over, along with Marguerite.

She woke up early and said goodbye to Angela, who was still half asleep, rubbing her eyes and yawning. She drove herself home and got back in time to get ready for church.

AFTER CHURCH, she got a call from a friend of Mark Tierney's, who told her Mark's dad had passed away unexpectedly of a heart attack the day before. Mark had been forced to cut short his Europe trip and was in Phoenix now with his two brothers, taking care of things and helping arrange the funeral. Marguerite had never met Mark's dad, who had been divorced from Mark's mom for as long as Marguerite had known him. She was shocked and worried for Mark, but at the same time thought to herself that at least now she might get to see him again before she went back up to school in Utah.

She set the portable phone down on her bedspread after clicking it off. She didn't want to think about leaving in two weeks. She'd probably never see John again, she thought. She was afraid already of the hole his absence was going to leave behind. Hopefully it wouldn't hurt for too long, and she'd be able to forget him. It was clearly for the best, anyway. As things stood now, she was on a collision course. She'd had no success at converting him to Mormonism, and he'd been equally unsuccessfully at converting her to agnosticism. In spite of this, she felt more attracted to him every time she saw him. How much longer could that go on?

It was definitely for the best that she was leaving, that it was coming to an end. She took her notebook out of her book bag and thumbed through it until she found the page where she'd written the poem about John and his strange, large soul. She read it over again and then turned to the back of the page, which was still blank. She wrote a note to herself.

Better to love him for eternity and not have him, than have him for a moment and lose him and my love forever. Still not sure what love means though. Troubadours? Should write a book about all this someday—if I can ever get it figured out.

She closed the notebook and put it away. Idly, she picked up and flipped open the birthday card everyone had signed, which she had set on top of her dresser when she'd gotten home that morning, next to a small stack of the postcards Mark had been sending her over the summer. Looking at the birthday card more closely, she realized John hadn't just signed his name. He'd signed it, *Love, John.*

CHAPTER 16

THE LAST SUPPER

THE DAY BEFORE THE German class final exam, Marguerite was sitting behind John, listening to Professor Liebmann review the material when she was seized with an overwhelming urge to poke John with a pencil, to touch or disturb him in some way. She sat on her hands for a while until she noticed a label was sticking out of the back of the loose surfer-style tank top he was wearing. After staring at it for several more minutes, at last she could hold out no longer, and, laughing quietly at the oddness of her compulsion, she reached out and tucked the label back inside the neck of his shirt.

John jumped a little and turned around to look at her with a wide smile spreading across his face. Pretending his modesty was offended, he joked in a loud whisper, "You're making me blush—touching my bare back!" But his cheeks were, in fact, bright pink.

"All right," Professor Liebmann announced, "enough lecturing. I'd like you now to drill each other in pairs." He went around pairing people up, and sure enough—"John and Marguerite—why don't you two work together?"

Professor Liebmann had earlier announced he was teaching an upper division literature class in the fall entitled "Women in Love," in case anyone wanted to sign up for it. Marguerite had since then begun to suspect that Professor Liebmann had been using this intensive German class all summer as a kind of petri dish in which to conduct experiments on the subject of the literature class he was preparing.

In spite of these misgivings on Marguerite's part, she and John dutifully pulled their chairs together and sat side by side to work, so close their arms were touching.

It was a good day. John was at his most charming and non-threatening, and Marguerite decided she'd been wrong in thinking she was on a collision course. She had thought she faced two alternatives that were equally horrible to contemplate. The first possibility was that John had no real interest in her and all her doubts about his sincerity were correct. The second was that he did genuinely care for her and at some point it would all come out into the open, and then she'd have to do the impossible and say No to him (impossible, because there wasn't any No in her where he was concerned). There was a third alternative, she saw plainly now—that they were really and truly friends. They could be friends without needing to be more or less.

It was in this state of mind that Marguerite made a confession to him as they walked together after class.

"I'm stressing out a little about going back to BYU."

"How come?"

"I'm afraid I'll be depressed and lonely there."

"Yeah, that place sounds depressing. If it were me, I'd transfer here."

"But it's more than that. I'm worried ... my depression can get kind of serious sometimes. Like more than the way normal people get depressed. I'm not really normal, I guess."

"What do you mean?"

"This summer hasn't been too bad. But there've been times in the past when it got so bad it scared me."

"The depression?"

"Yeah. If something sets me off ... it can spiral ... to the point where, in the past, I've felt like I almost couldn't take it anymore. But it comes and goes. Most of the time I'm fine."

John looked uncomfortable, but asked, "What kinds of things set it off?"

Marguerite jammed her hands into the pockets of her shorts and stared down at the sidewalk as they walked. "It can be different things," she said. "Like—feeling rejected if I like someone and they don't like me back, or maybe screwing up really badly on a class assignment. I just get to feeling like I'm worthless and nothing'll ever be better, like I'm unloveable, and it'll never be okay."

"Hmm," John said.

Marguerite turned her head to glance at him sideways, then looked forward again.

"I shouldn't have told you that," she said. "I don't usually tell people."

"No, it's okay." He caught sight of his car in the parking lot. "Well, that's me, I guess."

"Oh, there's your car." She stopped. "I'm a little further down. See you tomorrow then—good luck with studying."

"You too. And look—don't worry too much about going back. You're not going to be lonely. Guys'll ask you out. You'll have your friends there. It'll all turn out fine, okay?"

Marguerite smiled crookedly. "Okay," she said and waved goodbye.

THE LAST day of class came. They wrote their exams in the morning, and almost immediately afterward, the oppression of freedom set in. Marguerite walked with Pam, Angela, John, and the others to the bookstore to sell their books back, with a sinking feeling in her chest. From there they walked to Mike's Place. The last *Stammtisch*. Jesus's disciples must have felt much the same on their way to break bread and drink wine together with him for the last time. Only in this case, Marguerite hoped, no one was going to betray anyone or wind up crucified.

"So, are you going to remember any of this philosophy stuff we've been talking about all this time?" John asked Marguerite when they had settled onto their usual table with their glasses of beer and (in her case) apple juice. "Did I actually get anywhere with you?"

"Of course I'll remember. I don't think I'll be able to see my religion quite the same way again after this. Not that I've stopped believing. If anything, maybe I'm stronger now than when we started. But I feel like I still have a lot to figure out. Like, now I know better how much I don't know. And I'm a little clearer in my thinking. It's been good for me, overall." She paused. "What about you? Have I gotten anywhere with you?"

"No. I mean, I'm obviously not going to start believing in religion any time soon. But you've given me a lot to think about. Maybe I understand a little better what makes people want to believe. But I don't know if I'll ever really understand it. It's all so foreign to me. By the way, I was going to tell you—you should read Kierkegaard. I think you'd like him. He writes a lot about faith."

"Oh, sounds interesting. I'll have to check him out one of these days."

Later, as they talked, Marguerite reminded him of the time he'd come over for dinner at her house when the elders were there. "Remember, you were talking about how I needed to get away from dualism? I was thinking a little more about that, and I was curious about what non-dualism would entail, and whether you could square that with religion."

"Oh right, non-dualism. Well, I doubt you could ever square it with religion. Like I was saying, religion relies heavily on these simple binary categories: black and white, light versus dark, good versus evil. But the idea in a nutshell, if you want to get away from that simple dualism, is just that reality and truth are a lot more complex. Heidegger talks about truth as a kind of clearing where beings reveal themselves, and he also calls the clearing a *Lichtung*, a lighting. But truth in that sense is also untruth. Because, for example, when you shine a light onto a wall, it obscures the darkness that was there before. The lighting is kind of illusory, because some things are still half in shadow, and the light makes you forget what isn't illuminated, so it also hides the truth that way. Does that make any sense? I don't know if I'm explaining it clearly."

"I think I get the idea, more or less."

"And it's the same thing with good and evil, you could say. You can think of them both as being parts of a whole, instead of as separate from one another, so that you couldn't annihilate one of them without diminishing the whole, or falsifying things. It's not like there's a perpetual struggle between them, it's more like they belong together, they're in a relationship. They interact and play off each other. It's not an arm wrestle between them; it's more like ... like ..." He cast about for the right words.

"Sexual tumbling?" Marguerite suggested.

John looked like he was about to spit out a mouthful of beer laughing, but managed to contain himself and swallowed. "I can't believe you just said that. But yes, that's exactly it."

"But I don't agree."

"You don't?"

"No. I think good is good and evil is evil. Truth is truth and a lie's a lie. And I think it's dangerous to portray these things as less clear-cut and separate than they really are. It could be a way of rationalizing evil and lies. Maybe there are a few cases, once in a while, where it's more complicated, but a lot of the time it's not complicated at all, it's pretty straightforward and simple. Right and wrong look fairly clear to me most of the time."

"Yeah, well, that's because you let other people do your thinking for you. You speak with the voice of the Other."

"Excuse me?" Marguerite blinked at him.

"Sometimes that's what I think," he said. "You don't know who you really are. You're not speaking with your own voice. Your thoughts and your belief system, they're not yours—they come from outside of you. They're imposed on you by others, by the They. You're speaking with the voice of the They. You don't know your true self."

"What? *I'm* the one who doesn't know who I am?"

"That's just what I think."

"Wow." Marguerite didn't know how to respond. She found his words profoundly upsetting, without quite knowing why. They cut her to the core, even as she thought to herself it was an absurd accusation for him of all people to make. "And you think you know who you are?" she asked.

"I know exactly who I am. Well, no, I can't say that. I'm figuring it out, like everybody else. But I'd never let anyone else decide for me, the way you do. I couldn't, not without losing my integrity, losing my grip on who I am."

"And who is that?" She asked, looking intently at him for clues that might lift the sense of confusion from her. "Who are you, really?"

"I'm just ... a person trying to be honest with himself. A person who cares a lot about the truth."

She gave him another long, searching look. "You do care about the truth, I know that. That's what I admire so much about you, your love of truth."

"Yeah," he said simply. "And I couldn't give that up. Not for God or Heaven, not for anything or anyone. It's such a big part of me that—"

"It *is* you."

"Yeah, pretty much."

Marguerite felt afraid then, once again, of being in love with him. Unconsciously, she had assumed she could separate out his love of truth from him, and fall in love with his love of truth without necessarily falling in love with him. But if it went down so deep in him that it *was* him ...

Damon appeared as Marguerite was thinking this. He clapped an arm around John and greeted Marguerite, but didn't look happy to see her. He and John talked for a while, and Marguerite sat off to one side, half-listening to them in between talking with Angela and Pam. She made a few feeble attempts to comment on things Damon or John said, but she got the feeling Damon didn't want her intruding on their conversation. Still, they'd started talking philosophy now, and the snippets of dialogue she caught were too interesting to ignore. After a while she resumed making occasional comments, despite a nagging sense she was making herself obnoxious by persisting where she wasn't wanted. But John began responding to her intermittent remarks and questions, and gradually she wormed her way into their conversation despite Damon's resistance. Bit by bit, she went further and took the reins of the conversation, steering it in the direction she wanted it to go, so that now it was Damon who was sidelined, listening. She felt uneasy about this, but the great slouching beast that paced back and forth down in the black depths of her being had no care for anything but John's attention and that it be directed to her and her alone.

Damon stood up abruptly and told John they needed to go. There was school business they needed to take care of in the philosophy department, business they shouldn't postpone. Marguerite could only look on desolately as John stood up to leave with him, quietly dreading she'd never see him again. John looked at her uncertainly.

"Will you still be here when I get back?" he asked. "I don't know how long this'll take, but I'll come back afterward."

She shook her head. "I don't know. No, probably not. I don't know how much longer I'll be here." She couldn't stay there just to wait for him; who knew if he'd really come back? She would feel foolish and pathetic, lingering in that seedy bar all day when her main reason for being there was long gone.

"If you're not here when I get back, I'll call you this weekend, and we can go out," he said.

Marguerite, who had gotten up from her seat to say goodbye, brightened at his words. "Oh, okay, that'd be great." She stood there awkwardly, wondering if it would be all right to hug him before he left. He laid both hands on her shoulders for a moment, while she looked into his face, scanning it for promising signs. Then he patted her on the head, as he might have done a small child or a dog. They said goodbye to each other, and he left.

What was *that*? That pat on the head? she wondered. That was not a good sign, not at all.

She left as soon afterward as politeness allowed. If he came back and she was still there, his if-then statement would be invalidated, and perhaps then he wouldn't call her and they wouldn't go out. She hurried away, in hopes of making it come true.

SHE SPENT the days until the weekend aimlessly, trying to read and practice the piano and go through the motions of all the things she usually did, but with her attention elsewhere. Friday night passed, and John still hadn't called, and then Saturday morning came and went. A troupe of relatives had descended on her parents' house, and in the afternoon there was talk of going to see a movie that night, with the group consensus leaning toward *Buffy the Vampire Slayer*, in spite of Marguerite's vocal dissent.

Surely this was pretext enough for calling John, to be rescued from having to see some awful teen vampire movie. So, her heart beating furiously, filled with dread (a sympathetic antipathy and an antipathetic sympathy, Kierkegaard tells us), she dialed John's number. When he answered, she explained her predicament and wondered if he might want to do something together that night.

He'd already made plans, he told her. (Of course he had, she thought. She was an idiot. Unlike her he had a life, one that didn't revolve around visiting aunts and uncles from Nevada.) But he'd been thinking of calling her today to see if she wanted to go out Sunday, he said. It should be okay with her belief system, as no work would be involved.

Instantly cheered, Marguerite said that would be fine.

"Great," he said. "So then, would it be all right if I give you a ring after you get home from church tomorrow?"

"A ring? Why, John, this is sudden. We've only known each other for a couple of months. Silver or gold?"

A pause. "Ha. I was thinking gold."

"Actually, silver would be better," she said. "Gold doesn't go so well with my coloring. I'm a Winter, you know."

"Well, that's good then. Silver's a lot cheaper anyway, and I'm kind of broke."

"Just as long as it's got a diamond in it."

"Oh." Another pause. "No glass then?"

"No way."

"And probably no cubic zirconia either, huh? No CZ?"

She laughed. "Nope. Only the real thing. I don't know what size I wear, though."

"I could probably measure from my pinky finger."

"I don't know, your hands are big and my fingers are small. It'd probably still be too big even then."

"Okay, okay already. Let's just say you'll get a ring—of some sort or another—from me tomorrow after church."

They said goodbye and hung up. Marguerite fretted she'd made herself obnoxious again, but thankfully John didn't seem to have taken it amiss, because he called the next day only half an hour after she'd gotten home from church, at half past noon.

"So what would you like to do?" he asked. "I have a couple of errands to run this afternoon, but then I'm free."

"I don't know. What did you have in mind?"

"I was kind of hoping we could just ... go for a walk or something. It's supposed to be nice out tonight, not too hot, and it's not supposed to rain either. But I don't know where. There aren't a lot of scenic places for walking down where I live."

"You could come over. There's a nice patch of desert right near my house with a few good paths running through it. I go for walks there all the time. We could pack sandwiches and have a picnic dinner. It'll be fun."

"Aha, so that's your plan. Lure me out into the desert and have your way with me."

"Pretty much."

He laughed. "Okay. Well, that sounds great. I'll be over around six, if it's okay with you. Your relatives won't mind you running off with me? Will I have to meet them all?"

"No, don't worry, they left this morning. I'll see you at six."

HE WAS early, as always, and they talked and laughed in the kitchen, assembling peanut butter and jelly sandwiches and packing a bag with the sandwiches, drinks, and a picnic blanket.

"Are you wearing that to walk in?" he asked. Marguerite looked down at her flat sandals and short flippy skirt, above which she wore a short-sleeved jersey top that buttoned down the front. It was the most flattering outfit she'd been able to put together that was also casual enough for a walk in the desert.

"Sure," she said. "It's not a really strenuous walk. You think I should change?"

"No ... no, you look nice."

They set off down a path that led through the side yard of Marguerite's house, with John carrying the bag over his shoulder. The sun was setting and it was still hot, but the air was dry and a cooling breeze blew over them.

"There's a lot of shade along the path as we get further on past these houses," Marguerite said. "I like to go down to the wash and sit there under the trees and listen to the birds. I can do that for hours."

As the row of houses fell into the distance behind them, John asked, "Aren't you supposed to call it an arroyo, not a wash?" They were walking now in the shadows cast by palo verde and mesquite trees, as Marguerite had promised.

"Probably, but I've lived here since I was six, and my family and everyone I know calls it a wash."

They walked along the path for a while under the shifting colors of the sunset without saying much. Marguerite felt peaceful and at ease, in her element, with the scent of dust and brush in her nostrils and the birds cooing and chirping around them. When they caught sight of the wash through gaps between the trees and cactuses, they left the trail and made their way gingerly through ankle-high chollas and thorny brush down into its dry, sandy, shaded bed. They spread the picnic blanket out in a flat place next to a boulder big enough for both of them to lean back against as they sat.

Marguerite wasn't hungry yet, so they sipped their water and talked, leaning against the rock. She told him about the movie, which hadn't been quite as bad as she'd expected. They fell silent again, and Marguerite tipped her head back against the stone and closed her eyes. The birds were quieting down, settling in for the evening, but she could still hear a dove singing *too-WOO hoo-hoo-hoo*. She opened her eyes and looked over at John, who was looking back at her with an unhappy expression. Her pulse quickened, and she looked away.

"It really sucks that I'm leaving," she said.

"I think I'm going to miss you a little."

She looked over at him. His expression hadn't changed. "I think I'm going to miss you a lot," she said, and to her horror she felt tears well up in her eyes. She blinked and wiped them from her cheeks with the heels of her hands, sniffing and hoping he wouldn't notice.

"Are you *crying?*" he asked.

She shook her head, but felt two more drops course down the sides of her nose. She heaved a sigh. "Oh, jeez." Now her face was going to be red and blotchy.

He scooted closer and put an arm around her. "I'm glad at least we got to hang out one last time, and say a real goodbye."

Marguerite said nothing, as she was concentrating on stopping the tears.

"Damon tried to talk me out of it, actually, when we went out last night. He didn't think I should see you. He thinks you're not good for me."

She looked up in surprise. "He—really? Why?"

"He says I think about you too much, and it's keeping me from going out with other girls."

"He said that?"

"Yeah. I don't know. He's probably right."

He squeezed her closer and put his other arm around her. Marguerite's heart was beating so hard now she thought he could hear it. She looked up at him. His face and lips were close to hers. And then they were kissing. She couldn't tell if she'd started it or he had. She hadn't been pounced on, but here they were, kissing. She could taste faint traces of mint and cigarette in his mouth, but it wasn't unpleasant. Every part of her seemed to be trembling, falling.

His hands moved through her, down her arms, over the fabric of her shirt, her ribs, her waist, then her hip; she could feel his thumb press into the bone as he gripped her there. She didn't push him away, but drank him in like a man lost and dying of thirst in a desert drinks water.

He was kissing her all over her face, over her closed eyelids, her forehead, the side of her nose, her cheek, her ear, her neck. He rested a fingertip in the notch of her neck. After a while his hand drifted slowly downward to unbutton the top two buttons of her shirt. His fingers slid under the fabric, warm and gentle, hesitant, testing. His hand moved back and forth, and then after a while, further down into the cup of her bra, catching her nipple between two fingers. She gasped, but made no move to stop him. Her mind felt curiously blank, as if her thoughts had all slid down into her body and dissolved into the blood racing through her veins.

He took the hand away, unbuttoned the rest of her shirt, and slid it off her shoulders. He pushed her bra down, too, so that it rested down around her waist, and bent over her to kiss one of her breasts. He took the hard nipple in his mouth and bit it tentatively. She cried out again. She could hear both their breathing, heavy and ragged.

He took his mouth away and she heard him laugh low, and then he was kissing her on the lips again. Inch by inch, his hand began traveling up her thigh underneath her skirt. At last she felt his fingers come to a stop against the elastic of her underwear and then, after a few instants of hesitation, press themselves up under it. She stopped breathing for a long moment while his hand explored, working its way down the crux of her leg until it dipped into the pool that was gathering at her center, welling up like the tears that had sprung to her eyes. He inhaled sharply and drew his hand back. He moved away and took off his own shirt, and while he did this, Marguerite reached behind her and unhooked the bra that still hung around her waist. He pushed her gently down onto her back on the blanket and lay down next to her and put his arms around her, pulling her in close.

Skin against skin. The sensation was entirely new to her, a feeling of great and deep richness, as though some alchemistic process had transformed her body from cool flesh into warm gold.

He unzipped her skirt and pushed it down past her hips, and then pulled her underwear down too. She wriggled under him to pull them the rest of the way off. He sighed and propped himself up on an elbow at her side. With his free hand, he stroked the skin of her breasts and stomach and then her abdomen and all down the length of her thighs, and up again to feel the wetness between them.

As he rubbed there, a melting pleasure began to spread through her, slowly building and deepening in directions her body didn't recognize. When she started to moan softly, he left off and went back to stroking her thighs and abdomen.

Marguerite raised her arms over her head and stretched, arching her back and pointing her toes. Then, drawing herself back in, she put a hand up to his chest and traced its outline above her, framed by the tangle of black mesquite branches against the indigo sky. John sat up, unbuttoned his shorts, and pulled them off along with his underwear. He fished a condom out of one of the pockets and put it on, then lay down naked next to her in the gathering darkness. He stretched himself out all along the length of her and kissed her hard on the mouth again, nudging her legs apart with his knee. Lying on the blanket, Marguerite could feel the sand and pebbles on the ground beneath her digging into her back as his weight pressed down on her and then, startlingly, into her.

CHAPTER 17

A LETTER FROM THE ISLE OF NAXOS

THIS NEVER HAPPENED, OTHER than in Marguerite's febrile imagination.

Marguerite waited to hear from John that Sunday after she got home from church at noon, and when he hadn't called by 2:30 in the afternoon, she had a feeling of foreboding. It wasn't so late that he couldn't still call, but it was late enough for her to worry. You had to wonder about a person who would let you sit and worry.

She took a nap and then decided to go for a walk in the desert—the same patch of desert she had imagined walking in with John. If she couldn't go with him, she would go without him. Besides, that way she wouldn't have to hear the phone not ringing at home. She sat in the shade of a tree on the bank of the wash for a long time, but the heat and the smell of the brush and dust and the sound of the dove singing *too-WOO hoo-hoo-hoo* couldn't drive out her melancholy. Pain was mounting in her, stinging fiercely.

It was humiliating to have believed he would call. To have imagined he was attracted to her, or cared about her as a friend. She'd struggled hard against believing, and only lately had wavered in her doubts, only to have them all confirmed now, it seemed.

She came home late in the afternoon. There'd been no messages for her. She lay down on her bed with her hands clasped behind her head, and felt worse. Should she call him? It could all be a mistake—a lost phone number, some emergency that had come up. A thousand explanations chased each other through her brain. But they all came to circle around the thought that if he was purposely not calling, she had to let the silence take its course. He might still call, and all would be forgiven, but the later it got the less likely such a happy conclusion became, and the more it seemed to her it was best to assume the worst, to steel herself against the pain of it and begin grieving without delay. The longer she held out hope, the more painful it would be to give it up.

Darkness seeped through the blinds to fill her room, but she didn't get up or turn on the light. Her mom knocked on the door and asked if she wanted anything for dinner. Marguerite said in a faint, wobbly voice that she didn't feel hungry. She wasn't feeling well—she was tired and would probably go to bed early. She heard her mom go away again.

She cried and found her tears despicable.

In her overwrought state, she thought to herself that if he never called to explain himself or apologize, she would be left alone like Ariadne on her island, with no Dionysius waiting in the wings to come rescue her. Where would her thoughts go then, all her fragile newborn thoughts about freedom and morality, God, truth, and faith—if the friendship was ending and she couldn't give them to *him* anymore? She imagined the thoughts piling up like the sandy dunes in her old recurring dream, blowing into her eyes and blinding her. She would wander, lost among shifting hills of them. The words she'd heard and read so many times before in church came into her mind, even as she ridiculed herself for thinking them when they were so far out of proportion to her trouble. *My god, my god, why hast thou forsaken me?*

It was the other way around, of course. She was the one who had abandoned God, to worship false idols. And this was her reward, to be in hell—not an ecumenical hell of gleefully dancing devils brandishing pitchforks, but the uniquely Mormon vision of it: cast into outer darkness, cold, alone, imprisoned in silence, in the solitary confinement of her spirit.

NEAR MIDNIGHT, Marguerite began to come back to herself. Yes, it hurt. It had to hurt. But it was for the best. She should be grateful John had lost interest and rejected her when he did. If he hadn't ... she might have lost her soul. As it was, she had sinned in her heart, but it would have been even worse if she had sinned in reality. If he had only put his arms around her and kissed her, she might have betrayed everything she believed in. She should be grateful she'd been spared.

She knelt and prayed, thanking God. Then she took off her clothes, crawled into bed, and fell almost at once into a heavy, dreamless sleep.

THE NEXT day was another bad one. She managed a convincing imitation of a person who wasn't mired in self-pity and struggling against hope, a person who could get out of bed, shower, eat breakfast, dress, and curl up on the couch in the living room with a book in her hands. She didn't turn the book's pages, but apart from this and the puffiness around her eyes, it was a good performance.

At lunchtime, she padded into the kitchen, where Cate was seated at the counter eating cheese crisps. Marguerite warmed up a bowl of leftover soup in the microwave and sat down next to Cate, who acknowledged her by saying, "Hey."

"So what's new?" Marguerite asked.

Cate grunted in reply and after swallowing a bite added, "I'm going out in a bit. David's picking me up." David was Cate's latest boyfriend, a shifty-looking, older non-Mormon boy with a too-fancy car that Marguerite suspected was at least partly financed by the sale of pot. Cate had never had any trouble attracting guys, with her curvy figure and clear, fair skin, but in Marguerite's view her taste in boyfriends was poor.

Marguerite bit back a sarcastic comment about David and said, "Cate, can I ask you a question?"

Cate turned her blue eyes on Marguerite in surprise. "Sure. What is it?"

"Have you ever been rejected? You know, by a guy you liked a lot?"

"Well, sure. Of course I've liked guys who didn't like me back."

"I mean, did you ever ask a guy out, and then he just blew you off?"

"Oh. No, not that. Personally, I'd kill myself before resorting to asking a guy out. Why?"

"No reason."

Cate raised one of her perfectly arched eyebrows, but before she could say anything, they heard a car honking outside. Cate jumped up, leaving the rest of her cheese crisp for Marguerite, grabbed her purse, and waved a hurried goodbye as she ran out the door.

As Marguerite waved to the closing door and turned her gaze back to the half-eaten lunch in front of her, it dawned on her with fresh horror what she'd done. She had driven John away by being too forward. She hadn't waited for him to call her and ask her out, but instead had called him and asked if he wanted to do something. And she'd joked about *rings*. She'd practically *proposed* to him.

She went back to her room and lay down on her bed again, covered her face with a pillow, and wanted to die.

She didn't know how long she had lain there like that when she heard someone ring the doorbell at the side of the house. She heard her mom walk past her door murmuring, "Now who on earth could that be?" and answering it. She heard Mark Tierney's voice, laughing.

"Mark!" Marguerite shouted, launching herself off her bed and out of her room with a leap and throwing herself onto him in a giant bear hug.

"Wow, Marguerite, I didn't expect quite such a warm welcome there," said Mark, stumbling backward, laughing, and patting her on the back. If he hadn't been solidly built, like a football player, he might well have toppled over.

"Oh, I'm so glad to see you," she said. "What are you doing here?"

"Nothing. I got back into town last night. And then just now there was a beautiful sunset starting and no one to watch it with. So I thought I'd drop by and see if you wanted to hang out for a bit and watch the sunset."

"Of course, I'd love to. I'm so happy you thought of it."

They dragged two folding chairs out the side door and set them up in the driveway in front of the carport. While they watched the colors flare and dim in the sky, Marguerite asked hesitantly, "So ... how was the funeral? I heard about it from Ravi—he called and let me know you were on your way back. I'm so sorry. I can't imagine what it must have been like for you."

"You know, the truth is—you never met my dad, did you?"

Marguerite shook her head.

"The truth is—" Mark paused, then lowered his voice, grimacing as he spoke, "well, not that I didn't love my dad ... Your dad is your dad, after all, no matter what. But honestly … my dad could be kind of a dick sometimes. We were never that close. I only saw him every few months. And he was such a jerk to my mom, I had a hard time forgiving him for that. I mean, I loved him, *because* he was my dad, but he wasn't an easy person to get along with. He and his girlfriend were together for ten years, but I think he made her life hell sometimes."

Mark fell silent again for a minute, then went on, "I was glad we got to be part of the funeral, though. It was good to spend that week at the house in Phoenix thinking about him, helping his girlfriend go through his things, and being there for my grandparents and our aunt. It was good to have that chance to say goodbye to him. I guess I was lucky, too, because he and I got to have a good talk before I left on my trip. So I didn't feel like there was anything too unresolved in our relationship, or some unfinished business, like I guess a lot of people do when someone they're close to passes unexpectedly."

"Still … it had to have been hard. I was worried about you. It's such a relief to have you back."

No one close to Marguerite had ever died. She asked Mark how his brothers were dealing with it, and when it seemed he had talked about the funeral as much as he wanted to, she changed the subject, hoping to distract him, pressing him to tell her about his trip and the sights he'd seen. While he spoke, in the back of her mind, she tried to imagine what it would be like if one of her parents died, but it was impossible even to begin thinking about it. Nothing came to her. It was like trying to work out a complicated geometric series in her head that had been printed in reverse and upside down.

"So what's up with you that you were so glad to see me?" Mark asked, when she had run out of questions to ask him. "Is something wrong? You seem kind of down."

"I'm always glad to see you. But yeah, I was going through a bit of a rough patch before you got here. It's a long story."

"Hey, I have an idea. Let's go out for ice cream. There's this new place that just opened up on Oracle Road. My treat. And then you can tell me all about it."

———

THEY SAT in a booth with their ice cream sundaes, and Marguerite told him the story. How she'd become infatuated with John and started to think maybe he liked her too; how she'd made the mistake of being too forward with him more than once, with the result that she'd managed to turn any liking he might have had for her into disgust almost overnight, causing his abrupt disappearance into silence.

When she was finished, Mark shook his head. "I don't know, Marguerite. Maybe you shouldn't jump to conclusions. It's only been a day. Maybe something happened to him. For all you know he could be in a coma in the hospital. Maybe he'll still call."

"But I just have such a bad feeling about it. Like I did something wrong to make him stop liking me."

"It would be weird if it were that. I mean, sure, some guys are fickle—some girls are, too. But you generally have a sense of whether someone likes you, and normally that's not going to change overnight."

"I thought he liked me. I thought we were friends. But now I'm starting to think maybe I was deluding myself all along, believing what I wanted to believe because I liked him so much. Maybe he did like me, but just as a friend. And he didn't realize I was so crazy about him until I starting joking about the rings. And then he realized all at once, and it freaked him out."

"I don't know. If you thought he liked you, he probably did. The fact that you called him a few times shouldn't be such a big deal. He called you too, didn't he? If I like a girl, I think it's good when she calls. Most guys feel that way. Maybe it's not that he didn't like you—maybe he liked you too much. And you were treating him like you were just friends. Maybe he couldn't deal with that."

"But—no, that can't be it. I'd be living in a dreamworld if I thought that. I'm sure I annoyed him. We did have this flirtation thing going on for a while, but he flirted with everyone. That's just how he was. I don't think he was ever serious. For him it was all just fun. For me it was—" She looked down and broke off, folding her arms across her chest and shivering.

"Or maybe he's just more of a jerk than you realized."

"Yeah ... I guess he did have kind of a dual personality. He was really nice to us, the girls he was friends with in the class. But I got the sense he might not always have been so nice to the girls he dated. He and I weren't dating, though, so I never imagined he'd treat *me* that way. I'm wondering now if he ever even meant to call. When I talked to him on Saturday, if he really wanted to see me, we could have made plans for Sunday right then. Instead he said he'd call me back later to make plans, and then didn't call. It's almost ... almost like he set me up, to hurt my feelings on *purpose*."

"Well, guys can be jerks like that. I would never treat someone like that, but there are guys out there who do."

"But it all seems so unnecessary, so gratuitous. If he hadn't wanted to see me ... I mean, it was his idea to go out in the first place. If he changed his mind, all he had to do was make some polite excuse, like he was too busy. I'm leaving to go back to Utah in a week or two anyway. He'd never have to see me again. So why tell me specifically he was going to call, and then not call?" Marguerite could hear her voice creeping up into a high, whiny register.

Mark sighed and Marguerite could tell his patience was starting to wear thin. "Look," he said, "guys can be cowards. Maybe he just didn't have the guts to talk to you. It can be awkward, making excuses not to see someone. So he took the easy way out."

She moaned over her bowl of ice cream and covered her face with her hands. She was close to crying again. Mark frowned and gave her a hard look.

"You really like this guy, don't you?"

Marguerite only nodded with her face behind her hands. She clasped her hands together in front of her with her elbows propped up on the table, looking down at her plate and blinking to keep the tears from coming.

"Did you try calling him? Maybe you should just give him a call and ask him what's up."

"Oh, jeez, no. No way. I'd just make myself even more pathetic than I already am."

"Marguerite, I'm sorry. It sucks that you had to go through something like this. It happens to everybody at some point, but that doesn't make it any easier."

Marguerite looked up at him with a wavering smile. Mark's dad had just died, and here he was consoling her over some guy who wasn't calling. "I can't believe I'm bothering you with my dumb problems when you had so much to deal with last week," she said.

"It's not dumb. Well, okay, it is dumb to be freaking out so much over one phone call. But that's okay. We've all done it. I know it doesn't feel like it now, but in a month you're not even going to remember this guy's name."

Marguerite nodded silently, feeling it surreal and shaming that Mark could be so calm and philosophical about his dad's death, while she was falling apart over a thwarted infatuation.

ON WEDNESDAY, Marguerite met Angela and Pam for lunch at a restaurant called the Blue Willow. Although she'd spent most of the past several days brooding gloomily in her room, she couldn't help but feel happy to see them and chatted away almost as cheerfully as she normally would have. They talked about the final exam and what they'd been up to in the meantime. Pam was excited and nervous, because Shawn from the German class had finally asked her out. They had a date set for Friday night. Angela, on the other hand, was feeling anxious about the upcoming semester and had started a new diet that involved eating large amounts of grapefruit every day.

"So, have you heard from John?" Angela asked Marguerite after a lengthy disquisition on the slimming qualities of citrus fruits.

Marguerite took a deep breath. "No, I haven't. Well, actually, I talked to him on Saturday just for a bit. He'd said something about getting together, so I called to see if he wanted to do something. And he said he'd call me the next day, but then I never heard from him."

"Really? That's strange. He never called you back?" asked Pam.

"No. The truth is, it hurt my feelings. I think I must have annoyed him somehow or—or made him mad at me."

"Really?"

"Yeah. You guys haven't seen or talked to him, have you?"

"No, neither of us has," said Angela, looking at Pam, who shook her head. "I wonder what's up with him. I hope nothing happened—I hope he's okay."

"I don't know. But you'd think if there were some good reason for it, he would have called by now to explain."

"True. That's really strange. I thought you guys were friends. Actually, Pam and I kind of thought you and he might be secretly dating, after you showed up at the restaurant together that one night. We were trying hard not to be nosy and bug you about it, though."

Marguerite bit her lip and shook her head. "No, we definitely weren't dating."

"But that surprises me," Pam broke in, "that he'd blow you off like that. That's just weird. It doesn't seem like him."

"But he is kind of unpredictable, isn't he?" said Angela.

Marguerite laughed. "You could say that."

"Well, we'll let you know if we hear anything," said Pam.

LATER THAT afternoon, one of the last monsoons of the season blew in. Marguerite went out to the back patio to sit on the swing that hung from the rafters and watch the storm. Lightning draped itself in spidery folds over the mountains, splitting open the atmosphere with deafening cracks of thunder. The scent of wet creosote filled her nostrils with cloying sweetness as the rain drove down in sheets.

Her mom came out and joined her on the swing. They sat and watched together for a while without saying much.

"Do you want to talk about it?" her mom asked, when the thunder quieted for a moment.

"Talk about what?" Marguerite asked dully, as a tear slid down her cheek.

"I don't know. You've been hiding in your room for days. I thought you might've had a fight with one of your friends or something."

"No, Mom. It's nothing like that. It's nothing, really. I'm just a little down, that's all."

"Oh, sweetie." Her mom put an arm around her and hugged her, and Marguerite could tell from the way her voice sounded that she was tearing up as well. "I just hate to see you sad."

Marguerite leaned her head against her mom's shoulder. They stayed out for another half hour like that, watching the storm.

———

ON FRIDAY, Pam phoned to report that she'd run into John on campus. They'd chatted a bit, and then Pam had told him he should call Marguerite.

"Oh dear," Marguerite said. "I'm afraid he's just going to feel harassed now and be even more annoyed with me than before."

"Well, he didn't seem annoyed when I said it. He said he would call you."

Marguerite got off the phone with Pam and began pacing worriedly back and forth in the living room. The phone rang again. It was Angela, calling to tell Marguerite she'd also seen John a day earlier and, like Pam, had told him he ought to call her.

"Oh, no. Pam just told me she did the same thing. Oh, this is a disaster." Marguerite wrung her hands with the phone pressed between her ear and a hunched shoulder. "This is just getting worse and worse."

"But he said he'd call you. Cheer up, maybe he still will."

Marguerite knew he wouldn't. If he called now, lengthy apologies would be needed to set things right, and she couldn't picture John making them.

"He mentioned something about him and his brother moving into a new apartment," Angela said. "Maybe that's why hasn't called—he's been busy with the move."

WHEN SHE hung up after talking with Angela, she tried desperately to think whether there was anything she could do to rescue the situation and redeem herself from the crushing sense of shame that enveloped her. Things were so mixed up now, and her mind was weary and muddled from days of wallowing in self-contempt. The idea of simply calling John presented itself. She could tell him never to mind what Pam and Angela had said—it had all been a misunderstanding. In reality, it wasn't a big deal and she didn't care one way or the other. No other ideas as attractive as this one occurred to her, so at length, with pounding heart and trembling fingers, she dialed John's number.

It wasn't John who picked up, but his brother Greg. When she asked for John without saying who was calling, Greg told her politely he wasn't there. Could he take a message? he asked.

"Oh, well, it's … probably no one he would want to talk to anyway," Marguerite said, and knew even as the words left her mouth she'd made a dreadful mistake by saying them. There was silence on the other line. "Okay then, goodbye," she said and hung up.

She hated herself. She wished she were dead. Greg had been nice to her, and now she'd gone and said this pitiable thing to him. What had become of her ideals of charity and kindness, that she would drag an innocent third party into witnessing her moral degradation?

The moral thing was to be happy, she'd been taught all her life. As the scriptures said, *Men are that they might have joy*, and *Despair cometh because of iniquity*. The moral thing was to be sensible and get over it. It was wrong to be mourning instead as if someone had died. Or as if she'd fallen in love with someone who'd spent an entire summer undermining all her beliefs and then disappeared into thin air without warning, goodbye, or explanation. Or perhaps as if some thoughtless, charming amoralist had made her fall in love with him on a whim, then got bored and discarded her as soon as it was clear she was weak enough to fall for him. It was shameful to dwell on such thoughts, but Marguerite had sunk too deeply into her rumination to free herself from it now, however hard she struggled.

She thought she couldn't sink any lower, but she did. She wrote John a letter, an absurd letter—a hate letter in which she blamed her religious difficulties on his bad influence. She implied she had cast her pearls before swine. She had offered him her thoughts, and he had trampled on them; the only real prettiness she had in her, he'd despised. How had he dared to call her intelligent and nice-looking, when clearly he must have seen her as worthless all along? How could she have thought to learn anything from him about freedom or truth, when he'd been so dishonest with her? Now he would be free of her and her good opinion, and she was glad to be free of him too.

She wasn't one to hold a grudge, she wrote. He could redeem himself, maybe in few years, but she wouldn't be holding her breath. She signed the letter "Love, Marguerite," and added a postscript not to forget the challenge and the promise about reading the Book of Mormon and praying about it, because that was still true, whatever else might happen.

It was the sort of letter anyone would cringe to think they'd written, let alone sent. But Marguerite sent it. She didn't have his address, so she called information. If he was moving, she supposed the letter would be forwarded. The directory had a B. Haberman in it, an address down by the university, and this was the address she wrote on the envelope. (Now that she thought of it, it was strange he hadn't ever told her where he lived. When she'd picked him up to go to the Gasthaus restaurant, he had insisted on meeting her at Bentley's rather than having her pick him up at his apartment. Maybe, when you went around sleeping with girls you didn't care about and tallying them up as notches on your bedpost, standing up thirty-year-old women when you'd made dates with them, and pretending to be friends with girls only to hurt their feelings on purpose in the end, you learned not to give out your address, or you'd be flooded with hate mail after a while.)

The day after the letter had gone out, she was pale with horror at having sent it. There was no way of getting it back. But perhaps she could call and get his answering machine, and leave a message begging him not to read it, to throw it away unopened. She dialed his number, but no one answered, and there was no answering machine. She let it ring twenty times, carefully counting them out before hanging up. Maybe he had already moved. Maybe he was there listening to it ring and ring, not picking up, certain it could only be her. There was no way of knowing.

CHAPTER 18

THE GRASSHOPPER

THE DAY BEFORE SHE left for Utah, Marguerite awoke to the sound of something buzzing and rattling against her window. She peered through the blinds and saw it was a large brown grasshopper that had gotten itself trapped between the blinds and the glass windowpane. It was propelling itself against the glass over and over again, thinking it was moving toward freedom, only to find itself continually blocked and bruised instead. Marguerite felt instant sympathy for it.

"You're not going to give up, are you?" she asked it. The grasshopper didn't acknowledge her, but merely launched itself against the windowpane one more time.

"Hey, little buddy, that's not the way to do it. Let me help you." She took a tissue from her bedside table, lifted the blinds, and held out the tissue for the grasshopper to climb onto. Gingerly poking and prodding, she persuaded the grasshopper into the middle of it, and then, hardly daring to breathe for fear of scaring him off it prematurely, balanced the tissue with the brown stick-like thing in it in the palm of her hand as she went to the side door and opened it. She stepped out and set the tissue down on the ground outside. The grasshopper flicked an antenna cautiously in her direction, then bounded off toward the front yard.

THAT EVENING, she saw Mark Tierney again. They sat in a booth in an all-night diner and talked over plates of greasy food.

"Mark, can I ask you a question?" Marguerite said, when their food had come. "What do you want to do with your life, ultimately?"

147

He was quiet for a moment, thinking, then said, "Honestly? I'd like to make myself immortal."

Marguerite laughed, then realized he wasn't joking. "Immortal? But I thought you didn't believe in life after death or God or any of that stuff."

"What I mean is, if I could have anything I wanted, I'd try to make myself immortal by helping humanity in some way—being great and being remembered for it."

"So you'd like to be famous? As a physicist, or what?"

"Yeah, maybe. Not famous like a movie star or some idiot Top 40 group, but for something worthwhile. Like accomplishing something in physics, or just contributing in some way to human progress."

"Okay then, my question is, why be famous for doing something good? Why not be a Charles Manson, if the goal is just being remembered after you're gone?"

"I don't know. Because of my values. Because of the belief system my parents raised me with. They didn't raise me to be a Satan-worshiping serial killer. I value reason and knowledge and progress, and that's what I'd like to be remembered for, for being a part of that."

Marguerite picked thoughtfully at her plate of French fries. Mark said abruptly, "Marguerite, you shouldn't be going to BYU. You should be going to the U of A instead."

"What? Where did that come from?"

"You're too smart to be going to BYU. You're too open-minded for that place. You're a thinking person. Why go somewhere where you have so many constraints placed on you and on what you can think about and study? I think you'd do better here, where there aren't those kinds of walls around you. You'd be free to think whatever you want. You could be yourself here."

Marguerite ate another French fry. "It's funny you say that," she said after she'd swallowed. "I've kind of been thinking the same thing. The U of A has a really good comp lit department, from what I hear. It's too late to transfer this semester, but maybe after that ... maybe it would be better for me. It's hard to think of going back to BYU when I've changed so much this summer."

"How do you think you've changed?"

"I think I've gotten more analytical, more critical in how I look at everything. I try a lot harder to be objective now, especially about things like religion and values. Maybe I've gotten more honest with myself."

"I was noticing that a little when we were talking earlier. Why do you think that is?"

"I think it's because of that guy John—you know, the one I was all depressed about. Because I spent the whole summer talking philosophy with him, and it changed the way I think. It made me more careful and aware of my beliefs and my reasons for them. But he's one reason against transferring to the U of A. I'd be so embarrassed if I ever ran into him now. I made such an ass of myself over him."

"So he never called you? What ever happened with that?"

"Oh, jeez, it's a horrible story. I'm almost too ashamed to tell you." But she told him anyway—about feeling sorry and hateful toward herself longer than she could justify, her conversations with Pam and Angela, calling and talking to John's brother, writing a hate letter, and letting the phone ring twenty times.

"Oh, no, you didn't. You seriously wrote him a hate letter and sent it? Marguerite, you're supposed to write those letters and *not* send them. Haven't you ever heard of sitting on a letter for 24 hours first, so you have time to cool off and reconsider?"

"Yeah, that doesn't work with me. It takes me more like a year to cool off and reconsider things."

Mark laughed and shook his head. Marguerite went on.

"But it was awful, it was like each new thing I did only confirmed his wisdom in blowing me off in the first place. The worst thing is, some part of me keeps thinking it was all because I wouldn't have sex with him. Not that he ever asked me to. But I can't help feeling like if I'd only been open to it, I wouldn't have lost him—he wouldn't have disappeared on me like that at the end. Although maybe he would have disappeared either way, and it would have been that much worse. But I feel like I gave up a chance at love for the sake of religion, and I don't know if it was worth it, if the Church is even really true. And I keep agonizing over it, even though it's all over and done with and there's nothing I can do now. But then on the other hand, I think if he'd really cared about me as a person, he would have stayed friends with me. So I can't have lost that much. And then I think I probably only imagined there was any chance of a relationship there, or that there would have been a chance if only I'd been open to it."

"Oh, God, Marguerite, you're going to drive yourself crazy if you keep thinking like that. Just remember, you don't know what was going on with him. It could have been something totally unrelated to you. You never know what's going on inside another person's head."

"True. I know that, I do. But anyway. I've signed up for 19 credits next semester. I'm just going to throw myself into my classes and my work, and hopefully I'll be so busy I won't even have time to think about it."

"Well that's one way of going about it. But what you said just now—that's a sad thought, if you gave up a chance at a relationship with this guy for the Church, and you're not even sure if you believe in it. I'm just worried at BYU you won't be able to explore that and find out what you believe for yourself."

Marguerite tapped a French fry against the edge of her plate. "John was always saying he thought I wasn't free, that I wasn't thinking for myself."

"But in the end it doesn't matter where you are, whether you're here or at BYU. You can be free in your own mind if you choose to be."

Marguerite looked up at him and was quiet for a moment. "What does that mean to you, Mark—freedom? What do you think freedom is?"

"Well, obviously there are different senses of it. What I'm talking about is a freedom based on self-reliance. You rely on the power of the mind, your own mind, and you don't let anything or anyone else stand in your way or prevent you from going after what you want, intellectually or otherwise. That's such a powerful thing. It's so incredible, just to think, no one can stand in my way. That's been the driving force behind all the progress the human race has made in science throughout history—that courage and determination and belief in the power of the mind."

Marguerite leaned back in her seat, looking at him, nodding, and thinking what a good friend and a good person he was. *If anyone deserves to be immortal,* she thought, *it's Mark.*

———

THE NEXT morning, Marguerite, her parents, and Cate loaded up the car with Marguerite's luggage and set off on the twelve-hour drive to Provo. Marguerite watched out the window as the city dwindled to scattered buildings and fenced land and then turned to open desert.

They passed through Phoenix, Globe, down and up the twisting narrow highway through the Salt River Canyon, through Show Low and Flagstaff, past the Grand Canyon and the border towns into the badlands of Southern Utah. As they traveled down the highways into the heart of this believing country, Marguerite was going on a nearly opposite journey in her mind. She penetrated further than she ever had before into the country of unbelief, into the bleak, heartless, desolate world of Korihor and John, where there were no protections for weak and fragile people like herself and she would have to be strong to survive.

John had probably been right all along, she thought, remembering their conversations about freedom. It was true, there was no objective basis for her religion. The whole thing was probably a hoax. There were hesitations that tugged at her still, her sense of reverence and peace when the priests passed around the sacrament in church, the whiteness of the torn-up pieces of bread and of the men's shirts as they handed the silver trays around, wafting the odor of yeast through the pews; the whiteness of the temple walls and the clothes people wore there, the quiet way they shuffled down the chlorine-scented halls in their industrial white terrycloth slippers. But Marguerite was determined for once to set these hesitations aside, at least long enough to go forward and catch sight of what lay ahead of her if she let them go.

If she were to do as Korihor had urged and shake off the chains by which she was bound, the chains of the religious indoctrination she'd undergone since childhood, if she were to forge her own belief system independent of doctrine or dogma, what would it look like? What shape would it take, assuming you left God and religion out of it?

She wouldn't lie, Marguerite thought. She wouldn't want to add to all the confusion in the world. If your first principle was the love of truth—which was what Marguerite thought she had loved in John—if you loved truth that much, it made no sense to deceive other people.

She would still believe in being kind. Kindness was beauty, and this bleak, desolate world was sorely in need of it. Kindness was also another reason to be honest in her dealings with people.

She wouldn't steal or kill. She would try not to envy. She would try to do no harm. She didn't see any reason to take up smoking or drugs, or engage in heroic drinking bouts. And sex before marriage? She still wanted marriage, marriage as she had always imagined it. She wanted children and a faithful, devoted husband, someone who would love her enough never to leave her, someone who wouldn't disappear on her, someone she could trust not to abandon her as Theseus did Ariadne on some lonely desert island, to watch as his ship's sails disappeared over the horizon. What was there for someone like her in the short-term and the temporary? She didn't give her heart lightly. She couldn't imagine giving her body away without her heart in it.

It all ended up not so far away from where she'd begun. And yet it might as well have been a world away, she discovered when she tried to go back the way she had come. She had groped her way into this gray, lightless realm only to find that, after all, she had a small light of her own to cast on it. But the way back was no longer visible.

The Church had taught her a set of ethical principles that generally worked well for her, had given her a measure of happiness and health, surrounded her with protections throughout her life. The Church had produced a wholesome, lovely society of attractive, freshly scrubbed-looking people, a society she would be rejoining in a matter of hours. In Marguerite's view, the great advantage of Mormonism over other faiths was its demand that people actually practice its principles with rigor and generosity, or else call themselves something other than Mormons. But Marguerite had lost her belief in it and her conviction it was true.

Marguerite's mom stopped the car just past the border in Kanab to let everyone go to the bathroom, get food, and stretch their legs. While they were there, Marguerite tried to draw Cate into conversation with her. She seldom did this, because Cate tended to be taciturn and closed off around her family, even though her personality in other settings was bubbly and effervescent. It was clear enough that Cate found her sisters and mother overbearing, self-righteous, and judgmental, and felt the same about most practicing Mormons. Cate was always getting into trouble, hanging out with the wrong crowd, going out with boys like David who dressed like gangsters and wore their hair slicked back with gel, boys who did drugs or smoked or drank too much. Marguerite, by contrast, almost never got into trouble in high school and hung out with good, college-bound kids like Mark Tierney (who didn't smoke, drink, or do drugs). She'd been a model daughter, if you could overlook her occasional bouts of acting withdrawn and temperamental and the times she'd been secretly suicidal.

There in Kanab, though, as they sat in the McDonald's and ate their hamburgers and French fries, Marguerite tried talking to Cate, asking about her friends, her plans and goals for the coming year, her opinions of people and current events, her favorite music and books. And for once, Cate opened up to her. It was almost as though she could sense Marguerite had come to a humbling place of uncertainty. The two of them got along better with Marguerite in that place, perhaps because Cate intuited that Marguerite was being nice to her for once not just because Mormonism told her she should, but because she loved her sister without anyone having to tell her to.

IT WAS dark and all the stars were out by the time they arrived at the condo in Provo. The condo was in a new and fashionable set of buildings on University Avenue, constructed according to modern design principles to be airy and light-filled, with high ceilings and lofts. Marguerite's dad had bought the place, figuring that since at least two of his daughters and any number of their cousins would be going to school there, it would be a good investment. Marguerite's older sister Lisa had lived there for three years previously, the last year with her new husband. Now Lisa and her husband had graduated and moved into a smaller apartment of their own so Marguerite could live there with roommates.

Marguerite's parents and Cate helped move her things in and then stayed several more days to visit relatives in Orem. Sunday morning, Cate and her parents got back in the car and set out on the drive back to Tucson. Marguerite waved goodbye to them and watched the car speed away down University Avenue until it disappeared into the distance.

She went to get ready for church.

PART II

HISTORY
OF THE
CONCEPT OF FAITH

CHAPTER 19

FEAR AND TREMBLING

*S*EPTEMBER *15*

I've hardly written anything in this journal since last fall when I got so busy with school, but I've decided I need to start up again. Since I don't have John to talk to and criticize my ideas anymore, I'm worried that if I don't write I might get intellectually lazy again and fall back into my old habits of sloppy thinking. Hopefully writing things down will help me be strict and honest with myself and do a better job of figuring out what I believe.

I don't know how much time I'm going to have this semester, though. I think I may have taken on too much with this course load. It's only been two weeks, and already I'm exhausted. I've got Advanced German Grammar, French Lit, Greek 101, Honors Science Colloquium, History of Philosophy I, and New Testament. The idea was to drown my sorrows in work and be so busy with school I wouldn't have time for a social life and therefore couldn't get my feelings hurt from any more guys rejecting me for a while. The second part of the plan is working—I certainly have no social life—but not so much the forgetting John part. I still talk to him in my head when I read my philosophy assignments. I still think about him all the time and wonder what he'd say about the things I hear and think.

It's funny given how badly he hurt my feelings that at times I feel I'm almost becoming him, taking on his role when I talk with people and question their statements, as though his spirit were somehow inhabiting me. I kept hectoring my religion professor about how the virgin birth was supposed to have worked, the first week of class. Professor R. is highly respected in the Mormon community, a scholarly man who knows Greek and Hebrew and reads works of Biblical research in several modern languages. And here I was, trying to get him to specify whether Mary's hymen was still intact after she'd conceived Jesus. I mean, it's important, isn't it? If God or the Holy Spirit came down and had sex with her, wouldn't that invalidate the law of chastity, if God Himself didn't keep it? The professor's answer at first was, "It's none of our business." But given the implications of it for me in particular, I can't help feeling it's very much my business.

When I stayed after class to press him further on it, I was red-faced and embarrassed asking the questions, and he looked every bit as uncomfortable to be interrogated about the mechanisms of divine implantation. His argument was that we can't know the specifics, but we start from two presuppositions: God wouldn't violate His own laws, and with God, nothing is impossible. (Although, isn't that a contradiction, if it's impossible for Him to violate his own laws?) Also, in the Hebrew text the word that gets translated as "virgin" only means "young woman."

John's ghost in me, if that's what it is, must have been laughing his ass off.

Church last week was hard. It was my first time going to a meeting in our new ward with all my roommates. (I'm living with Rachel again, plus Ellen from our old dorm and Miriam, who said one summer of living at her grandma's house was enough for her.)

It's almost physically painful not to believe when everyone else does or seems to. It's as if I were the sole jarring, discordant note in an otherwise stately and balanced musical composition, as if I were singing in a choir and my voice stuck out, hoarse and toneless, grating on my own ears. But I started to feel hopeful in Sunday School when the lesson turned out to be interesting for once.

The teacher, a returned missionary a few years ahead of us in school, took a surprisingly philosophical approach. The lesson was on "Ways of Knowing," and he started by writing a list on the blackboard that looked something like this:

- *Authoritarianism*
- *Science*
- *Empirical Observation*

158

- *Mysticism (fabrication)*
- *Revelation*

I raised my hand and suggested reason or logic should go on the list, too. So he added that and then went through the list discussing each item. Authoritarianism was faulty and hard to trust; science, empirical observation, and reason-slash-logic were all capable of making mistakes, and mysticism was no good either, being basically knowledge of our own invention, as he saw it. Which left revelation as the most trustworthy source of knowledge.

He had us read a scripture in the Doctrine and Covenants: *You must study it out in your mind; then you must ask me if it be right, and if it is right I will cause that your bosom shall burn within you; therefore, you shall feel that it is right.* I raised my hand again and asked how we could trust our feelings any more than reason or our empirical observations. A couple of other people in the class raised their hands and suggested the answer was it takes practice to differentiate between feelings, to tell which are from us and which are spiritual and from God. The teacher asked what I thought, and I had to admit it didn't satisfy me.

The discussion went on, but everyone was staring at me as if they pitied me. I started feeling sorry for myself too, disabled by my lack of faith and understanding. As the teacher brought the lesson to a close, he looked me in the eye and said, "And I promise *you*, Marguerite, on a one-to-one level, it's true what the scriptures say: Seek and ye *shall* find."

When he said that, I felt pierced through but also uplifted. For a moment I caught a vision of myself not giving up, still striving to understand and believe in spite of all the difficulties that stand in my way, my weaknesses and flaws. It felt as though some invisible, graceful, bright-winged being were taking me by the hand to lead me forward through my blindness and confusion.

Then he asked me to say the closing prayer. I hesitated, but decided to try. I said, "Dear Father in Heaven, please help us gain understanding." I stopped, feeling all wrong, but then tried again. "We thank Thee ..." I tried to think what I was thankful for, but only felt empty and cold. I didn't know who or what I was talking to, and I resented it. So I finally said, "I can't ..." and sat down. Tears started rolling down my cheeks and dripping onto my blouse.

The teacher stood up and gave the prayer in my place, and Rachel, who was sitting next to me, put her arm around me and hugged me during it.

As everyone else was leaving the room, the teacher came over to me and Rachel (who was also crying by now) and asked if I was okay. I told him I had just felt too dishonest, praying in front of other people when I was filled with so much uncertainty. He said most people don't even think about it, so in that respect, I was a step ahead of them. But I think he just said that to make me feel better.

September 18

I've been thinking about conscience since that traumatic Sunday School lesson. I clearly have one with a strong voice that doesn't want me lying to myself or telling myself or others I know something when I don't. Is conscience like revelation at all? There's nothing that feels so trustworthy to me as this voice—what Socrates called his *daimon*, I suppose—but where does it come from? Is it God, or the Spirit speaking in me? Or is it the ghost of John again? Or am I just plumb crazy, hearing voices?

September 24

Church went better today. It helps that I still pray and read a chapter from the scriptures every night. If I didn't I'd be cutting off the lines of communication, and then how could I hope for answers? Meanwhile, I've decided the two provisional tenets of my belief system are, one, I will search for Truth (yes, Truth with a capital T) and will let nothing stand in my way, like Mark and I talked about the night before I left. And two, I will be loving toward others. That is, I'll be kind and try to help others find Truth also. Practicing Mormonism isn't inconsistent with either principle, so I'll keep doing it for now and hope someday I'll figure out how it all fits together. I only worry that someday the two principles might collide, and I'll have to choose between them.

September 26

There are some nice guys in my classes, but stupidly, I can't help comparing everyone to John. Stupid, stupid, stupid—comparing boys I probably couldn't have even if I wanted them to a guy I never could have been with under any circumstances, and who's gone now, probably for good. Stupid as it is, I'd be lying if I said I didn't miss him. No one here makes me laugh the way he did. Of course, I tend to remember his good side more than his bad side. I keep having to remind myself how awful he could be. Like when he joked about how all he had to do to get girls to sleep with him was pretend he cared about them. Even if it was a joke, I bet on some level it was true. Anyway, I'm sure it took him less than two seconds to forget about me. I bet he went out drinking with Damon, got trashed, hooked up with some random chick, and hasn't thought of me since.

It's funny—I thought I loved him for what he loved, for his love of Truth, more than for all his incidental, contingent qualities like being tall and having the body of a Greek god and making me laugh. I thought it came down to shared values. But here I am, surrounded by thousands of single guys who share my values at least in theory, and I don't want anything to do with any of them, or they with me.

If it was so easy for him to forget me, why is it so hard for me to forget him? I feel like something's wrong with me, like I'm one of those people whose blood doesn't coagulate, so they never stop bleeding if they get a cut. I can't stop obsessing over it. But then, how do you forget someone who changed you and the way you think, and made you see everything in a new way?

It's not surprising I can't get interested in anyone else. No one here can compare to him on his good side, and no one is as instructive or stimulating as him on his bad side.

September 27

Is it better to love or be loved? If you're the one who loves, you can take the high road, and you have a built-in defense if things go wrong or the other person doesn't love you back. You can say to yourself: At least I was loving. I was in the right. But it's different with being loved. Then it's something imposed on you from the outside, whether you want it or not. You're the victim. You might deserve it or you might not, but it's done to you regardless. You can only react but can't control it. So it's a strange thing.

I remember John saying the night of the pool party at Angela's,

"It's been strange." I suppose that's what I did to him—I made things strange for him, by imposing this being-loved on him.

September 30

I wrote another letter to John and sent it yesterday. I know, I know. Writing one letter was bad enough, and then to write and send a second one? But I needed to do it. I wanted to repent, apologize, and say goodbye. We never did say a real goodbye. If he wouldn't say it to me, at least I could say it to him.

I kept feeling I must have done something morally wrong with regard to him. If not, why would I still feel so unresolved and troubled by the whole thing, which objectively speaking was such a trivial, stupid business, just a silly summer flirtation that had to end, and did? Repentance is supposed to make you pure, whole, and clean again in God's eyes and your own. But before you can repent, you have to understand and feel sorry for what you did wrong. So in writing, I tried to make clear to myself what I'd done and why I regretted it.

For one thing, I lied to myself, telling myself he cared and it was possible for something to happen between us. Worse, I cared more about him and whether he liked me than about Truth, the truth of things like God, religion, and morality. If I'd cared more about Truth for its own sake, maybe I wouldn't have gotten so tangled up in that mess of wanting everything I couldn't have and he couldn't give me. I feel guilty, too, for having all those possessive, ulterior, ugly motives beneath the veneer of friendship. And I regret wanting to give in and be whatever he might have wanted me to be even though I hadn't lost the argument. He couldn't beat me fair and square by convincing me my views were wrong, but I still wanted to let him win. I tried to cheat, not in order to win, but to lose. At that point, I lost my integrity. That's what I'm most ashamed of, and that's what I needed to repent and apologize for.

Of course, there's only so much a letter can do to make me feel better. I know he won't write back, and all the stupid letters in the world won't change the fact that he's gone.

October 10

I think I've made a new friend. Her name is Amanda, and she's in my philosophy class. A couple weeks ago she called me to talk about one of our assignments, and we ended up having a long conversation about philosophy and our classes and the people in them and all kinds of things. A few days later I called her, even though I felt a bit shy about doing it, and we had another nice long conversation. Since then we've talked often and sometimes meet to study together.

Amanda and I have a lot in common, counting ourselves among the few female philosophy students here. We've both felt conflicted about being Mormon women with intellectual aspirations, wanting careers as college professors and yet also wanting to get married and have families. It seems like at every fireside and devotional we go to, one of the general authorities ends up talking about how mothers shouldn't work outside the home, and it always makes me want to tear my hair out. Now I can vent my frustrations to Amanda.

She grew up in a small town in Utah and hasn't had as many experiences with being out in the non-Mormon world as I have, so she's more conservative than me about some things. Like the other day we were talking about polygamy, and she was saying she thought it had actually been a good thing for the women who practiced it in the old days, including her great-great grandmother's family. In their letters and diaries the women said all kinds of positive things about it. But I find the idea horrifying. Amanda thinks that after the Second Coming polygamy will be restored and everyone will practice it again. I told her I was sure that was just folk theology, not official Church doctrine. But the nice thing about Amanda is that we can have these interesting arguments and she doesn't seem to get offended when I disagree with her or point out flaws in her reasoning, the way a lot of people would; instead, she stands her ground and tries to come up with more convincing arguments to persuade me.

She also makes me laugh, the way she gets so excited about things in our philosophy readings. She can be goofy and silly and tends to use dramatic hand gestures to illustrate her points when she talks. She's got that classic happy, glowing Mormon look about her, and she's pretty, with a beanpole figure, a round face, and wide pink cheeks. She always wears pink lipstick. I really like her.

I'm officially a philosophy major now. I'd been going back and forth between that and literature. What finally decided me was getting a lousy grade on my last history of philosophy exam. Afterward I went to see our professor, Dr. Gardiner, to talk about it. I said I worried I wasn't smart enough to study philosophy and wondered if I should stick with literature instead. He smiled and told me how when he was in college he started out as an English major, but at some point he felt he wasn't learning anything, so he switched to philosophy. His professors would tear his papers to shreds and tell him he contradicted himself all over the place, and he would know they were right. Philosophy was simply more demanding in terms of the rigor and the level of self-criticism it required, he said. It all depended on whether you cared about learning or just wanted to coast through school.

So that decided me. Besides, I'm passionate about philosophy in a way I haven't been with other subjects, because its questions affect my life so directly. Should I try to get what pleasure I can in the here and now, or give up things I badly want for the sake of religion and morality? Does God exist? How can I know, and what does it mean to know? Is my existence meaningful and valuable enough to make it worth enduring even when I hurt and feel alone and hopeless? I don't see how anything else could possibly be as important as finding answers to those questions.

October 11

My roommate Rachel is seeing a guy she met over the summer, the first guy she ever kissed. He comes over sometimes, and they sit on the couch or upstairs in the loft of our condo, hold hands, and kiss. When I see them together, I can't help but think of John and feel stupidly wistful again.

Was it for the sake of a beautiful illusion that I lost any chance I might ever have had to do those things with him? Even if it's too late to change the past, I want to know. That's the question I'm trying to answer by studying philosophy. I'd like to believe I didn't give that up for a lie.

If we'd just kissed. At least then I'd have that to remember and hold on to. But instead I have nothing but the bastard child, Doubt, he left me with, a child I'm slowly trying to drown so as not to have to bear the shame of it, like Margaret when Faust left her. And what prison will I languish in for that crime?

But I get myself all turned around with these grand, life-explaining metaphors. It's never clear, either, whether I'm supposed to be the boy or the girl in the story. I'm Ariadne, but I'm also Theseus, trying to find my way out of a labyrinth. I'm Margaret, but I'm also Faust, led on by lust and longing, restless and striving, trying to atone for my sins by building something worthwhile in the world.

Enough grandiosity for one day. I should get back to studying for my Greek exam.

October 29

I've started going to a series of lectures on campus called the Philosophy Club, where the philosophy department arranges for faculty members and sometimes visiting scholars or even the more advanced undergraduate students to present papers every few weeks. I don't understand much of what's said, but it's fun to go, especially when Amanda comes too and we can talk about it afterward.

There's a small clique of upperclassmen philosophy majors—all guys, of course—who I see at the lectures. They seem interesting, and I wish I could make friends with some of them, but it's much too intimidating to think of introducing myself. I run into one of them often after my Greek class, because he's in the class that meets after mine. There's something strange about the way he looks. I think it's his eyes. They look ... old somehow. Aged, ancient even. Although he's clearly an undergraduate and couldn't be that much older than the rest of us—he couldn't be older than twenty-four, maybe twenty-six at the outside. But the phrase that springs to mind to describe him is "Ancient of Days," like in a William Blake poem. He reminds me of the Edgar Allen Poe story about the guy who survives a maelstrom at sea and his hair turns white afterward. Except this guy's hair is black, and he's not really old; like I said, it's just the eyes. They're poetic eyes, sphinx eyes, the eyes of someone who's been telling riddles for a long time, guarding the secrets of a crumbling ruin half buried under desert sands.

He doesn't look much like a Mormon, in other words. Mormons tend to look untroubled, young, and happy, even when they aren't. Although I can't exactly say he looks like a non-

Mormon either; he doesn't look quite like anyone I've ever met. All the same, weirdly, I find I keep searching my memory for a face his resembles. It's like when you have a word at the tip of your tongue, but it won't come to you.

The strangest thing of all, though, is that he can see me. I'm invisible to nearly everyone here. I'm used to people's eyes passing over me as if they saw right through me. But whenever we run into each other, those sphinx eyes of his stop on me and take me in. The first couple of times, I thought I'd imagined it. But no, it's clear. The last time we passed by each other, he stared straight at me, to the point where it was almost rude, without smiling or saying hello. It's as if he were a medium, one of those people with the rare gift of seeing ghosts and spirits other people can't. Which makes sense, since I'm walking around like one of the living dead these days. (Or is it John's ghost he sees in me?)

I don't know what to make of him. I'm pretty sure he has a girlfriend, because I've seen him with the same girl a few times in the library, and they act like a couple. Oh well. We'll probably never meet anyway, and all this curiosity on my part is futile.

November 10

I finally met the Ancient of Days. His name is Matthew Godbey. I had heard some girls I knew at church talking about an older guy they'd met who was a philosophy major, someone named Jared Burton, and I asked what he looked like. From the description they gave—dark hair, thin, not so tall—I wondered if it might be the guy with the sphinx eyes. The next time I saw him, I thought I could use that as an excuse for talking to him, so I asked him if his name was Jared Burton, since if it was, we might know some people in common. And he said no, his name was Matthew Godbey. I said, "Oh, I was just wondering if you might be the same guy, sorry," and went off feeling embarrassed and transparent.

A few days later, I saw him again at a Philosophy Club lecture, and he asked what my name was and what year I was, and whether I was a philosophy major. I answered his questions, adding, "but I'm afraid I might be too dumb to major in philosophy." He laughed, and one of the other guys in the upperclassmen philosophy clique who had overheard us said I surely wasn't too dumb, he could almost guarantee there were people majoring in philosophy who were much dumber than I was. That made me laugh. And now when I see Matthew we say hi to each other.

November 18

I love my Greek class. The grammar and syntax and sounds of the language, and even the way the letters look on a page are all so beautiful. And the other students are funny—whenever someone mentions "copulative" verbs, they make sly jokes. I guess as Mormons we have to get our jollies where we can.

If you can believe it, I even got asked out on sort of a date by one of the guys in the class. His name is Jim, and he invited me to go to a Baroque classical music concert with him last weekend, as he happened to have an extra ticket. It threw me into a panic, but I said yes. In the end, I had fun going with him, although nothing will come of it. I know he has a girlfriend in Idaho, and I'm not attracted to him anyway. He's a mousy-looking, skinny guy, a bit geeky (not that I can throw stones there). Granted he does seem intelligent and kind, and even writes poetry. Before the concert we looked at some paintings in an exhibit hanging in the fine arts building, and he made witty remarks about them. It wasn't bad, being there with him. And if nothing else, it made me feel hopeful about forgetting John, the fact that I managed to go on a date at all. It's starting to hurt less to think about him.

The night after the concert, though, when I got home from studying in the library, I fell into an existential crisis, a brief but bad one. It was a Saturday, and my roommates had all gone out. I felt suddenly exhausted and lonely, and had all these thoughts about time and death and solitude—too incoherent even to bother writing down—and everything began to seem senseless and impossible and I curled up on my bed and lay there like a stone, inert and numb.

I couldn't sleep, so finally around midnight I got up and read a little in a book I'd checked out of the library just for fun—a book about German-Jewish intellectuals before the Second World War (yeah, I realize my idea of fun reading is not the same as most people's). I came across the story of Erich Mühsam, a poet and utopian socialist. The Nazis were starting to round up Jews to put them in concentration camps, and a friend was able to get him papers and a train ticket to leave the country just as the borders were closing. But hours before he was supposed to leave, a Jewish friend came to visit him, and Mühsam gave the other man his ticket to freedom. The next day, the Nazis took him away, and he wasn't just killed, but tortured horribly for years before they finally executed him. He refused to commit suicide, although the Nazis hoped to drive him to it with the torture. The book was so engrossing I didn't go to sleep until four in the morning.

I really don't have much to complain about, do I?

Jim seems like a decent person. Who knows, maybe he is interested in me in spite of the girlfriend in Idaho. And maybe if I made an effort I could be interested in him. But what I really want these days—my Greek-inspired fantasy—is to be Artemis. She's a virgin goddess, a huntress, fierce, chaste, wild, and free. I can totally picture myself as her, in flowing white Grecian robes and sandals, with my hair up in a cool tiara made of little white flowers, a bow and a quiver of arrows slung over my back, leaping through cold moonlit woods, alone and fearless.

And what am I hunting out there alone in the woods at night, in my fantasy? Truth (with a capital T), of course.

December 5

I keep feeling so frustrated with my religion—I just can't seem to make it fit, or make myself fit it. I'm starting to think reason—or at least *my* reason—just can't get me as far as I need to go. I'm beginning to understand its limitations. I had a conversation with Dr. Gardiner a few days ago about the relationship between morality and rationality. I'd gone in to discuss one of my terrible exam essays and was arguing in my usual bullheaded way that morality had to be wholly grounded in a rational principle of selfishness. You do the right thing because ultimately you perceive it as what will make you happier. Dr. G. was smiling while we talked, like he found the whole thing amusing.

Then yesterday, I went into the philosophy department lounge to find out about a new class that's being offered and ran into Matthew, the Ancient of Days. He was with Luke Young, another guy in the upperclassmen philosophy clique, and introduced me. Matthew had to leave, but Luke and I stayed and talked for a while.

Luke is another interesting type—has kind of a tubby, teddy bear physique with swingy light brown hair cut in a bowl shape and thick dark eyebrows that give him a menacing, scowling air. Until he smiles, that is; then his whole face lights up and you notice he has nice green eyes with long lashes.

I asked whether he'd read any Levinas, because right now I'm reading *Time and the Other* by him and finding it rough going. It's another book I checked out of the library to read just for fun, on my own, because one day Amanda and I were talking and I was telling her I thought there was no meaning outside of one's relationships with other people, either in language or existence generally. She gripped my sleeve and told me, "You *have* to read Levinas," in a tone that implied the world was going to end in a violent conflagration if I didn't go to the library *that instant* and check him out. So I did, and even found the French edition too, so I could compare the translation to the original for the difficult passages.

It turns out the book consists entirely of difficult passages, but there's a poetic undercurrent to it that I do get, if only on a subrational level. I can appreciate the imagery: consciousness as a kind of insomnia and feminine "otherness" as that which flees from the light, a kind of modesty, and the future and death and Eros as forms of radical otherness, ungraspable mysteries.

Luke said he'd read a little Levinas, so we talked about the idea of otherness as it related to irrationality. I brought up the question of whether morality might be based in irrationality at some level. Luke said the thing to realize was that morality was an intrinsic good, not an instrumental good, that is, it was a good in itself, not a good that was good for the sake of any other good it might get us. I liked his idea of morality being something to love just for itself, like a beautiful painting. It's easier to understand how it might not be wholly rational, if there's an element of love and longing for beauty in it.

Since we were on a roll, I asked him what he thought of the relationship between faith and reason, and whether the truths of faith could be proved by reason. He thought not; faith was more a matter of "spirituality" than philosophizing. I'll admit, I found this answer annoying, since I had no idea what spirituality was. I think maybe I used to know, back in the old days before John, but if I knew before, I don't anymore.

I asked, "What if a person were completely unspiritual, so far as she could tell. She wouldn't know the Spirit if it hit her over the head and knocked her down. But suppose this person loved the fruits of religion. What would you say to someone like that?"

He said, "Well, if this person loved the fruits of religion and the life of spirituality, I'd say that person must be spiritual without knowing it."

I thought that was a nice answer.

December 9

I went on another date this weekend, not with Jim this time, but with a boy named Ted from my New Testament class, someone I'd barely talked with before he caught up to me after class and asked me out. Again, my first reactions were surprise and panic, but I said yes. He's a botany major, a quiet, reserved, rumpled-looking guy. He took me to a play in Salt Lake Saturday night. It was a good play, but he seemed even shyer than me, and we never seemed to get past the phase of awkward small talk. The end of the evening was especially nerve-wracking, when we said goodbye at the steps to my porch. I was petrified, thinking he might lunge in and kiss me, but instead he only held out his arms for a hug. What a relief.

I guess John was right when he said guys would ask me out. But I don't know why I get so panicky over the idea of going on dates. Maybe it just happens so rarely I haven't gotten used to it yet. Whatever the reason, any direct, frontal approach seems to trigger a flight response in me on some primal, animal level, like a deer getting a whiff of human scent. Mentally, I'm bounding off into the forest even if my body is standing still. I'm just getting to the point in the Levinas book where he compares the otherness of death to that of Eros, and he talks about a sense of powerlessness, *impuissance*, that one feels, face with death. *Nous ne pouvons plus pouvoir;* we're no longer "able to be able." That's how I feel, I guess.

I suspect I was only able to fall so hard for John because there was never meant to be any possibility of it going beyond friendship. I was supposed to be safe with him, so there was no reason to have my guard up and nothing to trigger my flight response, until it was too late and I was caught and was no longer able to be able.

Last night, when I should have been studying for finals, I read this essay by Montaigne, "On Friendship," that my Greek professor talked about in class. The essay got me thinking how the important and unusual part of what happened with John was the friendship part, more than the infatuation part—because goodness knows, I had plenty of infatuations before him. William Blake says, "Opposition is true Friendship," and if that's right, I never had a truer friend than John. As short a time as we knew each other and as awfully as it ended, no one else has ever been so completely opposed to me.

The friendship with him wasn't anything like the Montaignian ideal, lofty, pure, disinterested, and so on. But Montaigne quotes a philosopher who says a man could be called happy if he met "even the shadow of a friend." That's what John was for me, I think, the shadow of a friend, of the best sort of friend, who challenges you to think and grow and be a better person.

When Montaigne lost his friend, he said everything became like smoke, it was all just "dark and dreary night." So maybe I'm not so crazy to grieve the way I've done, which Rachel and Ellen and Miriam all think is far out of proportion to what happened. It's as if the friendship sent light into me where there hadn't been any before and made everything around me look lit-up and golden. Then the light was snuffed out, and everything lost its sheen and went dull and colorless. It's as if I were seeing in black and white now.

January 4

It was good to be home in Tucson for a couple of weeks for Christmas vacation. I read a few novels, including some trashy romances I stole from my mom. I hung out a lot with Mark, too. He has a girlfriend now, and she sounds great, although I didn't get to meet her because she lives out of state and spent Christmas with her folks.

In the car on the way back to Provo, I started reading Kierkegaard's *Fear and Trembling*. I'd been meaning to for a while. One of the last things John said to me was that he thought I might like Kierkegaard. But ever since I started the book, I've been having the strangest thoughts and can't seem to get them out of my head.

Kierkegaard is this Danish philosopher from the 1800s who was engaged to a girl named Regina, but for reasons that aren't completely clear—something to do with his depression, or shame about his family, or a sense of ill-fate—decided he couldn't marry her and broke off the engagement. Regina "fought like a lioness" to keep him, arguing, crying, and writing letters. So Kierkegaard pretended for her sake he was a scoundrel and a seducer who had just been trifling with her affections. He thought his cruelty would make it easier on her in the end. In *Fear and Trembling,* he compares the sacrifice he made in hurting and betraying Regina to Abraham in the Old Testament being willing to offer up his only son Isaac as a human sacrifice.

The weird thought that sticks in my head now is this: What if John thought he was going silent for my own good, a bit like Kierkegaard with Regina? What if he could tell my resistance had crumbled and if he'd only put his arms around me and kissed me, I would have gone against everything I believed in? And then I would have been consumed with guilt and ended up throwing myself under a train like Anna Karenina ... or at the very least, I would have gotten kicked out of BYU and lost my scholarship. He didn't want anything like that to happen, so he disappeared without explaining why and let himself look like a jerk, thinking that would make it easier on me.

What if *that's* partly why he told me I should read Kierkegaard—so I'd understand later why he had to disappear? But it can't be ... I'm back to living in a dreamworld ... people in real life don't send each other messages through philosophy books. Unless they're Kierkegaard, of course, who meant to send Regina all kinds of messages through his books.

Anyway, I don't know if you can see how thoughts like that could drive a person crazy. Of course it's more likely he went silent because I wasn't worth bothering with. But if I believe what's more likely, I have to wrap my head around the idea of his being just really a jerk, even though he was so nice to me the whole time and I'd thought we were at least friends. I'd prefer to believe something kinder, but I don't want to delude myself. Besides, I'd feel worse if I believed the kinder thing, since the lost friendship is more of a loss if he thought he was doing it for my own good. I want to believe both, and neither.

Either way, I feel for Regina, who was unlucky enough to fall for a philosopher and then went half-crazy over losing him. She too had to convince herself of the seemingly impossible, that someone who'd seemed to care about her could abruptly turn around and behave cruelly with no explanation.

Then there's the story of Agnes and the merman. In the book, the merman is a seducer who sets his eye on an innocent girl named Agnes, catching her up in his arms as she stands dreaming by the seashore. But he has a bad conscience with respect to girls, so instead of plunging into the water with her to ravage her down in the depths, he sets her back down and says he only meant to show her how pretty the calm sea is. It makes me think of that strange moment by the pool at Angela's house, when John scooped me up into his arms and held me over the water, and after what seemed a long time set me down again very gently and said no, he couldn't do it.

There's no great genius without some madness, Kierkegaard says. If being crazy is the price of genius, I'm not interested. But to believe something obviously unlikely, that's a kind of madness, isn't it? And I'm always stuck having to believe unlikely things. That John was a jerk, or, even more absurd, that he went silent for noble Kierkegaardian reasons instead. And the same with religion: It's hard believing in Mormonism, because it's absurd. But I can't *not* believe it either, because not to believe is terrible; without belief existence looks as absurd and senseless as any religion could.

Here's something interesting, though: Kierkegaard talks about a "knight of faith," an ideal, perfectly faithful person. The way Kierkegaard describes him, he's not glamorous or very knightish-looking at all. Instead, he looks like a contented tax collector. He takes delight in everything, wanders around happily imagining the delicious meal his wife is making for dinner, and is capable of being completely absorbed in ordinary, everyday pleasures. The interesting thing to me is that this guy is the picture of mental health, a paragon of cheerful sanity. So I wonder—if I were able to have faith, *could I be sane?*

And if I have faith, do I get back the person I lost? The essence of Abraham's faith, according to this book, is that Abraham firmly believes he'll get Isaac back, even at the same time he's fully resigned to losing him. And Abraham *does* get Isaac back—but Kierkegaard loses Regina.

I can hardly talk of having faith, though, when I haven't even gotten to the point of resigning myself. But suppose I resign myself. Suppose I understand and accept that the person I cared about is lost. What does it mean then to believe in spite of this that "God will provide Himself a lamb for the burnt offering," as Abraham says—to believe you'll get Isaac back? Is there a spiritual meaning to it, so you get the sacrificed person back without really getting him back, and get the spiritual equivalent of him instead?

But it seems in asking that question I'm missing the whole point of this concept of faith, which is that such questions aren't the important ones. The important question is my relationship with God as a solitary individual. How do I stand in this relationship; do I have a relationship or not? That's the question I have to work out with fear and trembling before Him, before anything else can be resolved.

CHAPTER 20

EITHER/OR

*J*ANUARY 7

Tuesday night I did something stupid. Again.

I had been thinking how my life was so filled with Either/Or's... Either the Church is true/or it's nothing but a hoax. Either John was a heartless jerk/or he was a decent person but had other reasons for disappearing—maybe even noble Kierkegaardian ones. I was sick of it, sick to death of never knowing, of always having to question and doubt, sick of being stuck on that slash between the Either and the Or, kicking my feet against the "r" and the "O." I just wanted to *know* for once.

If I knew for sure John had just been a jerk, I could get over it and move on. If I knew for sure there was some nicer explanation, at least I could think kindly of him and hope he thought kindly of me, and find a sort of peace and resolve in that. That was my (obviously irrational) thinking, anyway.

I called information and got a number for him, and when no one else was home, I went upstairs into the loft and dialed it. I got his answering machine and hung up. Then, after thinking about it for a few minutes, I called back and left a message. I said it was me and that I'd finally gotten around to reading Kierkegaard. It had made me have all kinds of funny thoughts, and I just wanted to talk about it. I didn't leave my number, because I couldn't bear the thought of putting myself in the position again of waiting for a call back, only to be disappointed. But I said I would call back the next evening around ten, and if he wanted to talk he could pick up the phone. I was in a terrible state of agitation all the next day until I finally called in the evening from a phone in the commons room of the library. I got his answering machine again and didn't leave a message this time.

In the end, of course, all I got out of it was another Either/Or. Either John didn't want to talk to me regardless of whether he got the message/or he hadn't heard the message and would have talked to me if he could have. I'll never know. What I do know is, I can't do anything like that again; the stress of it nearly killed me. So here I am, still stuck on the slash, and it looks like I might as well make myself comfortable, as it's going to be a while before I find a way off of it.

January 10

My favorite class so far this semester is Keys to Scripture Study. It counts as a religion credit, but is required for philosophy majors, and the professor is Seth Mewes, the head of the philosophy department, who taught my writing class last year. He's the most cheerful, kind man, brimming with *joie de vivre* and as round as a planet. He makes me think of Kierkegaard's knight of faith, the happy tax collector.

The first day of class, Dr. Mewes handed out the syllabus, went through it, and asked if there were any questions. I raised my hand and said I had sort of a philosophical question. Dr. Mewes said, "That's allowed here," and everyone laughed. I asked whether he thought the basis for faith could be found in the scriptures, or whether you had to approach the scriptures with a pre-established faith in order to learn from them. Could the scriptures help a person make the leap of faith?

As if he'd been reading my thoughts, Dr. Mewes talked about Kierkegaard. He said Kierkegaard used a pseudonym when he wrote about how amazing and incomprehensible faith was because in his true identity as a Christian he couldn't write about his faith. (Kierkegaard wrote *Fear and Trembling* under a pen name, Johannes de Silentio. John of silence.) In the guise of a pseudonymous persona he could examine the movements of faith, but he couldn't explain his own faith. The answer to my question was no, the movement to faith isn't explained in the scriptures any more than it's explained anywhere else, because it's inexplicable. The scriptures can't direct us how to obtain faith, because there are no directions.

This gave me a lot to think about. If there are no directions on how to get to faith, either in the scriptures or outside them, maybe it's because the movement from doubt to faith isn't like a movement from Point A to Point B. Maybe it's more like a transformation of the way you see the point where you are. The movement is more like opening your eyes than taking a running leap across a chasm.

If that's the case, maybe it's an explanation, too, of why faith falls into the category of the absurd—because faith is at once the farthest and nearest thing to us, so what seems like an impassable abyss between Either and Or is crossed without taking a single step. As if you were in a country where there was no light, and you'd heard tales of a far off place of sunlight and colors. However far and fast you walk, you can't find this country. Then you open your eyes and realize you were in the country of light and colors all along, only you didn't know it because your eyes were closed.

So the movement of faith is incomprehensible, absurd, because it's a completely stationary movement, yet gets us across the abyss. And so, Kierkegaard says, the knight of faith is like the dancer who "leaps into a definite posture in such a way that there is not a second when he is grasping after the posture, but by the leap itself he stands fixed in that posture."

January 12

I'm trying to get a crush on a guy named Zach Sorenson who's in all my philosophy classes. He seems like he'd be a good candidate for a crush. Besides being a philosophy major, he's movie-star gorgeous and tall like a basketball player. He's got piercing Scandinavian blue eyes and thick, wavy dark hair that always looks insouciantly mussed. I sit by him in class and occasionally make lame attempts to flirt. He's much nicer about it than you'd expect someone so gorgeous to be. We've also started trading off textbooks, since I have one he's missing and he has one I'm missing.

I asked Amanda today what she thought of him, since she's been friends with him since last semester. She said her impression was that he's a bit quiet and reserved, but very kind and "morally upstanding."

Clearly he's way out of my league, but that's okay. All I need is to have a crush on someone so I'll stop thinking about John and Kierkegaard and mermen. It doesn't have to be someone who likes me back. At least with Zach I know he's nice and not some amoral heartbreaker, so my unrequited crush will be bestowed on a worthy object this time.

Of course, it would be even better if he liked me back. But there's no chance of that, since I already made a mistake with him. The other day before class started, he asked me how I got interested in philosophy. I said, "Because of a guy." He nodded but didn't say anything in response. I don't think it made a good impression.

January 17

Dr. Mewes's religion class always starts with an opening prayer, and this morning I volunteered to give it. I managed to do it, to pray in front of other people without breaking off or bursting into tears. That seems like progress of a sort. Admittedly, some part of me was probably just trying to impress Zach, who gave a beautiful prayer in class the other day.

I haven't gone out with Ted again, and goodness knows I'm not getting my hopes up with Zach. But I did have another date, so to speak, with Jim from my Greek class. A few days ago when we were walking together after class, he said he wanted to show me his business. That surprised me, as he'd never talked about having his own company or running a store on the side or anything. I asked what it was, but he was mysterious about it, and said I'd just have to see for myself. I figured that in any case, he must like me a lot if he wanted to show it to me, whatever it was. So we made plans to meet yesterday evening on campus.

I was mystified when he led me to an empty classroom, and even more confused when we sat down and he started telling me about his "dreams and goals" and asking what mine were. He said he dreamed of having a big, beautiful house and being well-off enough that when he got married his wife wouldn't have to work and would be able to stay home with the children.

Is he going to propose? I wondered. This is BYU after all, where you never know if someone's going to have a sudden revelation that you've been destined for all eternity to be their future spouse.

Finally it emerged that his business was multi-level marketing. He works for Amway and wanted me to work under him. I said no thanks, I was too busy with school and was getting by okay on my scholarship and with my parents' help. This morning in class, he was noticeably cooler toward me.

It's easier to have faith in God, and probably easier for a camel to go through the eye of a needle, than to believe I'll ever get a real boyfriend and be in a normal, stable, healthy relationship.

January 20

The crush on Zach is coming along nicely. Today he offered me a ride home after our Logic class. It took nearly as long to walk to his car as it would have taken me to walk home, but I told him I was glad for the ride anyway, as I always feel like I'm taking my life in my hands when I cross University Avenue—there's no light, only a crosswalk, and the cars never stop for you.

"So I'm actually saving you from grave danger by giving you a ride?" he asked.

"Yes, I'd probably be squashed flat as a pancake if you hadn't come to my rescue," I said, batting my eyelashes. He laughed. When we got to my house, I gathered up all my courage and asked if he'd like to come in for a cup of chamomile tea. He looked uncomfortable—I could almost swear he blushed a little—and said he was sorry, he couldn't, he had to go meet a friend. Probably that meant he had a date. Ugh, I'm such an idiot.

At least we had a nice talk on the way to his car. It turns out he's interested in photography. He does it as a hobby, but has also read a lot of aesthetic theory on it. He seems to know a ton about Heidegger and other philosophers I find opaque, and besides that, he's double-majoring in math. It seems unfair that someone who looks like a movie star should be that smart and talented, too.

I've been trying to get a feel for how he thinks, and it strikes me that his thinking is a lot like the way he walks. Being so tall, he has kind of a slow, meditative, loping gait, and likewise, his thoughts seem to move at a gentle, steady pace. My style of thinking is hungrier, more predatory. I tend to stalk answers, sniffing out the ones I can't have among all the scents that hang in the air, and going after exactly those ones single-mindedly and obsessively.

Amanda's style is loopy and digressive. She's always going off on tangents, circling around and away from the questions she starts out with.

January 25

Zach gave me a ride home after Logic again, and this time, I asked him about his mission. He went to Chile. He told me some parts of being a missionary were hard and some parts he loved. It was hard learning the language and having to concentrate all day, every day, on spiritual things. But on the other hand, the people he met were wonderful and inspiring, and he felt like his testimony grew a lot through teaching them and seeing the way their lives were changed by the Gospel.

I asked if he thought of himself as more conservative or more liberal as far as the Church went. He said that if he'd understood my question right, he was probably more liberal in some of his interpretations of the scriptures than your typical so-called "Utah Mormon" (he grew up near Berkeley). But he tried to be conservative when it came to practicing the principles.

He asked, "What about you?" Against my better judgment, I ended up telling him a little about my struggles with faith, worrying all the while he might think badly of me for it. But he just listened quietly (politely?) and said he was sure I wasn't the only one who struggled with questions like that.

January 28

This morning before our history of philosophy class started, I gave Zach the outline of a philosophical argument that I'd been thinking about and had typed up and printed out, about Plato's concept of knowledge. I used to do that sometimes with John last summer—bring him little essays I'd written, or diagrams, or outlines of arguments.

It just wasn't the same with Zach, though. I could tell he wasn't very interested.

February 1

Monday afternoon when I went up to study in the philosophy section of the library, I found Zach and Amanda sitting at a table together, working on the Logic homework. It occurred to me for the first time that *Amanda* might like Zach. After all, she was friends with him before I was. And she's prettier and a more devout Church member and a nicer person, so of course he would like her back, and she'd be much better for him than me. I hastily excused myself and went off to sit alone in one of the carrels. After Zach left to go home, Amanda came and found me and asked if something was wrong.

"No," I lied, "why would something be wrong?"

"Why didn't you come sit with us?" she asked. I tried to think of a diplomatic answer. She said, "Let's go get a burrito in the cafeteria."

In the cafeteria, I asked her if she liked Zach. She laughed and said, "Oh, so *that's* what that was about." She said no, he wasn't her type, and in fact she'd just been thinking the other day what a cute couple he and I would make. But so far as she knew, he was dating a friend of her roommate's named Heather Matheson.

"Heather Matheson?" I said. "She's in my Latin class!"

Heather, unfortunately, is one of those paradigmatic, beautiful blond BYU girls with long wavy hair. And I can't even hate her, because she's nice and one of the few Latin students besides me who's always prepared.

Yesterday after Latin I struck up a conversation with her and said I'd found out we had a few mutual acquaintances, Amanda's roommate, and Zach. Her face brightened when I mentioned Zach.

"Yes, we've gone out a few times. He seems nice. Kind of quiet, but really smart."

"He is," I said warmly. "I'm a bit jealous, in fact. He's a great guy. Quite a catch." I kept my tone light and joking, trying not to let on that I really was jealous.

Later, when I saw Zach in class, I mentioned casually that I knew Heather.

"Yeah," he said, "we've gone out a few times, but she's been dogging me lately. I think she's actually going out with a friend of mine this weekend." He sounded like he was hurt, but was trying to keep a light and joking tone so as not to let on that he was hurt.

How ridiculous—as if any girl wouldn't want to go out with Zach.

February 2

I asked Amanda who she would date if she could pick anyone, and to my surprise, of all people, she said Matthew Godbey, he of the sphinx eyes. I would have thought he'd be even less her type than Zach, but she said he's "devastatingly handsome" and is always teasing her. She would never date him in reality, though, she added, for one thing, because of course he has a girlfriend. And for another thing, she thinks he's very liberal in his views about the Church, and she isn't.

February 9

After Latin class today, I was talking to Heather Matheson again, and she said she had mentioned to Zach that she knew me, and he'd spoken highly of me. He told her he thought I was "very open and honest."

For a minute, I felt like Christmas, Thanksgiving, and my birthday had all come at the same time.

Then I came to my senses. Whatever nice things he might say about me, still, he's clearly not interested in dating me. He asks plenty of girls out, and if he wanted to go out with me he'd have asked long before now.

February 19

Midterms are looming, and I've been procrastinating on all my assignments. The crush on Zach isn't helping my productivity much, and I'm beginning to think talking myself into it may not have been such a bright idea after all. I'm starting to sympathize with Young Werther, it that tells you anything about my state of mind.

We discussed *The Sorrows of Young Werther* in Dr. Gardiner's class when we studied Romanticism last week, and I giggled when Dr. G. made fun of him, so this is probably some kind of karmic payback. But Zach and I are friends like Werther and Lotte were, and Zach is sort of the male equivalent of Lotte: sympathetic, funny, intelligent, well-read and wise, a good listener, and has a profound, solid faith in the Gospel. Which is to say, he's close to perfect in all respects. And like Werther, I'm agonizingly aware it can never go anywhere, yet I spend tons of time around him so things can only get worse.

Maybe the crush has partly served its purpose, though. Yesterday afternoon I was in the library studying in the philosophy section, and Zach came in and sat down across from me. I looked up and saw he'd gotten rained on. There were raindrops clinging to his insouciantly mussed black hair and his brown leather jacket, and he smiled at me, and his lips and cheeks were pink and his eyes that piercing Scandinavian blue. When I looked up and saw all this, I realized I was seeing in color again. At least for that moment, the world wasn't all in black and white anymore.

But the old pain over what happened last summer hasn't completely gone away, and I have a bad feeling I've just added a new ache onto the old one.

February 25

Today I was sitting on the floor in the library halfway down an aisle among the stacks, reading a book I'd pulled out, when I saw some of the books on the shelf in front of me move, seemingly of their own volition. Then the row of books parts, and Zach's face appeared in the gap where they had been, wearing a puckish grin.

"What have we here?" he asked.

I laughed, then told him to go away, as I was busy working, although I phrased it more nicely than that. I've been trying to avoid him lately, because I don't want to be Werther.

The library is my sanctuary these days, more than church or home or anywhere else. When I'm procrastinating doing homework or writing a paper, I can spend hours wandering the stacks. I trail my fingers over the spines of the books and occasionally stop and take one out when I see an interesting title or an author I've heard of and want to read. So many books ... I get a sense of infinity browsing through them; there's an infinite pool of knowledge out there for me to play in. I let myself get lost in a kind of wonder and give myself over to it without restraint, the way I've never been able to do with a person.

Sometimes I think the books and philosophy and wonder are all becoming a kind of refuge for me from the temptation of letting myself be loved, or of loving someone who might actually love me back for once. With philosophy, I don't have to be vulnerable. If anyone were to come too close to me, or if someone I care for doesn't care in return, I can just retreat into this beautiful, shining, solipsistic world of ideas, and I'm safe there.

It reminds me of another Greek story I came across the other day, about Galateia the sea-nymph. As Ovid tells the story, she's in love at first with a handsome boy named Acis. Meanwhile, the cyclops Polyphemus is in love with her, but she thinks he's an ugly, uncouth brute, so she rejects him. Polyphemus is jealous of Acis and crushes him to death with a rock. Galateia mourns for Acis and turns his blood into a river.

In the same way, any guy who might actually be interested in me would look like a brutish, one-eyed monster, and I'd only want to run away. I want Zach, who I can never have, or John, who I'll never see again. The only way I can have either of them is by writing about them, so that's what I do, turning them into a river of words, which I love more than I could ever love a real person.

March 12

Matthew Godbey has taken to lurking in the corridors and abruptly shouting "Hey!" in a loud voice to scare me and Amanda as we pass by unsuspecting. I nearly jump out of my skin every time, although the effect is funnier with Amanda since she has the strongest startle reflex you ever saw and blushes furiously. Then yesterday, after Logic got out, I was walking alone to my next class, and out of the blue Matthew appeared at my side. I'd barely said hello when with no preliminaries he asked me, "What do you do? What do you think about? Does philosophy just *define* you?"

Taken aback, I couldn't do more than sputter in response. Matthew seemed to realize he'd shocked me and started over more gently, asking, "Okay, so tell me ... what do you do in your spare time?"

I had trouble answering this question, too, and told him I didn't really have spare time. (What was I supposed to say? I read books about Weimar-era German-Jewish intellectuals and mope over unrequited crushes past, present, and future?)

But he persisted. "Well, then ... what kind of music do you listen to?"

"Classical."

"What kind of classical?"

"Modern." I named some of my favorite twentieth century composers, Heitor Villa-Lobos, Charles Ives, Arvo Pärt.

He nodded as if these were all familiar names to him, then went back to his earlier line of questioning. "So, what do you think about?"

"I don't know. I guess you could say my life is a life of the mind."

"But what does *that* mean?"

"It means everything that happens to me is mainly in my head. But mostly I just think about banal, normal sorts of things."

"What kinds of things?"

"Well, things like—I've never had a real boyfriend, for example. I think about things like that. My life goes on mostly in my mind, maybe because I'm too socially inept to really live. I make all kinds of mistakes, and then I retreat into my thoughts to try to figure out why I'm always going wrong." I told him I thought it was the way I grew up. As a child I was freakishly sensitive, especially to sounds. My mother had a flair for the dramatic and sang opera in college, and had an operatic sort of voice, so when she would yell, even though she was only saying normal mom sorts of things like "clean your room," I would tremble and feel she hated me. My parents were happy when I did well in school and praised me for being smart, so at some point I decided being smart was the way to avoid making mistakes and getting yelled at, the way to be safe from threatening things.

Finally I stopped and said, "But why am I telling you all this? Do you even care?" I told him I hated having the urge to reveal myself constantly.

"Everyone needs someone who understands them," he said. "Everyone needs to be understood."

He was looking for a mailbox to mail a letter to his sister. While we walked and looked, I told him some of what I wrote in my last entry. Philosophy wasn't what defined me, but it was my refuge from the temptation of being loved. I told him I was never interested in philosophy before this summer, when I fell in love with a guy who was into it. The guy disappeared on me, but philosophy stayed, and now whenever I was afraid of not being loved I could just retreat into it and say: I don't care, because I love philosophy and not some stupid guy.

"You *do* need a boyfriend," he said.

We found a mailbox and he stuck the letter in the slot. He told me he adored his sister—she was a missionary, the only one in his family who ever served a mission. I asked Matthew why he didn't go on one (almost every guy at BYU is either going on one or has gone on one). He told me he wasn't a Mormon, really. I wasn't surprised. It fit with what I thought about him before we met, his having sphinx eyes and looking like he'd survived a maelstrom. But I was disappointed, just because I'm always hoping to find someone who believes in the Church and understands both it and me well enough to be able to convince me beyond doubt it's true—someone who'd be the antithesis of John, in other words. But Matthew is clearly something else altogether.

"Do you believe in God?" I asked him.

"Yes."

"Do you love God?"

"I *respect* God," he said.

March 19

Zach has a new girlfriend. Her name is Ashley, and I happen to know her, because she's in my ward at church and is a music major. I'd seen them together a few times. Then this afternoon I was down in the basement in the fine arts building practicing the piano, and I ran into her on the way out. We chatted a bit, and I asked if she and Zach were an item now. She said yes, they'd been seeing a lot of each other. I guess my face must have fallen, because she asked, "What's wrong?"

I didn't answer, and she said slowly, like she was putting two and two together, "You like him a lot, don't you?"

I wish I'd denied it convincingly, laughed it off and said something like, "Oh, no, we're just buddies." But instead I nodded and felt like crying. My face was probably getting all blotchy, too. She gave me a look full of pity and said, "I'm sorry."

Then I did manage to laugh a little and said, "Oh, no, don't be sorry. It's a happy thing. You're lucky—good for you, for both of you. Zach is terrific." Then we changed the subject and talked about church and the music department. But before we left each other to walk in different directions, I asked her please not to say a word to Zach about that conversation. She smiled and said she wouldn't. Thank goodness. It'd be more humiliation than even I could stand, if I knew they'd talked about me. I'm sure he has some idea of how much I like him; subtlety was never my strong point. But the last thing I need is to picture them together discussing how pathetic I am and shaking their heads pityingly over me.

March 27

Since that conversation Matthew and I had a couple of weeks ago, I've felt anxious and vulnerable around him. He knows things no one else knows about me. It doesn't help that he can be an awful curmudgeon. There are days when you say hi to him and he will growl at you in response. You can't help laughing, but it's unsettling all the same.

Luke Young teases Matthew that his way of winning friends and influencing people is by being openly abrasive. He says if Matthew says something rude to you, it means he must really like you. Matthew has other ways of winning friends and influencing people, though. When he's in a good mood, he says hilarious things, and sometimes tells long, mesmerizing stories. He's done all kinds of unlikely things. Driven all across the country on a motorcycle. Won a roller skating contest. Worked at an amusement park where he had to wear a costume with lederhosen. Knows how to knit his own scarves and sew his own underwear. Has smoked cigarettes and even tried pot, which no one else I know has done. And he's read everything. Plus, his knowledge of every genre of music, from rap to twelve-tone, is encyclopedic. So when he gets going telling stories in the philosophy department lounge, everyone in the room ends up stopping what they're doing and listening to him. There's a general sense around the department that he's one of the smart ones, one of the promising students who'll go on to grad school.

Anyway, today he and some of the other upperclassman philosophy guys were sitting around in the lounge talking, and I came in to meet Zach to trade books. The conversation sounded so interesting I couldn't help butting in and asking a question, something only tangentially related, having to do with Camus.

A few of them started to answer, but then Matthew said I was obviously asking the question just to make myself look smart. It was mean, the way he said it, and it wasn't even true—not really. But I didn't know how to defend myself. I said he was right and I was sorry. I opened my mouth to say something more, but Matthew said irritably, "Oh, just drop it, Marguerite."

I tried to be funny and said I couldn't drop it since I'm obsessive-compulsive; I'd probably obsess over it for the next three weeks at least.

"You seem more neurotic to me." Again, his tone was mean. He wasn't even joking, he was dead serious.

"I'm sure I'm that, too," I said, feeling terrible. I took Zach's book under my arm, said goodbye to everyone, and left.

I brooded over this exchange the rest of the afternoon, thinking I was mainly upset because Matthew had told me some ugly truths about myself. When I got home, I told my roommate Ellen about it, and she pointed out that my being upset probably had more to do with the fact that he'd been a jerk.

Then a couple of hours ago, as I was sitting up in the loft doing homework, the phone rang, and it was Matthew, calling to apologize. He said he knew he was a real asshole sometimes, but he was the one who had to deal with it. I tried to explain without sounding accusatory that I was thin-skinned and didn't have some of the psychological defenses normal people have. So when he acted like that with me, he was more likely to do damage than with other people. All the same, I liked him and wished we could be friends. I said I wanted to understand him better.

So he told me a few things about how he grew up. His late father was an artist, and instead of talking, his father would always point out beautiful things to him and say, "Look, look at this, look at that." I wonder if losing his father is what made his eyes look so old and sad.

Later in the conversation I asked, "So, do you like me okay, then?" But he didn't like the question and wouldn't give me a straight answer. I said I always felt unresolved and never knew where I stood with him. He said he knew he was a very private person. I said maybe he was like a poem, one of those opaque ones you read and wonder at without hoping to understand it, and I supposed I would just have to be okay with that. He didn't disagree.

April 28

Spring term is starting now, and during the short break between terms, I skimmed through the first volume of Kierkegaard's *Either/Or*. The seducer's diary part was deeply disturbing. I kept coming across passages that seemed to describe me, for example:

"I can picture him as knowing how to bring a girl to the high point where he was sure that she would offer everything. When the affair had gone so far, he broke off, without the least overture having been made on his part, without a word about love having been said, to say nothing of a declaration, a promise. And yet it had happened, and for the unhappy one the consciousness of it was doubly bitter because she did not have the least thing to appeal to, because she was continually agitated in a dreadful witches' dance of the most varied moods as she alternately reproached herself, forgave him, and in turn reproached him. And now, since the relationship had possessed actuality only figuratively, she had to battle continually the doubt whether the whole affair was not a fantasy. ...

"Such victims were, therefore, of a very special kind.... No visible change took place in them ...and yet they were changed, almost unaccountably to themselves and incomprehensibly to others. Their lives were not cracked or broken, as others' were, but were bent into themselves; lost to others, they futilely sought to find themselves."

It brought back a flood of memories of last summer. Had *he* read this passage, I wonder, when he told me I should read Kierkegaard? Can he have known then he was doing something like this to me, getting ready to leave me lost and bent into myself? I can't believe he deliberately set out to do that, but even so, the effects are almost the same as if he had. And in retrospect I sometimes hate him for it. He didn't want me, and now I'm ruined for anyone else. No one faithful and good like Zach could ever love the lost, bent, wandering, unanswerable thing I've become.

CHAPTER 21

PHILOSOPHICAL EROS

JUNE 29

I know it's been a while since I've written. Spring term brought an avalanche of work, and I've been too busy and sad to write much. My head is crammed full of Greek grammar, Xenophon, and Plato. With Amanda and Zach's help this term I'm managing to keep my head above water, just barely, in Advanced Logic.

I've been so lonely. I talk with my roommates and Amanda and the other people in my classes, but it doesn't help. I'm restless and keep wishing I could go somewhere, anywhere but here; I never want to be where I am. Since the weather's been nice I've started going on long walks by myself, walking for hours, just thinking and watching the houses as I pass by them, trying to imagine the families that live in them. Mothers, fathers, children, normal people living out their lives, going to work, cooking dinner, having the kinds of conversations normal people have.

Yesterday I walked so far I ended up at the foot of the mountains around Provo. I climbed up a little ways, and from the mountain I could see the whole city and the lake shimmering in the sun. Then I headed back home, coming down behind the Temple, passing by the Missionary Training Center. It gave me the sense anything was possible—to see a point far off in the distance, the base of those mountains, and then walk there on my own two feet. It made me feel more powerful, somehow, to find the distance was conquerable, traversing a space wasn't an impossibility, whatever Zeno's paradox might say. Those hills that looked so unattainable became mine once I'd walked to them and taken those miles under my feet. To make the impossible possible, all I had to do was move.

July 25

Zach and Ashley are engaged, following the typical speedy trajectory of BYU romances, and I feel more Wertherian than ever. I see them constantly, run into them everywhere, together and separately. I have my two summer classes every day with Zach. Even when he and I and Amanda don't study together after class, on a typical day I'll bump into him four or five times in the library. I see Ashley in church and in the fine arts building and in the philosophy department lounge when she comes to meet Zach. I can't seem to escape them, and I can't stop being friends with Zach. I've tried, but it feels too unfair to be anything but grateful and kind to him in return for how kind he's always been to me.

You'd think at least I would find some refuge from these Wertherian torments on my walks. The other day I had been walking for an hour or two on a path by the road that leads into Orem and joins the river trail. I was feeling more alone and miserable than ever. The sunset and clouds were so beautiful it hurt to look at them. I wanted to disappear into them, to walk and walk until I came to the ends of the earth and found a path up into those clouds. Then as I was passing by Will's Pit Stop, a gas station out in the middle of nowhere, I heard someone call my name.

"Marguerite ... what on earth are you doing out here? Are you just ... walking?" It was Ashley. She and Zach had stopped to get gas just as I was walking by.

I said, yes, I was just walking. I asked if they knew where the river trail picked up. She pointed it out to me, and I thanked her and said goodbye. They drove off and I kept on walking. I didn't get home until long after dark.

As long as I don't run into Zach and Ashley, though, the walks do seem to help with my moods.

August 14

Summer term is over, and I'm home in Tucson for another week or two on vacation.

I came *this* close to not turning in my final paper for my Plato class. I'd changed topics at the last minute and decided to write about the relationship between classical conceptions of tragedy and philosophical eros in Plato. I think I understand the meaning of philosophical eros better than most people, given what I've been through, but it was a bad topic for me, for exactly that reason. Six pages in, the night before it was due and the night before I was supposed to leave town, I got stuck and couldn't finish.

I was writing about how Socrates, like Galateia the sea-nymph, was always loving an ideal and fleeing from real love. Socrates was in love with Alcibiades but pushed him away as soon as Alcibiades turned out to love him back. Socrates is ugly and sensual and strives to attain an inner beauty, a beauty of the soul, to compensate for his outward ugliness. He seduces the object of his erotic love, the physically beautiful Alcibiades, with talk of virtue, temperance, and wisdom. But in the *Symposium*, when Alcibiades wants to surrender himself to Socrates, Socrates rejects him, because philosophy is what Socrates really loves. It's a tragic situation both for Alcibiades, whose life is ruined ("I had no idea what to do, no purpose in life; ah, no one else has ever known the real meaning of slavery!"), and for Socrates, who had to be aware of his own cruelty in seducing someone only to reject him as he's on the point of succumbing.

My argument was that Socratic philosophical eros is tragic because of its limitations. The lust for knowledge, certainty, and beauty can never be satisfied, yet wonder's embrace leaves the Socratic lover too full to accept any imperfect, mortal love. The Socratic lover loves beauty and wisdom because he lacks them, and can't let himself be loved in the fragile, contingent way of things that are real because he's too enamored of the ideal.

I got stuck because it was too depressing to think all that through. If I followed this line of thinking to its logical conclusion, I would have to acknowledge that in some sense philosophy, instead of helping me solve my problems, had become the problem. But there was no way out, no way of undoing what had been done, my falling in love with philosophy, my eros for Truth, the waking up of my conscience. I could never see the world again the way I saw it before.

I went outside and walked down to the park a few blocks from our condo. I swung on the swings while a large, charming family with children ranging in age from maybe three to thirteen played around me and took turns pushing each other on the swings on either side of me. I was a stranger to them and to everyone else in the world. I cried and swung and cried, and finally walked home. I nearly collapsed on the floor when I came in, and my roommates asked what was wrong. Crying even harder, I tried to explain to them what philosophical eros was and what a jerk Socrates had been to Alcibiades, and how this all related to my own life. I was completely incoherent and they probably didn't understand a word of it, but they were kind and tried to console me with hugs.

After that, I called my professor and left a message on his answering machine: "Hi, Dr. Fillmore? This is Marguerite. I'm having a philosophical crisis. Help. I can't write my paper, so I can't turn it in." I hung up and breathed a sigh of relief.

Admitting defeat seemed to clear a space in my head. Some sentences came into my mind for the paper, the next sentences I needed to go forward. So I went to the computer and added them to what I'd written. As I typed, more and more sentences came, and I wrote them all down. My roommates turned on the TV to watch *Star Trek*. They asked if I wanted them to keep the volume low so I could concentrate, and I said no, not to worry about it, I'd be joining them to watch in a minute. But *Star Trek* came and went, and I was still typing sentences. Around 11pm, I started feeling drowsy, so I stopped and went to bed. I woke up at 6 a.m. without having set the alarm, with more sentences in my head. I went straight to the computer, and the rest of the paper tumbled out onto the keyboard. Just as I finished printing it out and stapling the pages together, one hour before my ride to Tucson was supposed to get there, the phone rang. It was Dr. Fillmore.

"What's your status?" he asked.

"I just finished. I'm bringing it over."

"All right, I'll see you in a minute then. If I have to leave before you get there, you can just slip it under my door." His voice was surprisingly sympathetic-sounding, as if the idea of a philosophical crisis wasn't anything new to him. I walked to his office and slipped the paper under his door without knocking, even though his light was still on. When I got back home, I only had fifteen minutes to pack, but I threw everything into my suitcase and was ready when my ride got there.

I'm still not sure what the solution to my problem is, the problem of philosophical eros with its tragic limitations and its inability to accept real love that falls short of the ideal. But I think writing the paper got me a little closer to an answer. It has something to do with grace, which is what I ended up saying in the conclusion to the paper, too. In Greek, the counterpart of *eraomai*, to love, is *kharizesthai*, to gratify, grant favors (e.g., to a lover)—whence *kharis*, favor or gift, the equivalent of Latin *gratia*, grace. Eros seeks, grace gives. The answer has to do with accepting grace. It has to do with giving up, clearing a space in my head, and letting things come to me as they will. In a larger sense, maybe it also has to do with inspiration, with art. In the *Ion*, Plato depicts the artist as the vessel of divine inspiration; art is graceful. Philosophy can't solve the problems of life all on its own. It works better when it's allied with art, intuition, creativity, the non-rational, grace.

August 24 (Tucson)

A few days ago, I borrowed my dad's car and went down to the U of A library to check out some books to read over the rest of the vacation. I ended up walking through the courtyard of the building where I had my German class last summer, and then, to complete the trip down memory lane, I walked past Mike's Place and looked through the iron bars at the patio in back, where I spent so many hours talking with Pam and Angela and John last year. People were sitting at tables drinking and having conversations just like we used to, just like people normally do.

John's ghost was everywhere, standing in the shade, smoking cigarette after cigarette, and laughing.

Then I drove home and got out my old journals and photo albums from high school and my first year at BYU. I tried to remember who I used to be, and to figure out what's happened to me in the past year. I remember always feeling afraid when I was younger, afraid of what people would think of me if I wasn't who they wanted me to be. I was supposed to be thin, charming, orthodox in my religious beliefs, free of doubts. I was supposed to meet a handsome returned missionary, marry young, have kids, stay at home, forego a career. I was supposed to be like them, like the others. There were always silent voices in me, the voices of the others, telling me what to do and what to believe. Then a year ago, John told me I was speaking with a voice that wasn't mine, it was the "the They," or something like that, involving oddly capitalized pronouns I could hear even in speech. But he was right. All summer, he'd been goading me to listen to a different voice, the voice of reason, the voice that came from inside me, the one that was really me and no one else.

In the past year I've done almost nothing but struggle to learn to listen to that voice. It's clear to me now the most liberating thing in my life so far has been philosophy. Philosophy and friendship. Philosophy has been the erotic side of the equation, and friendship has been the grace—my friendships with Mark, Amanda, Zach, Matthew, Luke, and even people long dead, Goethe, Socrates, Kierkegaard. And of course, John.

September 5

Back in Provo. A rough first week. Driving into town and seeing the familiar shape of the mountains around it, I felt I'd come full circle. There I was again, back at BYU, and there I was again, full of new doubts about Christianity and God. It was that day of wandering around the U of A and looking at old photos that did it, all those thoughts about finding and listening to my own voice. When I listened, that voice seemed to tell me none of this was true, this whole shining edifice, the foundation of this town and university, of this way of life, of so many families and romances and friendships, of this network of communities that spans the globe, of all these literally shining edifices like the Temple standing out white at the foot of the mountains.

Added to that, I still had the other despair, the despair I find personified in Zach. In his physical and inward attractiveness, he's been a constant reminder of everything in me that's ugly and unworthy of love. Like Socrates in the paper I wrote on the tragedy of philosophical eros, I'm ugly and foolish, and love beauty and wisdom, *his* beauty and wisdom, because there's none in me.

As the week went on, I fell into a state much like when I tried to call John and talk about Kierkegaard last January—one of struggling against an impulse to talk and reveal everything. I was exhausted by the silence and ambiguity. I wanted to break the silence with Zach, to clear the air, to make everything bright and unambiguous (as if it were the silence and ambiguity that had hurt me, rather than his lack of interest). I know, stupid. But I've never exactly been a genius when it came to relationships. And you have to understand, I was half out of my mind at that point.

So, Friday I found him in the library—alone, thank goodness—and asked if we could talk. Heart pounding, blood all drained from my face, even the skin across my knuckles looked white, thin, and stretched taut. I was in a state.

We went to the cafeteria, got something to drink, and sat down facing each other in one of the small padded booths. Being so tall, he looked cramped and uncomfortable sitting there, like a grown man who's been made to sit at a kid's school desk. Finally I came out with it and told him I'd had a crush on him forever. It had been hard on me and probably made me less of a good friend to him than I ought to have been. I can hardly remember now what else I said, as I've tried steadily ever since to block out the memory. But there was probably a lot more nonsensical stuff of the sort you can imagine a terrified, besotted girl saying.

Of course he was kind—of course he was. This is Zach we're talking about. And nothing I said came as any surprise to him. He said Ashley had told him about the conversation she and I had that one time in the music building about me liking him.

I went cold with horror and said, "But she promised me she wouldn't say anything to you about it."

"We tell each other everything these days," he said.

I decided at that moment I don't like Ashley. It's not as if he couldn't have figured it out on his own, but still, it was a dirty thing for her to do, telling him. Apart from that, nothing he said came as a surprise to me, either. I already knew he cared about me as a friend, and all the rest.

I asked him what he thought of me, and he said, looking up at me with those piercing Scandinavian blue eyes and toying nervously with a paper napkin in his hands, twisting and shredding it, "I think you're a person who's trying to figure out who she is."

Which is true, of course. But I felt the implication was that I was incomplete and immature. Which, again, is true, but hurt.

Here you're not supposed to have to figure out who you are. As a Mormon, you're supposed to know from day one. You're a child of God, a man or a woman. As a woman, you're a future wife and mother; it's all simple and clear-cut. It's a failing, a flaw, to be trying to figure out who you are. Everyone is pulling for you as though you were sick with cancer, and they all hope you'll get it sorted out, but no one wants to date or marry or be too intimate with a girl who has this failing, any more than they'd want to woo a terminal cancer patient. Add to this being flat-chested and funny-looking, and you have a recipe for eternal solitude.

But maybe I'm too hard on BYU and Zach. Probably, trying to figure out who you are is a problem no matter where you do it, and would be a turnoff to any guy, Mormon or not, who wasn't in the same position. And would I want to be with someone in the same position? No, because I love the certainty and beauty of people who already have it figured out.

Zach and I parted on good terms, and despite my despair and embarrassment, I don't regret the conversation. Who knows, maybe Werther also would've done better if he'd only sat down and had a real heart-to-heart with Lotte, instead of blowing his brains out with a revolver.

September 6

Last night, Amanda came over and we went for a long walk together. I told her about the conversation with Zach and also about my paper on Socrates, my philosophical problem with ugliness and trying to compensate for it with moral and intellectual beauty, but never really being able to get beyond the ugliness—in short, all my doubts about the value of my ugly existence.

She said she thought the yearning for beauty was itself a beauty. I liked that.

Seeing I was still sad, she asked, "What do you want? What would make you happy?"

I thought about it and after a while said, "I would be happy if, just for once, someone would come up to me and say, 'You know, Marguerite, I've seen your work, I see what you're trying to do, and it's beautiful.' If only someone saw beauty in me."

"So, in other words, you want a boyfriend to tell you you're beautiful?"

"No—It doesn't have to be a boyfriend. It could be a professor, maybe."

"Hmm. A professor or a boyfriend ..."

"No, I mean, it could be a girl, too—anyone. If you said it, it would make me happy."

"But Marguerite, isn't it obvious? Isn't it obvious I think you're beautiful?" She told me some of the things she loved about me and said she had always admired my honesty.

I suppose I shouldn't have been so surprised to hear that. We are best friends after all, so it only made sense. I guess I had just gotten so used to feeling alone in the way I see and value things, valuing my own idiosyncratic search for redemption in a way no one else seems to understand or believe in. And then to have Amanda say that gave me the sense at least for one evening that I wasn't alone, despite how much my vision had been clouded and dimmed by solitude and hurt.

September 7

They say Joseph Smith received his famous revelation, the one where God and Jesus appeared to him, because he had prayed and asked God which church was true. He had read in James 1:5, *If any of you lack wisdom, let him ask of God, that giveth to all men liberally, and upbraideth not; and it shall be given him.* So he went to the Sacred Grove and knelt down and asked the Lord for wisdom on the question that had been troubling him. If it worked for Joseph, it seems it should work for everyone, even me. The problem comes with the rest of scripture, which says, *But let him ask in faith, nothing wavering.* How can a person ask for wisdom concerning faith if she doesn't have faith to begin with? My whole being is a wavering. There seems nothing steady or constant in me *but* wavering.

What else can I do but try, though? I need to have it out with God, the same way I did with Zach. I'm sick of silence and ambiguity, of being stuck on the Either/Or. But it doesn't seem fair simply to call myself an agnostic and leave it at that. I have to give God one last chance, to confront Him and see if I can't find out for myself if there's any truth in the idea I have of Him, if I can't have a testimony of the truthfulness of the Gospel.

I talked to my roommate Rachel just now about dropping me off in a place where we went hiking once before, a beautiful, secluded area a little ways up into the mountains, near where Rachel's older sister used to live. We're going after lunch.

***

Back and too tired to write more, except: I'm resigned to my fate. I understand the renunciation I take on myself, going forward.

CHAPTER 22

THE MOUNTAIN

THAT AFTERNOON, RACHEL HAD dropped Marguerite off by the side of the road, and she'd made her way through the brush further up into the hills until she couldn't see the road anymore. She'd brought a backpack with water, a few granola bars, and her scriptures.

The day was sunny and hot. She wore a hat but had forgotten her sunglasses, and the glare reflecting from the rocks was harsh in her eyes. This was desert country. There weren't the cactuses or mesquites or palo verdes of the Sonoran desert she knew so well, but the trees were short, stubby, and thorny, and the brush was dry and scratched her bare shins.

She sat down on a rock in the shade of a tree, pulled out her scriptures, and opened them at random. The passage her finger landed on was nothing insightful, one of the bloody battle scenes in the Old Testament. She closed the book again and got down on her knees on the rocky soil under the tree. She folded her arms, closed her eyes, bowed her head, and prayed aloud.

"Dear Heavenly Father, I don't know if you've been watching or listening. I don't know if you exist at all. That's why I'm here. Tell me, what am I supposed to do? Can you understand why I'm tempted to give up on you, to give up hoping I'll ever hear an answer? If you choose to be silent, can you blame me if I struggle? I don't understand you and I don't understand why you would want me to suffer.

"I don't know how much longer I can bear to hurt like this. I'm alone. I have friends and family, and I'm grateful for them, but still, you know what I mean when I say I'm alone. I don't have a husband, and I don't see how anyone could ever love me in that way. Why give me this body, if it's only there to make me unhappy and fill me with wanting what I can't have? Why did you make me so ugly and unlovable, so unworthy inside and out?

"Can you really be so cruel—if you even exist at all? I want to believe in you as a loving Father. I want to have faith your reasons are loving ones, even if they're hidden from me.

"But how can I, when I don't even understand what it means to have faith? Please give me the wisdom to understand how to have faith. I don't want some mystical revelation. I don't have to see you or hear your voice. I'm not asking for you to show yourself and explain yourself to me. I'm not worthy to stand in your presence. All I want is enough wisdom to understand how I can believe and still be honest with myself.

"Surely you couldn't want me to lie to myself. You are Truth itself, so you couldn't want anything from me but absolute honesty. But I need to understand how you can ask for both faith and honesty from me, when I can only give you one or the other.

"I need both, as much as you do. Try to understand why I want so desperately to have faith in you. Do you remember when I was thirteen years old, and so depressed I thought all the time about killing myself? Remember that night I tried to do it by swallowing a whole bottle of Tylenol? And after I got home from the hospital, I knelt and prayed to you, and promised you I'd never try to hurt myself again, no matter how bad it got.

"I've held up my end of the bargain. I've endured these days of despair where every step I take is like walking on knives and every breath is like breathing poison gas, and it's agony just to be. But you have to hold up your end of the bargain too. If you don't exist, *I don't have to either.* If you don't exist, anything is allowed. It doesn't matter what I do, and there's no reason anymore to endure what I've suffered.

"If I just had some reason to hope, Heavenly Father. I've been waiting for you my whole life. How long can you expect a person to wait for you, without a word or a sign? Please, just answer me. Surely you can give me a way to believe in you without lying to myself. How can I be true to you without disbelieving in you? You're the only one who can tell me."

201

The tears were streaming down Marguerite's face, and her eyelids were swollen and sore. She stopped speaking, but remained on her knees in the shade with her eyes closed. She listened, and heard birds twittering in the branches above her. Cicadas keened, and wind stirred the brittle leaves and dry bushes. Far off, she heard the faint woosh of a car passing on the road. Underneath all these sounds, there was silence, beating like a heart.

She opened her eyes and lay down on her back on the rocky ground with her face turned up to the sky between the branches. How could He not be up there in that clear, bright expanse? But appearances had deceived her before.

She felt an ant crawl up her leg and sat up quickly to brush it off. A bee floated by, humming. She got to her feet, trudged a few yards over to a rock in the sun, and sat down on it, crossing her legs underneath her. She sat for an hour there, soaking in the heat, listening to the sounds of the mountainside and the silence underneath.

Silence was an answer. That was the trouble. People said things to each other through silence all the time. You might not understand what it meant, but you understood it meant something.

God was never more human than when He was silent and invisible, Marguerite thought to herself. Maybe he was like the seducer in *Either/Or*. He made people fall in love with him in indirect ways, letting them think He loved them, hinting they might find a kind of ecstasy and transcendence with Him. Then He abandoned them to silence. But He did all this only in order to bring out something extraordinary in them.

Silence. As long as there hadn't been a negative answer, technically speaking, there was hope a positive answer might come. Practically speaking, the longer a silence lasted, the more likely it became that silence was the only answer you'd ever get. How long did you wait before giving up hope? A year? Twenty years?

Marguerite looked down at her watch. Still a couple of hours to kill before Rachel would meet her back at the road with the car. She got up and started walking uphill. She climbed under the sun's harsh glare, pressing on until the minute hand on her wristwatch had gone a full circle around and then some. She turned around and headed downhill, back the way she had come, although there wasn't a path, so she couldn't be sure she was following the same route.

God remained silent, but she didn't want to give up listening yet. From a practical standpoint, silence as an answer usually meant nothing good. But that was the thing with silence. You never knew if *your* silence might not be the exception. She wasn't ready yet to give up on listening, and that meant she wasn't ready to give up on existing, either. To listen you had to be alive. Her existence might be full of senseless pain, but the silence didn't render her any more decisive about ending it. She could end it, really and truly she could. She could stay out here in the hills and let herself die of hunger and thirst. Instead, she was walking forward, heading down to where the road would be, to meet Rachel.

The hand on her watch had passed the hour mark again a while back, and still the road didn't appear. Marguerite began to worry she had come down the wrong way. Her feet ached and her skin was gritty with dried sweat. Still, she kept walking.

Maybe this was what she was, she thought as she walked, a separate category all to herself. Not a Christian, not an agnostic, but a person waiting for an answer. She knew what it meant, to call herself this and admit it once and for all. It meant she couldn't serve a mission, couldn't go to the temple, couldn't bear her testimony in sacrament meeting. These things required a certainty she didn't have. She would live as a Christian while she waited for an answer, in the hope it might all be true. She would be an outcast within the fold. And she would be alone, eternally alone. No faithful man would want to be with an outcast, and no unbeliever would have the patience to wait for her while she waited for God. This was the fate she was taking upon herself with every step forward.

She caught sight of the black line of the road below her, and Rachel's dark blue car, its dusty roof glinting dully in the sun. She hurried down to it.

CHAPTER 23

WORKS OF LOVE

SEPTEMBER 18

Zach and Ashley have broken off their engagement. It's so strange. I was used to the idea of them together, or at least I'd gotten used to not getting used to it. It must have happened just a few days after my declaration of doomed unrequited infatuation to Zach in the cafeteria. I remember running into each of them separately right after that, out with their other friends. At the time I thought to myself it was odd not to see them with each other, but I was impressed they were autonomous and self-possessed enough to spend time apart instead of acting joined at the hip like engaged people normally do around here.

I guess I couldn't be blamed for wondering, when I first heard the news, if it had anything to do with our conversation in the cafeteria. But the way I found out about it laid that doubt to rest pretty quickly. It was Amanda who told me, and she heard it from Zach directly. He came over to her house to look at grad school brochures, explaining that his plans for next year had gotten more settled since breaking off the engagement. The reason he gave for the breakup was that "eternity is a really long time." Which is understandable I guess. But I believe that in telling Amanda, he knew she'd tell me, and that was his way of communicating indirectly to let me know it had nothing to do with me.

I'm not so sure, however, that the breakup had nothing to with Amanda. And to my own surprise, I'm okay with that. I must finally be getting over him.

September 19

I went to a Philosophy Club talk today that Dr. Mewes gave on faith and reason. It was very Continental and Heideggerian in flavor, which is to say, I barely understood a word of it and couldn't make heads or tails of what the thesis was supposed to be. But I kept catching intriguing, fleeting phrases that piqued my curiosity and gave me the impression it would all be deep, relevant, and insightful if only I understood it.

Thinking about the lecture afterward, I came to a decision: I need to learn enough so that I can understand these kinds of talks. I need to understand faith, by any means possible; I need to read and study and understand everything that's been written about it, all through the ages. I have no talent for believing, that much is clear, but I can read, think, talk, and write. Maybe that's my slow path to faith. If it's a task for a lifetime, if I have to have to become the world expert on faith in order to understand it, then that's what I'll do. There are worse ways to spend an intellectual career than trying to understand faith.

September 21

Today after our Nietzsche class got out, I went to Dr. Mewes's office and asked if I could talk to him sometime. He said I didn't need an appointment; he could talk with me then and there. So I came in and sat down. I wonder if I didn't look a little desperate to him. I probably look that way a lot these days.

I told him about going to his lecture on faith and reason, and how I was always struggling to understand faith and didn't think I could serve a mission or have a testimony. Even if I got so far as believing in God, I wasn't sure how one got the rest of the way to believing in Christianity.

He said he thought I was wrong about not understanding faith. Maybe I understood it better than I realized, and probably I had a testimony, too. A testimony was based on "spiritual experiences," and I must already have had at least a few of those, or I wouldn't be here at BYU in the first place.

That was true, I said. I'd felt things often that seemed to fit with what people meant when they used the words "spiritual experience."

I'd felt it reading the scriptures, hearing other people bear their testimonies in church, seeing people behave Christianly to each other, and so on. But maybe on some level I was afraid of letting those experiences be valid for me, afraid of taking them at face value. I was hesitant to rely on my feelings rather than reason and didn't see how I could overcome that fear.

He said it clearly wasn't a matter of my not being able to, but of my refusing to. I always wanted to be in control, I willed not to have a spiritual witness. It was my will that was the problem. The difficulty I faced was wanting to have Cartesian certainty, a "clear and distinct understanding." I was playing Descartes, falling prey to the seductive Enlightenment project of attaining total knowledge.

I brought up the paradox I'd been thinking about with regard to James 1:5 and asking for faith, but needing to have faith already in order to have the prayer granted.

He said, "There isn't anyone who doesn't already have faith." Right at that moment, I was putting my trust in him by talking to him and confiding in him. Wasn't that already a form of having faith in someone? I trusted things and people all the time, on a daily basis, without having exact knowledge of them. That, too, was faith.

We talked about commitments. I asked, how did I dare commit myself to Christianity and this particular form of it? How did anyone dare to make such commitments?

His response was essentially that there wasn't any "how" to it. One could only reflect and intellectualize it after the fact. When it came down to making the commitment in actuality, one either did it or didn't. That was true of any commitment or promise. Overall my tendency, as was the case with many "bright" people, was to want to be in control and intellectualize everything, just as I was doing with my past spiritual experiences. When these experiences occur, they occur as what they are, something fleeting and ungraspable. But after the fact, you want to assign intelligible physical causes to them, to bring them within the grasp of your reason and power. Why not just let go and simply accept these experiences as "givens"? Why be so eager to explain them away?

We ended with those questions. Not with him telling me what I was supposed to think, but giving me those question to mull over and answer for myself. I liked his Socratic approach, and I think there was a lot of wisdom in what he said. But in a bizarre way, it reminded me of what John's friend Damon said to me so long ago. "Don't you want to be able to just let go, don't you want to feel someone *inside* you?" The idea is the same. To succumb, to give in to what I want, give in to passion.

I'm not sure it gets me any closer to faith. I agree reason can't do it all; that much is obvious. But surely it has more of a role to play in questions of both faith and passion than just getting the hell out of the way.

November 17

I worry I'm getting sick. My depression is starting to seem chronic now. I used to feel okay most of the time, with occasional bad spells. Now it's the reverse. It's the good days I notice, the days I don't feel like crying or wish I were dead. I can't always tell if the sadness comes from cognitive or physiological causes, or a combination. I feel lonely, despairing; I think pessimistic thoughts, and my body is stressed by too little sleep, bad food, and anxiety about school.

I talked about it recently with Amanda, and she thought I should see a psychologist. She said a therapist could help rid me of the burden of guilt, and that I'd probably be much happier if I weren't neurotic.

"Do you really think I'm neurotic?" I asked her, surprised. When Matthew had called me that I'd felt hurt, although I wasn't even sure what it meant other than being crazy in some way.

Amanda shrugged her shoulders, sighed, and said she didn't know. The next day I looked up "neurosis" in the encyclopedia in the library. Some of it sounded like me. Feeling guilty all the time: check. Feeling responsible for everything, thinking everything is my fault: check. Worrying too much about what other people think of me: check. Obsessing over boys, morality, and God: check. The occasional anxiety attack: check. And of course, my depression. But other parts sounded too extreme to fit my case.

In a way, though, in spite of the pain and despair, I feel I'm moving forward in a dialectical progression, a dialogue with myself. This sickness feels like a step in the dialectic, a valuable step, and I'm not sure I like the thought of some facile counselor trying to lift the burden of guilt off my shoulders. Dr. Mewes keeps telling us that in Nietzsche's writing, he's always playing on the double sense of *Schuld* in German. It means guilt, but also a debt. I'm willing to pay my debts. I wonder if you can really get out of paying them without losing some part of your soul.

I don't feel like I'm progressing toward an end-point, a place of rest, either. The destination is Christianity, if you like, or faith, which itself is a whole new journey. So I'm journeying to a journey. Maybe that's a good definition of faith: every journey that only ends in another journey is a type of faith.

December 2

Two good things have happened. One is, I have a job. Dr. Fillmore hired me as his assistant. I've never had a job before, and I like it. It feels good to earn my own money, to be that much more free and independent.

I started by helping Dr. Fillmore organize his files, and funnily enough, I found my own paper in one of his folders, the one I wrote on the tragedy of philosophical eros for his Plato class this summer. He said he'd kept a copy for his files because he thought it was interesting.

The other good thing is, I may have found a solution to the problem of faith, or at least to *my* problem with faith. It's in a book by Kierkegaard called *Works of Love*. We've been reading chapters from it for the seminar on Kierkegaard I'm taking with Dr. Udall this semester. It's a different sort of book from the others I've read by Kierkegaard, more a series of sermons than a philosophical work. But they're interesting sermons, full of stories and poetic images, and all of them are about the ideal of Christian love.

One of the sermons is called "Love Believes All Things—And Yet Is Never Deceived." In it, Kierkegaard writes about how easy it is to mistrust people. No one wants to be made a fool of. But often, the exact same set of appearances and evidence we take as the basis for mistrust can serve equally well as the basis for giving someone the benefit of the doubt. When the evidence is ambiguous, we have to choose whether to trust or mistrust, and our choice shows whether there is love in us or not. It's more loving to give someone the benefit of the doubt.

Loving is the greatest joy, the highest good in life, and the person who is truly loving can never be deceived. If someone tries to deceive the true lover, he's only deceiving himself. He's cheating himself out of the highest good by not loving, and he's on the way to cheating himself out of the next highest good too, which is being loved by someone who loves truly. Meanwhile, no matter how much anyone might try to deceive the true lover, the true lover still has the highest good and can't be cheated out of it.

I don't know if I've explained it clearly enough, but it's exciting, because this is the solution not only to the problem about God, but also to understanding all those confusing things that happened with John the summer before sophomore year. Love believes all things and is never deceived. I can believe in God *out of love*. Not because I've reasoned my way to belief, and not because I've thrown away reason, but because I've *chosen* to be loving. I've chosen to give God the benefit of the doubt, out of love for Him, as a work of love. It's not irrational, because only a rational being can make a choice of this kind, but it's not wholly rational either, because I choose based on what I desire and value. The difficult part is becoming transparent to myself, so I can see clearly what my desires and values are.

And what happened with John was that I loved him. That was a good thing; I wasn't just fooled or deceived into loving him based on false pretenses. Love believes all things and is never deceived. I'll never know what his intentions were, but it's okay for me to give him the benefit of the doubt. It's okay for me to trust and hope that whatever was going on with him, he didn't mean to hurt me, at least not as much as he did. It's not just crazy wishful thinking on my part, to believe that. In its own insignificant way, it too is a work of love.

February 4

Something strange is happening with Matthew. Yesterday we were sitting in the philosophy department lounge, just the two of us, and he said something about there being sexual tension between us. He was joking, but still it shocked me a little, because I've never thought about him that way. And it's *odd* that I've never thought about him that way. It's not as though he isn't handsome. I've thought so much about him in other ways, obsessively trying to understand him and earn his approval, you'd think it would at least have occurred to me to fantasize about him. But no, it never had until he mentioned it.

We're both taking a class in Greek Lyric Poetry together this semester. Today as we were sitting in class, going around the table taking turns translating lines of Sappho, I heard a quiet, shrill scraping sound behind me. I looked over and Matthew was twisting the blunt end of his pen against the table with one hand. He looked up and our eyes met, and I felt a jolt of electricity go through me. Good God.

February 28

I can't believe it—I'm going to Germany this summer! I got a scholarship from the German Academic Exchange Service to study for six weeks in Regensburg. My mom and dad said they'd pay for the plane tickets. I'm almost in shock. This was something I applied for at the last minute in a "what the hell, why not" kind of mood, figuring I had no real chance of getting it. Wow, wow, wow.

Thank God, that gives me something to live for the rest of the semester. In all seriousness, I've worried sometimes I might not make it. For a month or two, December and January, I was doing really well. That was after I read *Works of Love* and realized it was possible for me to have faith. But then my sickness, this depression, came back, and I still have to fight it all the time. I worry I'm always going to have to struggle with it; no matter how many times it seems to go into remission it will always come back, like a killing cancer.

I asked Matthew the other day what he thought of psychotherapy. He said it helped some people, but from a philosophical standpoint you had to take it with a grain of salt. He asked, why, was I thinking of it for myself? I told him a little about my depression and anxiety, and how Amanda thought I should see someone about it, but I didn't feel comfortable with the idea. Matthew said I should only go if I did feel comfortable, and if I went I should take it with a grain of salt. He promised not to tell anyone, and said if I ever wanted to talk about it, I could always talk with him.

March 6

Today after our Greek Lyric Poetry class let out, Matthew and I were walking back to the philosophy department lounge together. As we turned the corner, he asked me in sort of a furtively lowered voice, "What do you want?"

When he asks me blunt questions like that, there's never any way for me to dissemble or hide from him the truth of what I think. So I said, "I want to fall in love." We walked along in silence again for a while, and at last I asked if I he thought it was bad of me to want that. We women were socialized to think love was the most important thing, when in reality ...

But he stopped me and said he thought it *was* the most important thing.

March 21

I've become completely infatuated with Matthew. I go back and forth with myself almost daily as to whether this is a good or a bad thing. Obviously it's a useless crush, since he's still with the same long-term girlfriend he's always had, and we'd kill each other if we were ever a couple anyway. He hurts my feelings all the time. With a single word, or a glance, or silence, he can fill me with terror. We'd be the worst imaginable combination, because I'm so sensitive and he's so intense. I'm a sort of emotional hemophiliac; where other people heal, I just bleed and bleed. And in his intensity he affects me as if he weren't one but three of himself.

I can't help loving him, though, precisely because of the intensity. He's frighteningly brilliant and passionate, with a large, labyrinthine soul, full of every imaginable beauty once you get past the prickliness and moods. Even his insults are so insightful you want to thank him for them. He's sort of a caustic, fiery cleansing agent. Plus, he always comes back to apologize and put things right in the end. You can never trust him, but you can't help believing in him.

March 26

Matthew knows how I feel now, more or less, because I ended up confessing it to him on Friday, a bit like I did with Zach and that declaration of doomed unrequited infatuation in the cafeteria.

Matthew and I share an office hour in the T.A. office Friday mornings, and since no students showed up, we got to talking. I wanted to tell him how I felt, if only to explain why I always take the things he says so much to heart, but I was so nervous I almost chickened out. Finally I blurted out that I was infatuated with him.

He wasn't exactly nice about it, not the way Zach was, but I liked his reaction better than Zach's niceness. He didn't seem surprised, but just listened with a grave expression on his face. I couldn't even tell if he was pleased or not. When I finished he said not to worry about it. These things happened, and he wouldn't hold it against me. He said he was prone to infatuations, too; he had them all the time. Sometimes they lasted for a few hours, and sometimes for a long time. He'd been infatuated with his girlfriend forever.

I felt a little foolish afterward, but I think it's going to be okay. I think we'll still be friends, although I don't know if I've exorcised the crush the way I was hoping I would. These declarations of doomed unrequited love are never quite as helpful they're meant to be.

April 8

I have a crush on Luke Young, now, too, albeit a more modest one than Zach and Matthew have had to endure. Luke is awfully nice once you get over those intimidating eyebrows. I love his comforting teddy bear shape and pudding bowl haircut. His hair always looks so soft and clean and swingy, it's hard to keep from running my hands through it.

We had a good conversation today. We went to lunch together after our German Lit class and got to talking about our families. He told me his mom had problems with anxiety and depression, but things had worked out well for her. His dad was understanding, so even though it wasn't always easy, his parents had a good relationship.

I said I liked that story, because I had worried that if a person (e.g., me) had problems like that, it might be unethical for her to marry and have a family. Luke said he didn't think so. It was hard sometimes with his mom—he would blame himself when she got upset, and his sister rebelled a lot. But he loved his mom and wouldn't have wanted her not to have a family. He said for a person like that, if it worked out, having a family could be the best thing in their life.

It was a good perspective for me to hear. It gave me hope that maybe the things I want most *are* possible, after all.

April 14

You know how in *Fear and Trembling* Kierkegaard talks about Sarah from the Book of Tobit? She's the one who tries to get married seven times, and each time on her wedding night, a jealous demon who's in love with her kills the bridegroom. That's what I feel my despair has become, a demon lover who threatens to hurt anyone I get close to. The terrible thing about the sickness is that it doesn't just hurt me, it has the potential to make me hurt everyone around me, the people I least want to hurt.

It's not a one-sided love affair, either. I'm drawn to despair and the idea of death as to a lover. There have been terrible nights when I so desperately wanted not to be anymore, to go to sleep permanently. I try to reason my way out of it and come up with all kinds of arguments as to why suicide is not a good answer and I shouldn't take my own life. But the lust for not-being threatens to overwhelm all logic and reasoning and arguments. It's not unlike that summer two years ago with John when, after reason had done its proper work, the desire remained and would have driven me to betray everything I believed in if I'd just had the opportunity.

A kind of grace protected me back then, when John went silent and I didn't have the opportunity. And in the same way, grace has come to my rescue more than a few times and kept me from losing my grasp on reason to the point of being able to hurt myself.

Last week, Amanda was out of town interviewing at grad schools. I missed her and started to feel terribly alone and powerless to help myself. I didn't think there was anyone I could talk to without doing damage to myself and them. Then I remembered how Matthew had once said if I ever needed to talk, I could talk to him. I thought, if anyone could understand what I'm going through, it would be Matthew.

You see, this is what I meant about not trusting him but believing in him. I couldn't trust him not to hurt my feelings from day to day, but I believed in him enough to risk calling him, and only him, when I was in real danger. When he answered, I told him I was having another bad spell. I was so tired of having them, I wished I could just die and be finished. He was worried and said maybe I really should think about getting professional help. Maybe I should look into my options for medication. We talked about it for a while, and finally I said, "Look, I'm lonely. If I go see someone in a clinic or if I take drugs, that's not going to change. I'll still be alone."

Once I'd finally admitted to him what the real problem was, he said, "Well, what are you waiting for? Bring your homework and come over. We'll study together."

I'd never been to his place before. It was a shabby but immaculately clean basement apartment. He lived there by himself. I sat down in an old battered armchair and tried to study while he sat at his desk and worked. It felt awkward and too quiet. But then we got to talking about music, and he played some records for me, things I'd never heard before, jazz songs by Chet Baker and some symphonic pieces by Penderecki and Messaien. So I got through that night and came home and slept. It must have seemed like a small thing to him, but probably saved my life.

April 17

I think all this pain and misery and danger, perversely, has helped me get a clearer idea of what I want in its place. I want a simple, poetic vision. I want to see the world without explaining away its mystery by calling things "wicked," "righteous," "sinful," and "good." I want to erase in myself the easy explanations, the always mendacious explanations about why things happen the way they do, and in this way, come to know the mystery of being—not by any approximation in thought, but *by being*. I want to be and not be ashamed of being. I want to forget myself in the hurry and bustle of existing, to love, speak, question, respond, caress, push away, shout, laugh, cry, sing, dance, walk, run, sleep, wake, eat, go to the bathroom, copulate, bear children, and sing them to sleep. I want freedom to grasp what I want, and I want what I want to yield to me.

Maybe Plato was right, and the Good is Being. And *this* is the highest: God, truth, love—they all end up as this.

CHAPTER 24

THESES ON FAITH

JUNE 19

I've been here in Regensburg for a couple of days already, and the jet lag is finally starting to wear off. I had no idea what to expect, but it's beautiful here. Today the program leaders took us on a field trip to the cloister at Weltenberg, with a boat trip on the Danube afterward. The countryside is green and picturesque, with rolling hills and farms dotted with fluffy white sheep, like something out of a book of fairy tales. The other students are outgoing and friendly, and I've hardly felt lonely at all since I've been here.

Thank goodness for this trip. I was getting so dangerously depressed before I left. They say traveling is helpful for taking your mind off things, and I do feel better here. Maybe all I needed was a change of scenery.

It was sad saying goodbye to everyone before I left. Amanda, Matthew, and Zach are all graduating, so Luke and I will be the only ones left next year from our small circle of friends in the philosophy department. Matthew got a fellowship to study at Oxford, so there's not much chance of seeing him again any time soon, but Amanda and Zach will both be in New York City. Zach is going to Fordham, and Amanda to The New School. So theoretically it might be possible to come out there for a visit at some point. In any case, I'm meeting Amanda in Leipzig in August after our programs let out—she got a German Academic Exchange Service scholarship, too—and we're going to travel together for a couple of weeks. We'll go to Prague and Vienna and then head back home.

My goal is not to write anything more in English for the rest of the summer, so I think this is goodbye to you too, journal, at least for a while.

September 3

What wouldn't I give to be back living the high life in Regensburg right now, instead of here in godforsaken Provo, UT, with my second-to-last semester looming over me. Being in Germany was such a contrast, it made me realize and finally admit to myself how much I just plain don't like Provo or BYU. I'm suffocating, smothering here. But I'll write about the time in Regensburg, since it's a lot more enjoyable to think about than the present.

It was hard settling in at first. I guess there was more in the way of culture shock than I expected. I thought it would be no problem, since I'd already been to France when I was seventeen. But so many small details of daily life were different that it was stressful and frustrating. The windows open differently, the washing machines boil your clothes, you have to bring your own grocery bag to the supermarket and a coin to deposit for a cart. All these little daily stumbling blocks and frustrations, along with my shyness and the difficulty of understanding spoken German, combined to make me terribly homesick and lonely. It wasn't long before I was as depressed as ever.

Then the trees saved me. It's the kind of thing that's hard to write about. If I try it'll end up being in a kind of private language. But I might as well try, since it's not like anyone but me is ever going to read this, and I don't want to forget it.

The program leaders had assigned each of us a local student volunteer to be our *Kampuspater*, to take us out and show us around. One was named Reinhold, and he ended up spending a lot of time with us, me and a handful of other American students who all hung out together. One weekend he said he wanted to show us some local historical sights, *Geisterschlösser* or "ghost castles," places you might only hear about if you'd grown up there.

Five of us squeezed into his tiny car with him, and we drove out to some nearby small towns, like Wolfsegg, where the castle was rumored to be haunted, and then to a village on the edge of the

Black Forest. We had lunch in an old-style Bavarian restaurant next to the river. It was a golden afternoon, sitting outside at trestled tables in the shade of leafy trees, watching the sunlight slant across the water, which was black-green with moss, while birds twittered and waterbugs glided over the surface. After lunch, a young boy in shorts ferried us across the stream on a wooden raft that he pushed with a pole.

We took a path that went uphill into the woods, and before long there was no sign of anyone but us. Reinhold told us this part of the forest was ancient; some of the trees were centuries old. They looked like old men, thick-trunked, stooping low, draped in beards of green moss. It was unlike any forest I'd hiked through in the mountains of Utah or Arizona, those forests filled with thin trees, flowering meadows, and plenty of light. This was a dim, mysterious place; it felt like being underwater, with the sunlight filtering down through the crowding cover of branches, splaying and refracting through floating motes of dust and moisture. There was a density to the air and a hush that lay over everything like an invisible blanket, ominous but entrancing, as though the ground were breathing under our feet, as though we were walking over the pelt of some enormous sleeping animal and had to step carefully so as not to wake it.

The smell that rose up from the trees and moss and the black soil was intoxicating. A rich smell of life, decay, old sunlight, and even older darkness. I felt it working its way deep into me like a drug, binding up places that had come apart, knitting together the lips of ruptures, healing me. It filled me with a happiness I hadn't felt in years—a wakeful, peaceful confidence in my own health and well-being. I had forgotten feelings like that even existed and that I was capable of them. The trees and their scent woke me up and brought me back to life.

We went higher and higher among the dwarf-like trees with their knobby faces and green beards, until we came to the crumbling remains of a small medieval fort. There were no signs or plaques or ropes; we could climb up and sit on the stone walls as we liked, and so we did. When we'd rested and seen enough, Reinhold led us up by another path to what he called a *mystischer Ort*, a mystical place. We found it, high up in the deep woods, a grouping of enormous rocks carpeted with thick moss. At the foot of the boulders, someone had set up a thin gold crucifix, about shoulder-high. Reinhold told us in ancient times, long before the Romans came there, the inhabitants of these woods held pagan ceremonies in this place. The crucifix was set up by Christians much later to ward off any evil spirits that might still be hanging around.

No question, there was something magical in the air, something wild and untamed about the place. I could well understand the pagans wanting to honor it with rituals and coming back to it time and time again over the centuries.

We got back to the campus after dark, tired and footsore but well-satisfied with our day of ghosts and trees. A few days earlier I had gone to the pharmacy and bought a huge bottle of sleeping pills, which I'd kept under my bed, trying to get up the courage to swallow them all and get it over with. When we got back from the woods, I threw it in a dumpster.

After that trip, Reinhold and I had a little flirtation going. He was a lot older than me at 29—I've only just turned 21. But it turned out we had some things in common. He was Christian (Protestant, that is; they're a minority in Bavaria), a bit shy, a teetotaler, and even still a virgin like me. We didn't have a lot of shared intellectual interests, and admittedly he wasn't movie-star gorgeous, but he was good-looking enough that it was fun to flirt. One night a bunch of students from our program went out in a group, and I got a ride with him in his car. On the way home afterward, he got sentimental and held my hand. It felt so good and so unfamiliar at the same time, to have affection turn physical like that. Small and simple as the gesture was—it would seem like nothing to any normal person probably—to me it was an amazement, almost as enlivening as the smell of those trees.

Among the Americans, the coolest girl I met was an accounting student named Heike. I always had this prejudiced idea that anyone studying accounting must be dumb and boring. But she was bright, interesting, and sweet. We were both in the philosophy seminar, and since she didn't have any background in philosophy, she asked if I could explain some of the history of it to her. So one evening we sat on the bed in her dorm room and had a marathon session of talking philosophy. I was in the middle of trying to explain to her what little I understood of Hegel when she stopped me and asked what I personally thought of all this.

I told her about my own dialectical progress, as I saw it, and the strange role philosophy had played in my life for the past two years. It turned out she'd had some similar experiences with struggling to figure out who she was and what her beliefs and values were. She'd read Ayn Rand at some point, and it had made her question whether she'd been seeing things wrong her whole life. She was fascinated that I would still choose to be religious even after having been exposed to all these alternate views and said she wished she could find something like that to hold on to. She was tired of "always floating." She didn't want to do that forever. We stayed up until midnight talking about religion, faith, and morality.

A few days later, she introduced me to an American guy named Josh, a German literature grad student from New York, and I fell crazy in love with him for a week or so. He and I sat together on a five-hour bus ride, coming back from a weekend trip to Weimar and Erfurt, and had an intense, passionate conversation about the meaning of life that lasted most of the way home. I don't remember many of the details apart from my impressions of him as bearded and slightly depressive, with the sort of eyes and mind that attract me: gentle but hungry. I remember when I told him about Mormonism he laughed in my face and asked how anyone in their right mind could believe all that. And we talked about me being a virgin. He asked whether it was by choice. I honestly didn't know how to answer the question. Later, I wrote a Sappho-inspired poem about it:

"By choice?" you ask, but I don't know what to say.
Did the ripening sweet-apple choose to blow first
Upon a high and dangerous branch,
A slender bough where every breath of wind
Sends her trembling and quivering on her stem?
Did any gentle gatherer draw her in?
No, but all shook, and she who if she fell, fell bruised and crushed
Unripe, untouched, to her branch clung.
And why should any climb?

Is she redder or sweeter than fruits close to hand?
Her pride is to be closest to the silver-fingered moon,
To be first touched at dawn by the light of the sun.
The gatherers pass by; she is scorned and left alone.

Sadly, like me, my poems are never opaque enough and lack all subtlety.

Later, Josh told me he loved to cook and was good at it, too. I immediately proposed marriage, telling him I needed to marry a guy who could cook, because I loved to eat but couldn't cook to save my life. He said he couldn't even tell if I was joking or not about the marriage part (I was completely serious). But he found it sad I wouldn't take the time to learn to cook well. He called it "self-abuse," to deny myself the enjoyment of one of the most sensual and essential parts of life, food.

I told him how, growing up as a Mormon girl, you were supposed to learn to be a good cook so you could stay home and be a proper subservient housewife later on. Maybe it was just my way of rebelling against these strict gender roles. If I never learned to cook, I could never be made into the one everyone relied on to do the cooking. I wanted to be a human being first and a woman second, like I'd read of Hemingway's mother, who sang opera and had an egalitarian marriage with a husband who did the cooking. I liked the idea of role reversals, playing up the "masculine" or androgynous qualities in myself sometimes, and seeing men play out "feminine" roles, being emotional, sensitive, compassionate, gourmet cooks, etc. I thought of Matthew Godbey and how he wasn't afraid to say love was the most important thing, how I'd loved him for saying it.

I could tell Josh was pleased when I said all this. Understandably, as it obviously described him, too. He said role reversals could definitely be a good thing; it was a huge turn-on for him when his girlfriend took the lead in the bedroom, for example. (Yes, he has a girlfriend back in New York. In my defense, I didn't know this at the time I proposed marriage to him.) In any case, I decided he was right about it being silly to deny myself the pleasures of cooking good food, so this year I'm going to learn to cook.

After that bus trip, we hung out often. One night he and Heike and I went to see an American movie dubbed in German, called *Threesome*. It was about three college students, a gay guy, a straight guy, and a straight girl who, for reasons I couldn't understand, ended up having to live together in campus housing. They all fell in love with each other and started having a passionate affair that involved group skinny-dipping and later sandwich sex with the girl in the middle. The story and mechanics of it were a bit mysterious to me, given my lack of analogous experience and the fact that I only understood half the German. We talked about it afterward (it turned out the others were nearly as confused as I was), and I admitted the movie shocked me, but not as much as you'd think. It reminded me of a line from a Tennessee Williams play, *Night of the Iguana,* when an old maid, a virgin like me with almost no experience in relationships, says, "Nothing human disgusts me." That line always struck a chord with me, because there's a sense in which I feel the same. I might not choose to be in a threesome sex sandwich myself, but seeing it didn't disgust me. If I'm honest with myself, there was a kind of beauty to it.

Those were some of the most important things that happened, but I'm leaving out a lot. All the evenings sitting outside in *Biergärten* strung with fairy lights, Reinhold and I drinking *Apfelsaftschorles* while the others drank beer, walking around the *Altstadt*, sitting alone in the dark cathedral and breathing in its cool, stony smell, riding to church Sunday mornings on an old gearless Hollander bicycle one of my German roommates lent me. Lying in the grass under the shade of a tree one afternoon, reading a book Josh had given me, *Narziß und Goldmund,* by Hermann Hesse. Crying because Hesse's language and the day were so beautiful; golden sunlight, soft breezes, leaves shimmering under the cloudless sky, the little meadow green and golden. And then Josh riding up on his bike and sitting down next to me; talking, laughing. We went for a walk and got ice cream. A nearly perfect day.

When the Regensburg program ended, I took the train to Leipzig and met Amanda there a few days before her German classes got out. She had a cool roommate named Harriett, a girl with short dark hair and little round glasses who dressed in baggy cargo pants and tight retro tee shirts. I loved talking with

Harriett—I'd never met anyone like her. She was smart, well-read, and funny, and told me she was the editor of a radical lesbian feminist literary journal back at her home university in Canada.

Somehow I didn't put two and two together. It was only after Amanda and I left for our trip to Austria and the Czech Republic that it dawned on me Harriett was a lesbian, when Amanda started telling me how uncomfortable and embarrassed she'd felt all summer about having a gay roommate. She was also convinced Harriett had been flirting with me like crazy. I had to laugh, at myself for being so clueless, and at the irony of Amanda, this conservative Mormon girl who'd grown up in a Utah town where cows literally roamed the streets, being assigned to room with the editor of a radical lesbian feminist literary journal. I had never met a lesbian before. I have to say, if I were attracted to girls, I would totally have asked Harriett out, and was secretly flattered to think she might have been flirting with me.

When I got back to the States, I got my hair cut short like Harriett's, because lesbian or not, it was a really cute style, kind of pixie-ish. My mom said it made me look just like Audrey Hepburn. My first day back in Provo, I went to buy books, and the girl at the bookstore checkout counter said, "Wow, that's a daring haircut. Cute, though." Only here would short hair on a girl be considered daring.

December 22

I knew this year was going to be a difficult one, and in some ways could only be a sterile time, with my old circle of friends gone and me stuck in this airless bell jar of a place. And it has been. The campus is like one enormous sensory deprivation chamber. I'm starved for affection and as invisible as ever.

My demon lover, Despair, still finds me and undoes me, day or night, in public or alone. It's a secretive, revolting, corrosive relationship from which I can't seem to disentangle myself. Some days I'm strong and can keep him at bay, but when I'm weak I give myself up to him and let him shove me apart with his cruel limbs, filling me with gangrenous secretions that leak back out as tears.

The other half of my life goes on as normal. I have good days. I recover from the harms people do me, not knowing I'm like a person without skin, an emotional hemophiliac. I find safe places, safe people. I go to my classes, I study and do my work. I make jokes, do the dishes, watch the *X-Files* on Friday nights with my roommates. I go to church and sing hymns, I pray, I read the scriptures, I live my faith. I try to have courage in the face of my illness that's like a killing cancer. Pieces of grace fall over me.

Sometimes I have what I call healing dreams. I dream of people putting their arms around me, of feeling safe, wanted, loved. Sometimes it's people I know, sometimes they're strangers. One night I dreamed I had given birth to a baby girl. I held her in my arms, newborn from inside me, and my breasts were heavy with milk. She slept, warm and with weight on my shoulder. She had long, dark, curly baby hair, and my mother, who was there too, said it was unusual for a baby to have so much hair. Her eyes were dark blue, but I knew they would turn brown, and watching her face I could tell how pretty she was going to be when she grew older.

I've been learning to cook, as I promised myself I would. One day I made boeuf bourguignon in the Crock-Pot. It was quite a production. I had to go down to the State Liquor Store to buy the wine. The recipe called for fresh thyme, which I'd never used or even seen before, but they had it at the grocery store. I stripped the leaves from the stems with my thumb and forefinger, and I could smell it on my hands for the rest of the day while I was in class and studying on campus. When I got home, the stew was done, and it was delicious. My roommates and I ate it for dinner that night, and I finally understood what Josh had meant when he talked about the sensuality of preparing good food. It was more than just the fact that it tasted good, but that it came from my own hands, and the smell of fresh thyme lingered on them all day.

I've made a couple of decisions. One is, I'm not going to start a grad school program next year. I'm going to take a year off and live in Tucson. I'll give myself some time to rest, work, and explore outside the structure of school life, some time in the sun. I agonized over the decision, but now that it's settled, I know it's a good thing, a way of being kind to myself. When I do apply to grad schools, I'll apply to programs in religious studies as well as philosophy. I still have this idea of learning everything there is to know about faith, everything that's been said or thought about it. I'd like to write a history of the concept of faith someday. A bit like Heidegger's *History of the Concept of Time*, whose title I always thought intriguing, although the book itself isn't anything like the title would lead you to believe, being terribly dull and nothing at all like a history. The book I want to write would be a real history, not some unreadable philosophy book. And I want to do more than just talk about what philosophers have said about faith; I'll write about what theologians, prophets, novelists, utopian socialist poets, rabbis, pagans, politicians, and accountants have said, too.

My illness strikes me at times as an extreme form of faithlessness, a despair and doubt that reach to the core of my existence. If only I could understand faith, maybe I could also understand a little better how to cure myself and heal from the sickness, what Kierkegaard calls the sickness unto death. (Sadly his book on that subject was totally unhelpful.)

I think I'll have to attack the problem of understanding faith from two sides: on the one hand, take a historical approach, to learn where the idea of it came from and how it came to be so problematic and rife with contradictions. On the other hand, assess it in the present, to show whether and how it's tenable and can coexist with intellectual integrity.

Another decision I've made is I'm going to swallow my pride, go in to the student counseling center next month when the new semester starts, and ask for help. I can't count on any amount of thinking or studying or even prayer to get me through this. Maybe there is no cure, but I owe it to myself to seek every avenue of help, no matter how shameful it feels to admit I'm sick and crippled and crazy enough to need it.

March 16

All kinds of news, all at once. I knew that Amanda and Zach had started seeing each other after they both moved out to New York. I figured it was only natural they should; after all, they are probably the only two Mormon philosophers in the whole tri-state area. And now they've set a date for getting married! Amanda called last night and asked sheepishly if I could ever forgive her, and would I possibly consider being her bridesmaid? I said of course, and not to be ridiculous, there was nothing to forgive. I'd been over

Zach for ages, and I couldn't be happier for them, two of my favorite people in the world ending up together.

But I had just found out some news of my own, I told her, which meant that I wouldn't be able to make the wedding next fall. Just the day before, I got a letter from the Fulbright Commission, offering me a fellowship to study in Hamburg next year, and I sent back my acceptance the same afternoon. This was something I applied for way back in October, before I made the decision not to apply to any Ph.D. programs. Dr. Mewes and Dr. Fillmore both encouraged me to send the application in, but never in a million years did I think I would actually get it. So it looks like my year in the sun in Tucson will have to wait, as will my congratulations in person to Zach and Amanda.

March 20

I'm excited to go back to Germany—I was so happy in Regensburg last summer. At the same time, though, I'm scared. Northern Germany will probably be completely different from Bavaria, and I don't know anyone there. I'll be plopped down in the middle of a big anonymous Northern city all alone and I'll be stuck there for a whole year, whether I like it or not. I'm fearful that without any kind of support network, I could go downhill quickly.

I told my counselor, Anna, today that I was afraid of moving to Germany by myself, and she pointed out that even if I am miserable there, I could always still come home. If I got into trouble there, my health had to take priority over the program organizers' convenience and everything else. She's made it clear she thinks I worry too much about pleasing other people and not upsetting them; apparently this is a common problem in the Mormon community. I understand she's right, my health has to come first. But these old habits of thought are hard to break.

I don't feel cured, although the counseling seems to have helped some. Every time I go in there, I cry buckets. It's wrenching and draining. But Anna seems to think I'm not so bad off. I told her I wasn't comfortable with the idea of taking antidepressants, and she didn't seem to think I needed them. She said I was learning all kinds of wonderful things about relationships and making great progress.

I'm not sure I've learned anything about relationships. My only male friend these days is Luke. Having watched me go through crushes on Zach and Matthew, he eyes me warily, as though he's afraid I might pounce on him at any moment (a fear that's completely justified). Still, it's a relief not to have to take pills.

One thing I've come to understand, though: In part my despair arises from a paradox, a conflict between two truths that place my existence in the realm of the absurd. First, the truth that I have no claim on anyone for anything, for any kind of help or support or kindness. Second, the truth that I can't make it through life on my own. I need the help, support, and kindness of others to survive. The paradox damns and paralyzes me, renders my existence impossible.

There is a way out of the paradox and it involves faith. The solution is to ask for help, even knowing you have no claim to it. To hope that when you ask for help, you'll get it, even though you might not. The fact that help comes sometimes when we ask for it is something beyond our control. When it comes, it's grace. Asking for help is a way of putting faith in people. It means taking a risk, gambling on their kindness, their goodness and mercy. When you gamble on their kindness, you're being kind to them, too, by giving them the benefit of the doubt, showing you think highly of them, showing that you trust or even love them. Putting faith in people is a work of love. Not something that can be done blindly, of course, but with eyes wide open to the risks involved, having courage and kindness enough to run the risks in spite of seeing them clearly.

The same goes for my relationship to myself. I have to ask strength of myself and take risks, even knowing my strength might fail me.

I have an intellectual understanding of the way out of the paradox. The difficult part is putting it into practice and taking the right risks. I have a bad track record with risk-taking. I've taken foolish risks that didn't pan out, trusted people who ended up hurting me, and failed to trust people who might have helped me. Taking the right risks, putting faith in the right people and things, that's what I still have to learn.

March 21

A propos of my idea for a history of the concept of faith, I'm slowly piecing together a rough thesis to base the narrative on. It's nothing too original—I've been reading Martin Buber and some Christian existentialist theologians like Rudolf Bultmann, as research for a paper I'm writing on views of faith among the early Church fathers, Justin Martyr, Irenaeus, and Clement of Alexandria. This is more or less how the story will go:

In the beginning, there's a primordial "Hebraic" sense of faith as *fidelity*. The God of the Old Testament cares less about what people believe than whether they're loyal and obedient to Him. In the Old Testament setting, everyone believes in some type of deity; belief is not the problem. Rather, the question is *which* deity you put your trust in and how loyally you serve it.

This primordial sense of faith as practical fidelity gets corrupted when Semitic culture meets Greek. Alexander the Great conquers the East, ushering in the age of Hellenism. The Hebrew Bible is translated into Koiné Greek. In Judea, a young rabbi named Jesus breaks off from mainstream Judaism and starts a messianic movement. He and his earliest followers speak Aramaic, but within a few generations only Greek versions of his story and teachings are available. The new Christian religion spreads among Greek-speaking Gentiles.

Among the converts are men educated in the Platonic tradition like Justin, Irenaeus, and Clement. When they read about faith in the Greek Bible, they are faced with a paradox: Faith is the key to salvation. God is pleased when the Israelites are faithful, obedient, and loyal, and He is angry when they behave faithlessly—when they're disobedient and disloyal. But to these Platonists, reading the Bible translated into Greek, it sounds like faith in the sense of *belief* is what God values so highly.

In the Platonic tradition they come from, belief is not a virtue. It's an abstract intellectual concept that's one small beam in a whole elaborate scaffolding of theories about knowledge and truth. These men struggle to understand how to integrate the Biblical conception of faithfulness with their Platonic conception of belief. In the process, they invent a whole new concept of faith that melds the mistranslated primordial Hebraic fidelity with Platonic epistemological abstractions. The version of faith they come up with is an incoherent mess, rife with paradox and absurdity. We are asked to assent mentally to propositions we don't know are true, by an act of will—in other words, wishful thinking combined with groundless certainty, leading to arrogant, hubristic dogmatism. It's this conceptual mistranslation way back in the third century A.D. that ultimately necessitates Kierkegaard. Kierkegaard represents the full flowering of this concept in all its absurdity, the dawning awareness that it requires an intellectually untenable leap.

The question for faith in the present day becomes how to get back to that primordial fidelity and still remain faithful to the best parts of the Platonic tradition. That's what my senior Honors thesis will be about. I'm going to write it this summer while I'm home in Tucson, and then I'll graduate in August. I've talked a lot about it with Dr. Mewes, my thesis advisor. The thesis is going to center around that passage in the Book of Mormon about how faith is an experiment and is like a seed that grows and thrives as you give it time and nurture. The idea will be that faith as experiment is grounded in uncertainty and consists in taking a risk of active commitment. As such, it's a work of love, involving us in a relationship of mutual nurture with God. We nurture the seed of faith by giving God the benefit of the doubt, and in turn God nurtures us by giving us the benefit of the doubt.

I remember several years ago John criticized that passage, saying it was circular and conflated the good and the true. If the seed is good, it grows, and if it grows, it's good. And if it's good, it must be true. But that's just it—in this context, goodness *is* truth. It's a different sense of truth, not truth as an ahistorical, unchanging principle or as the correspondence of a statement to reality, but rather as an ethical quality that unfolds over time, historically and dynamically, in a lived relationship between persons. In this sense, it has almost the same meaning as faithfulness—truth as *Treue*, the quality of being trustworthy, loyal, dependable, dependably kind, good, loving, and present. *I pledge my troth*, say the lovers in medieval ballads. *Troth* is faithfulness; later it becomes "truth." When truth is understood as trustworthiness, the true and the good become one and the same.

August 24 (Tucson)

My thesis is done. I've graduated with University Honors. I never have to see Provo or BYU again, for the rest of my life. And I leave for Hamburg in a couple of days. Haven't even started packing yet, so I'd better get to it. Again, I've resolved not to write or read in English for the whole year, so I'll pack this journal away and take it up again when I get back.

CHAPTER 25

GERMANY BY THE NUMBERS

*S*EPTEMBER 6 *(one year later)*

I just got back to Tucson a week ago. It's strange, being back. Everything looks so different, all washed out and flat. But I suppose it's the same, it's my eyes that have changed.

The Fulbright people gave us this book in our orientation packet when we got there a year ago, *Germany by the Numbers*, filled with every imaginable sort of statistic. Here's my own statistical update to sum up my year in Hamburg:

Friends made: Too many to count

Gay friends: 1

Communist friends: 2

American friends: 0

Average daily hours spent hanging out with friends in smoky cafés: 4

Cups of coffee consumed: 0

Cigarettes smoked: 0

Cigarettes smoked secondhand: Unknown, but likely enough to cause slow, painful death by emphysema/lung cancer

Times late to church or classes because stayed out too late dancing or bar-hopping with friends: Too many to count

Latest time returning home from same: 10 a.m. the next morning

Alcoholic beverages consumed: 0

Sex shows seen in Red Light District: 0

Nights playing tambourine in an impromptu samba band till dawn: 1

Bicycles stolen: 1 (from me, not by me)

Cool female flatmates with culinarily gifted boyfriends: 1

American-style hamburgers consumed at faux "Tex-Mex" restaurant: 2

Guys fallen in love with: 2–3, depending on how you count

Declarations of doomed unrequited infatuation: 1

Recipient's occupation: Lutheran pastor in training

Hours spent debating points of Lutheran theology with recipient: Too many to count

Seminars taken on Kierkegaard: 2

Hours spent debating Kierkegaard's views on faith with Lutheran pastors-in-training: Too many to count

Hours spent looking at Kierkegaard exhibit in museum after five-hour train ride to Copenhagen: 0.5

Requited infatuations: 1

Age difference between self and requiter: 14 years

Requiter's occupation: Former sex therapist, currently studying for Ph.D. in Psychology. (Seriously.)

Degree of guilt felt by requiter over age difference: Considerable.

Acts of fornication: 0

Instances of heavy petting: 0

Kisses on lips: 0

Highly arousing kisses on neck in dark stairwell: 1

Times I wished I could stay in Hamburg instead of coming back: Too many to count

CHAPTER 26

DEVIANCE

SEPTEMBER 10

I'm all moved in to my cozy little converted garage room. My sister Cate, her best friend Kendra, and I are renting a house together near the U of A campus. Since my room used to be the garage, it's detached from the rest of the house. It's nice to have my own small domain, bright, peaceful, and quiet. The inside of the house is pretty, too—it's an older adobe one with wood floors, a fireplace, and arched entryways between the rooms. We have a decent-sized yard with a lemon tree and mesquite in back. The previous tenants even planted herbs in one corner of the garden, so I can use fresh herbs in my cooking—all I have to do is step outside to get them.

It's fun living with Cate. We get along so much better these days, now that I've gotten to be more open-minded about everything. She's left behind the last vestiges of her Mormonism and behaves like your average normal American college student: respectable amounts of drinking, boyfriends who sleep over, and a big collection of Ayn Rand paperbacks. The me of just a few years ago would have been horrified. But it seems the more decisive I've become in my commitment to Christianity, the less threatened I am by other people's choices. The more I understand of faith, the more I understand that it's grounded in uncertainty; it's my own risk and experiment that I've chosen to take upon myself. I can well understand other people not wanting to take that risk or make such a commitment; it's a fearful, lonely thing between myself and my silent, invisible God. The relationship makes me into a solitary individual before Him. I am alone with my conscience in the darkness of my soul's ignorance and blindness. Which is to say, I understand well that I could be wrong, terribly wrong about the whole thing, even as I throw the whole of my life into it.

"You made me confess the fears that I have," says Stephen Dedalus in *A Portrait of the Artist as a Young Man*. "But I will tell you also what I do not fear. I do not fear to be alone or to be spurned for another or to leave whatever I have to leave. And I am not afraid to make a mistake, even a great mistake, a lifelong mistake and perhaps as long as eternity too."

I'm not so fearless as him, but I'm prepared to make my own great mistake. Except mine involves not leaving my religion, perhaps, but remaining faithful to it.

September 12

I've started going to church at the campus singles ward. There are a few cute guys, but no one I'm interested in. Oh well. It probably doesn't make sense to date anyone seriously, since if all goes well I'll be leaving for graduate school in a year. I've requested a ton of prospectuses from different Ph.D. and masters' programs, and will have to get started on the applications soon. Meanwhile I'm taking a few classes—beginning Modern Hebrew, Medieval Latin, and Ancient Near Eastern History.

Mom and Dad are paying my tuition and rent, but they wanted me to get a job to cover the rest of my living expenses. So I've started working at the coffee shop down in the basement of the student union. My first minimum wage job ever. I guess it's good to have the experience, but I hate pretty much everything about it—wearing that stupid brown polyester visor, emptying the trash bags with their nauseating stink, wiping down slimy tables, wrapping bagels and muffins in plastic, clocking in and out and getting yelled at when I'm even a few minutes late, which I usually am.

There are only two things I don't hate. One is when I get to grind the coffee. The smell is so good, it makes me want to get in a big vat of the stuff and roll around in it. Which is ironic, since I can't stand the bitter taste once it's brewed into liquid coffee, at least as far as I can judge from my experiments with decaf.

The other part I don't hate is my coworker Ron. He looks

European—wears little square black-framed glasses and has close-shaven hair, kind of ash-blond and peach fuzzy looking, and he dresses all in black every day. He's studying engineering and Russian literature, and has a quirky sense of humor. Every morning we sit and wrap bagels and muffins together in the back of the shop and talk. He's really friendly. I got my hair cut even shorter than before—almost a buzz cut—because I thought it would make me look chic and sophisticated. Then I wasn't sure I liked it; I thought maybe I just looked butch. But he complimented me on it first thing when I came in the next morning, so that was nice.

September 19

Shoot, Ron quit working at the coffee shop already. He said he found a better-paying job delivering pizzas. I'm going to miss our morning chats. Now all I have is the ground coffee smell to show up for.

I miss Hamburg. Somehow it was so easy to make friends there, and I was constantly going out and getting invited to parties. Here I haven't met anyone besides Ron, and now he's gone.

I had such a strange dream about Hamburg last night. I was in church, standing in the chapel with other people milling around. I thought it looked like my ward in Hamburg, although it wasn't so different from my ward here. An eerie, scary-sounding organ music started playing, and all the people around me became hypnotized and possessed. I wanted to leave, but the others looked at me and silently shook their heads no. In spite of them, I started walking toward the exit, trying to leave. A man I didn't know stood in front of me to block my way and said, "No." He looked 50 or 60 years old, balding and out of shape with close-cropped gray hair, very ordinary looking. I looked him in the eyes and said, "I love you." Then I stepped around him and kept walking in the direction I had been going.

The man followed me and again stood in front of me to keep me from leaving. We did the same thing over and over—each time, I said, "I love you," and moved forward, and each time he came to stand in my way again. The words had a curious effect on him. Every time I said them, he looked more and more like a devil. His face got redder and blacker, and he got more and more ghostly, till he began to float in the air. At last he disappeared in a blast of hot air and red light, and I woke up.

I should read Freud on interpreting dreams. Or maybe the meanings of my dreams are obvious, but I just don't want to understand them. I remember back in Hamburg, I dreamed one night I was trying to light a cigar with matches, but the matches kept flickering out. I couldn't get a fire started no matter how hard I tried. It was very frustrating. Then I looked around me and realized I was in a cage, but the door was open.

I told Matthias, my Lutheran pastor in training, about the dream, and he said it couldn't be more clear what it meant. I had put myself in the cage, and only I could let myself out.

I was a bit disgruntled to hear that from him, since how was I supposed to let myself out of the cage and light the cigar on fire if he'd made it clear he didn't want me? Then I wondered if he meant he would have wanted me to light his cigar if only I hadn't put myself in the cage from the beginning. Oh well. It's too late now, and I'll never know.

September 26

I ran into Ron today on campus randomly. I was happy to see him again, and I guess I showed it. We sat down on a bench together and talked for half an hour, and before we said goodbye, he asked if he could take me out for sushi Friday night. I said I'd like that. We traded phone numbers, and I gave him my address so he could pick me up at my house.

I'm happy even though this obviously can't go anywhere. I'll just be honest and straightforward, casually mention that I'm Mormon, and let him draw his own conclusions. At least I'll have the chance to talk a little more with him and have a fun night out for once, instead of sitting home reading Kierkegaard discussion group threads online, like I typically would be doing on a Friday night.

October 10

Ugh. I wish Ron would call me. Our sushi date was nice. He was all in black as usual, and seemed nervous. His car smelled strongly of coconut air freshener, and he apologized for it. He said he was worried it would smell like pizza, so he'd hung one of those coconut-shaped cardboard air fresheners from his rear view mirror, but the coconut smell had gotten to be overpowering.

It was the first time I'd ever had sushi. Ron was a sushi connoisseur, so we talked a lot about food, and I told him how I'd gotten into cooking. He also plays in a band. Apparently they're very avant-garde and experimental, and Ron plays every imaginable instrument, but mostly base guitar and accordion. I said I'd go hear him play sometime.

He didn't bat an eye when I said I didn't drink, and I did manage to slip into the conversation the fact that I was Mormon. He didn't ask me any questions about it, and it wasn't clear from his reaction what he thought of it.

The end of the date was a bit awkward. He drove me back to my house and walked me to the door. In the movies, that's usually the point where the girl invites the guy in and they have sex. But clearly I wasn't going to do that. So we just kind of stood there uneasily with our hands in our pockets and said goodbye, and he drove off.

Afterward I was sorry to think he would assume I didn't like him. So a few days later I called him and invited him over for dinner the following weekend. He said he'd love to.

I made this elaborate mushroom *velouté* soup from *Mastering the Art of French Cooking*. When he got there I was still putting the finishing touches on it. The recipe book was lying open on the kitchen counter, and Ron read aloud the introduction to the recipe, where Julia Child says this is the soup to make for a grand, special occasion. He looked up at me with a hopeful expression. I tried to downplay it and said, oh well, it was a recipe I'd wanted to try for a while, because it sounded good, so I was using him as kind of a kitchen-experiment guinea pig. I didn't want him to get his hopes up too much.

He said the soup was delicious. Just as we finished eating, Cate and Kendra got home, so I suggested to Ron we eat dessert in my room, where it would be quieter. I had bought a pint of good pistachio ice cream. I took it out of the freezer and brought spoons, and we sat cross-legged on my bed and ate it right from the carton. When we'd finished, we sat there talking for a long time, until it got late. When it was close to midnight, I said I was sorry, but I had to kick him out because I was turning into a pumpkin. I couldn't tell if he was disappointed or not. I walked him to the door and gave him a hug goodbye.

Since then I haven't heard from him. I wonder if it was too forward of me to invite him for dinner. I feel like it would definitely be his turn to call now, if he were going to, and it's driving me crazy that he hasn't, even though you can't blame a guy for not being into the whole platonic dating thing. I'm sorely tempted to call him, just to say hi and hear his voice. But that would probably be even more forward and pathetic, and he'd despise me. I don't know, I don't know. But if I haven't got anything to lose anyway?

October 13

I finally broke down and called Ron this afternoon, and it was one of the stranger conversations I've ever had. I was so nervous calling him, afraid he would be annoyed to hear from me. But after a few minutes of small talk, I decided just to be completely frank. I said I missed him and wished I could see him again. He asked, "Why? Why would you miss me?"

"I don't know," I said. "I just like you. I don't know why exactly. I enjoy talking with you, I guess."

He laughed in a strange-sounding way and said, "You don't know who you're talking to."

"Who am I talking to? What?—what is it?"

"You'd be shocked if I told you."

"Maybe not. Maybe I'm more open-minded than you think."

"Just how open-minded are you?"

"Try me. Go ahead, you can tell me," I said.

"Did you know I'm bisexual?"

"Oh. No, I didn't know that." I didn't know how else to respond.

He laughed again, and said, "Did you know I also queen?"

"You queen? Is that a verb? I wasn't aware that was a verb."

"It means I dress up in women's clothing and go out."

"Oh. Wow. Hm. Do you do this often?"

"Every now and then."

Then I couldn't help myself and started laughing.

"What's so funny?" he asked.

"You don't know who *you're* talking to."

"Who am I talking to?"

"You're talking to a girl who's not just a virgin, but who's so sexually inexperienced she's 23 years old and has never even French-kissed a guy."

"Whoa. Whoa. That's *incredible*."

"Why incredible? I mean, I know it's not normal, but ..."

"You're talking to someone who enjoys being beaten during sex. As in, I couldn't date a person unless they'd be comfortable sticking a six-inch pin in my thigh."

"Wow. Yeah, I don't think I could do that." A pause. Then I ask, because I'm genuinely curious, "So ... were you always bisexual? Or is it something you discovered over time? Do you prefer one gender over another?"

"I used to be straight, but then I decided gender shouldn't make a difference in who you love. It doesn't matter who's on top. I like being on top, but I also like being on the bottom."

"There's a logic to that."

"I like to transgress. I think of myself as a transgressor."

I said, "Now I'm wondering if you asked me out because I seemed androgynous to you." I was remembering how he'd complimented my butch haircut.

"No, it wasn't just that. Oh, no. I knew the minute you stepped into that coffee shop. From the first minute I saw you, I knew there was something off about you, that you were different. You're really, really different. You should know that. You're incredibly intriguing to me."

"I am? Why? What could possibly be intriguing about me?"

"You're like ... *chaste*."

My breath stopped for a moment. There it was—he had summed up my existence in a word.

He said he was attracted to me because I was different, exotic, a freak. He was a freak too, he said. But he thought I was *fantastic*, and I should know just how different I was.

"I know," I said.

"Sometimes, I love you." He said he was very clear on the nature of his relationship to me, but wasn't clear on what my relationship to him was. What would I have to do with him?

I wasn't sure myself, and didn't know what to tell him.

I've hardly thought about anything else since our conversation, and a few things have become clearer. Even if I were free, I don't picture myself with him as a lover. I found his declaration bewildering, and I haven't had enough time for anything like desire to grow. And I certainly am not prepared to stick pins in his legs. But he's intriguing to me. I would like to understand him, listen to him in the way that lets people unfold and stretch out into themselves, the way Mark Tierney always listened to me.

Am I so different from him? No, masochism is something I understand. And he's right—we're both freaks, sexual deviants. He's deviant by virtue of what he does, while I am by virtue of what I don't do. Of the two of us, I'm probably the weirder. I can't even be deviant in a straightforward, normal way. I'm deviantly deviant.

The incident made me realize, too, that for a long time already, my chastity hasn't been a Christian sort of chastity, but a fierce, pagan kind that has more to do with freedom than obedience. I don't want anyone on top of me, and I don't want to be on top of anyone. I don't want to be dominated or dominate anyone. I want to be free of all the nets and traps and cages that lie in wait for me there. Like Stephen Dedalus in *A Portrait of the Artist As a Young Man*, to fly past those nets while my soul undergoes its slow, dark birth.

November 24

I've started corresponding regularly by e-mail with an Australian philosopher named Ben Halloway, whom I met on the Kierkegaard discussion list. He's not a philosopher in the usual sense, a professor with a Ph.D. in philosophy, but I'm not sure what else you could call him. He's unemployed and lives on the dole—apparently Australia has a generous social safety net that accommodates even cases of full-time enlightenment seeking. Ben is a Buddhist and lives as a hardcore ascetic. At 40, he is proud of still being a virgin and believes all forms of sensuality and attachment are wrong. Apart from Buddhism and Kierkegaard, he talks constantly about Otto Weininger.

This Weininger is a strange figure. I'd never heard of him before I met Ben online. He was a contemporary of Freud in Vienna, a philosophic *wunderkind,* and killed himself at the age of twenty-three, the age I am now, after writing a book called *Sex and*

Character. The book argues against all forms of femininity as spiritually degraded and degrading and has nastily anti-Semitic parts, too. He was one of those self-hating Jews, sadly.

Ben makes my deviant deviance look like plain old everyday ordinary deviance by comparison. In our letters we argue over the value of normalcy, sensuality, gender differences, love, marriage, and family life. I advocate all these things passionately, while he excoriates them. He's almost as opposite to me as Ron is, but in the reverse direction. I'm enjoying being opposed in both directions. It's sort of the philosophical equivalent of a threesome sex sandwich.

February 2

I ran into Ron on campus again a week or two ago. I was delighted to see him—it had been a long time since we'd had a good talk. Mostly when I see him these days it's because I go to hear his band play, or I'm hanging out at an underground club called the Airport Lounge, which I mainly go to because I have a good chance of running into him there. We talked about books, and he told me his recent reading was all "filth"—the Marquis de Sade, Charles Bukowski, and some Russian Symbolist whose name I forget. I asked him what attracted him to this literature, and he said, "It's human."

I thought again of that line from the Tennessee Williams play, *Nothing human disgusts me.*

Ben Halloway says a sage could spend all his days in a brothel and be none the worse for it, but of course a true sage wouldn't be interested. *Unto the pure, all things are pure.* That's one of my arguments in favor of marriage, but Ben equates marriage with adultery, because you turn away from God in committing yourself to another human being.

I've been reading voraciously in both directions, the Ben direction and the Ron direction. Weininger, Simone Weil, Meister Eckehart, and the occasional Buddhist text Ben sends me. And on the other side, Lermontov's *A Hero of Our Time* (amoral soldier seduces captured Circassian princess) and George Bataille's *Le bleu du ciel* (people having sex in the mud).

A Christian is supposed to be in the world, and yet not of the world—a Both/And as perplexing and demanding as the Either/Or that precedes the life of faith. I'm at once a pure, beautiful, genderless soul, but at the same time, a gendered body full of flaws, sins, and wanting. This contradiction, the Both/And, is the cross.

May 4

I've been accepted to the Ph.D. program I applied to at the University of Chicago in cultural history, with funding no less. I'll finally get to write my history of the concept of faith. Already I've started compiling a massive bibliography of all the primary texts throughout history that might be relevant, from the Ancient Near East, Classical Greek and Latin civilizations, the Hellenistic Era, and on through to today. I've already got pages and pages and have started a collection of index cards with notes on important passages, which is quickly getting out of hand. I feel a bit like Mr. Casaubon in *Middlemarch*, with his endless notes on an all-encompassing Key to All Mythologies that never coalesced into a coherent work. But hopefully this project will be different, since it will at least have to coalesce into a dissertation, even if it's too ambitious to complete in the ideal multi-volume form I envision for it.

Ron tells me he has a girlfriend now and is in love with her. I can't help but feel sad and jealous, however irrationally. I admitted that to him, and he laughed. I think he took it as a compliment, which it was. Later I was trying to get him to explain his ideas about God to me. He has some, but will only drop oblique hints about what they are. So far as I can tell, they involve some sort of mysticism related to higher math or theoretical physics, but that's only a guess on my part. He says if he tells me I'll just analyze it, which apparently would be missing the point completely.

He asked if I enjoyed debating with him. I said, "No, when have I ever debated with you? I enjoy interrogating you."

"That's an interesting basis for a relationship."

"I like listening to people. It makes me feel kind."

He said yes, he understood.

I said, "I wouldn't want to debate with you, it's too erotic for me."

"How is it erotic?"

"It's just another way of trying to get on top of someone, only mentally instead of physically," I said.

May 9

From Pascal's *Pensées*:

"*Trop et trop peu de vin.*
"*Ne lui en donnez pas: il ne peut trouver la vérité. Donnez-lui en trop: de même.*"

(Too much and too little wine.
Don't give him enough of it: he can't find the truth. Give him too little of it: the same.)

Faith, in one sense, is a balancing—like the dancer in *Fear and Trembling* who lands without a moment of stumbling, perfectly graceful. To walk the Middle Way, astride the Both/And, without falling to one side or the other. To be faithful and true to both sides of oneself, human and divine, uniting oneself in being.

May 25

Dream: I am in love with a man condemned to die. He is tied up on a cross. I climb up on the cross with him, and start to kiss him on the mouth. I feel him grow hard under me. I straddle him, and he pierces me through. We make love on the cross; I cry out. Then they take him away from me.

Freaky. I've been reading too many weird books, I think.

June 3

From Umberto Eco, *Foucault's Pendulum*: "'Not bad, not bad at all,' Diotallevi said. 'To arrive at the truth through the painstaking reconstruction of a false text.'"

My thesis on faith?

June 8

Had a funny conversation with my older sister Lisa today, who's here visiting from Provo with Tom and the baby. She asked if I'd ever had an orgasm. I said I wasn't sure. I admitted that I'd tried a few times, by myself, but the results had been disappointing. She said probably not, then—if I had one, I'd definitely know. I asked her if she liked having sex with Tom, and she said yes, it was nice, although the first time it hurt. I wanted to ask her if she ever masturbated, or how exactly it was supposed to work if you did it by yourself, but was too embarrassed.

June 28

So I finally figured out how to masturbate. It was surprisingly unintuitive. Who thought this up? It's almost as impressive as the fact that at some point people figured out you could bury wheat in the ground, water it, fertilize it, let it grow, cut it, thresh it, grind it up, mix it with water and cultivated yeast, bake it, and get bread out of it.

Of course, once a secret like that gets out, it can't be put back in the dark. It becomes a life-sustaining staple food, and whole civilizations grow out of it. All the same, for a while I did try to stop, because I was worried about it being a sin. You'd expect it to be merely a matter of deciding whether or not to do it. But I found it wasn't so much a matter of deciding whether or not to as of how long I held out before giving in. So instead I'm following Oscar Wilde's advice, "The only way to get rid of a temptation is to yield to it," and William Blake's, "He who desires, but acts not, breeds pestilence." No pestilence breeding here, nope, we can all rest easy on that score.

It's hard to fathom just why it'd be a sin anyway. It doesn't seem any worse than cooking a delicious dinner and eating it by myself, which I do all the time. Sure, it'd be nice to have someone to share it with who would appreciate my cooking, but that doesn't make it selfish and evil to enjoy it by myself when I get the chance, does it?

If nothing else, it's teaching me the importance of timing. Timing is everything. If you draw it out too long, you can lose your momentum, but you also don't want to get there too soon, because getting there is most of the fun. The best part is the moment of being *almost* there, right on the brink. The longer the *almost* lasts, the better. Maybe that's why that Summer of Platonic Love with John all those years ago made such an impression on me—it was like an entire summer of *almost*.

When I get to Chicago, I think I've got to at least try to get a boyfriend. It's about time.

CHAPTER 27

IS

SEPTEMBER 19

Yesterday I went to the University of Chicago library for the first time. My classes haven't started yet, but I wanted to check out the Marquis de Sade's *Justine, ou les infortunes de la vertue*. It's a good library, so they had it in the original French.

This time it wasn't Ron, but Ben who gave me the idea of reading it. He said I reminded him of Justine/Therese because I was too passive and trusting; I had too much faith in human nature.

When I got to the checkout counter at the library, the guy behind the counter took the book out of my hands, looked at it ... paused ... then looked back up at me and asked, "Is that the Marquis de Sade?"

I blushed and stammered, "Um ... yes?"

The guy chuckled, handed me the book back, and said, "Have fun."

That tells you a little about the place I've come to. At the U of A, I checked out some pretty strange books, let me tell you, and nobody ever batted an eye at the titles. But this is the U of C, and everyone is interested in books, and they all know about the Marquis de Sade.

In any case, *Les infortunes de la vertue* is supposed to be *Justine* with less obscenity and porn than later versions. There's still no shortage of rape and torture, but for me the effect is somewhat dulled by reading it in a foreign language, a bit like seeing the scenes through a veil. I know what's happening, but it's all slightly blurred and filmy.

I can see what Ben meant, though, about the resemblance between me and Justine. Through everything that happens to her, she clings doggedly to her faith in a benevolent God and holds fast to her ideals of virtue, no matter how much misfortune they bring her. But the ending is interesting—even when she dies a miserable death, Justine dies still believing she has chosen the right way. I don't think the ending is convincing with respect to the point Sade wants to make. His point is that virtue is stupidity, and the smart and right thing to do is whatever brings you the most pleasure and the least pain.

Admittedly, Justine is not the sharpest knife in the drawer. But even knowing that and knowing how it ends for her, I'd still rather be her, living with the courage of her convictions, uncorrupted despite all the corruption around her, than anyone else in the story. She loses pleasure and fortune, but keeps her sense of who she is. There's a way in which she wins, even when it looks like she loses. She remains herself. She keeps hold of her ownmost being, as the existentialists might say. She *is*. She wins by being.

She's a personification of faith, of fidelity to her own authenticity, just like Erich Mühsam, that utopian socialist poet I read about in college who was tortured by the Nazis but refused to kill himself. And so this book is going into my massive Casaubonian bibliography on faith with all the rest.

October 18

I had a date last night. It was with a guy named Izaäk who I met in the park a couple of weeks ago. I walk through the park every morning and afternoon on my way to and from campus, and often see him walking his dog there. One day we got to talking—he had seen me in the classics lounge, which my History of Culture program shares with the classics students, and asked if classics was what I was studying. It turns out he's a philosophy grad student. He's Belgian and Jewish, with curly brown hair, a long nose, and round wire-frame glasses. I think he's good-looking.

After we'd talked in the park a few times, he asked if I'd like to go to a play with him Friday night. So last night we went to one at the Steppenwolf Theater. The play was about a woman who used to be a nanny and had been having an affair with the married father of the kids she looked after. She left the position and her married lover to get away from the whole mess, but then her ex-lover (still married) found her and tried to persuade her to come back. They argued and fought and made love.

When the play got out, we took a cab back to Hyde Park and talked about the story on the way back. I said I thought it was a good play, but it was hard for me to understand how people could act that way. Why had they done and said so many crazy-seeming things? Izaäk leaned in close and whispered in my ear, "Do you know why?"

I shook my head.

His breath was hot on my neck. "Because passion makes people insane." I found myself aroused by this and at the same time frightened and uncomfortable.

We got out at a cafe in Hyde Park and went inside to sit down. We talked for a while about neutral, safe things, classes, our academic departments, things to do in Hyde Park. Then the conversation swung back to the play and the topic of relationships, emotions, and rationality. I told him I was a great fan of friendships. I liked their reasonableness, sobriety, and egalitarian nature. But then there was a lot I didn't understand about the other sort of relationship, the passionate, erotic kind, just because I didn't have much experience in that area.

"You don't?" he asked. I explained about being Mormon and how you were supposed to wait until you were married. He laughed and said, "I see." I said I didn't like how with dating—judging from what little I had done of it—it seemed there was always so much pressure to get physical right away, and it rarely seemed possible in the U.S. for a guy to accept being friends at first and take the time to really get to know you. I had liked how in Germany, friendships between men and women were accepted and valued, and there was no such thing as dating per se. I asked Izaäk how he felt about these things. Supposing he knew nothing physical could happen between us, or at least not right away, would he still want to see me?

He laughed again and said, "Can I be honest with you? I mean *really* honest?"

I nodded.

He looked me in the eye the way a cat might stare down a cornered mouse it's about to eat. "I don't think I'd want to go out with you again if I couldn't do some pretty depraved things to you."

My body responded, against my better judgment. As if it were a machine, things were whirring and clicking into place, lights were coming on, gears were turning, equipment was primed and ready, all systems were go. My body, it appeared, was enthusiastically in favor of having Izaäk do depraved things to it.

But when he asked if I would come home with him, I said no. Even if I weren't still Mormon, even if I hadn't made the commitments I've made, I still would have said no. There was something too heartless and mechanical about the whole business. My soul was cold and unmoved, not caring that every On switch in my body had been flipped.

He walked me home politely, and we said goodbye without touching.

November 3

The girl I was supposed to share my campus apartment with got homesick and dropped out after only a couple of weeks, so now I'm living by myself. It's quiet, which is good for studying, but also lonely. So I've started eating dinners and Sunday brunch at one of the student co-op houses in the neighborhood. That has been a good arrangement—there are about twenty other people in the co-op, so I only have to cook dinner every three weeks, and now I have people to talk to while I'm eating. The other co-opers are smart and interesting, and most of them seem nice enough.

I've been going to the Hyde Park Ward on Sundays, but haven't really hit it off with anyone there. More and more I feel like I'm just going through the motions at church. If I'm honest with myself, I don't believe the doctrines anymore. I decided it was dumb to be studying cultural history and yet know so little about the history of my own church, so I've been reading church history from outside historians' perspectives, including Fawn Brodie's controversial biography of Joseph Smith, *No Man Knows My History*. Brodie grew up Mormon and studied history here at the University of Chicago, just like me, back in the 1930s. At any rate, thanks to Brodie's and others' work, the pieces are falling into place and the story is getting clearer in my mind. And it's not a pretty one. It's clear to me now Joseph Smith was nothing more than a creative, charismatic shyster.

Meanwhile, in my Intermediate Biblical Hebrew class, Professor Cordy has been initiating us into the mysteries of "higher Biblical criticism," pointing out the different layers of the text, the J, E, D, and P sources. The consistencies between the passages in each of these four distinct voices are clear once you have a sense of what to look for in the Hebrew. And this broader narrative, too, is beginning to make more sense to me than everything I was taught about the Bible growing up. There's no longer any honest way for me to go on believing it's divinely inspired. There's too much of the piecemeal, the propagandistic, and the folkloric about it. It no longer speaks to me as a scriptural document, any more than the Epic of Gilgamesh or the Ugaritic Ba'al legends do.

Still, I keep going to church, and when I'm there I keep these thoughts to myself. I go for the sense of community, out of a sense of responsibility to the other people there, because I can serve and help them. There are a lot of new converts in the ward. Some come from the lowest stratum of Chicago society: former drug dealers, prostitutes, welfare recipients, people with obvious mental illnesses. It was like that in Hamburg, too—the converts were all people on the outskirts of society, immigrants from Africa, Brazil, Iran, the poorest, sickest, and most desperate. In Utah and Arizona, most of the church members were white, clean-cut, successful, and middle or upper class. Their families had been in the Church for generations. It's been eye-opening to see what wards full of new converts look like.

I can see the appeal for them. In church they get social support; they can access the Church Welfare System and get job counseling. They feel they're part of a community and finally belong somewhere. But they're not there because it's true, any more than I am.

I've been filling in most Sundays as chorister, leading the hymn-singing in sacrament meeting, and there have been hints I'm going to be called to that position permanently. If I stop going to church, I'll be letting them down—they'll have to find someone else to do the job. If I leave, I might shake others' faith, the faith of these new converts who need the Church's help so badly. On the other hand, the longer I stay under false pretenses, the more responsibilities they'll ask me to take on, and the more damage I'll do if and when I finally leave.

I've been talking about it a little with some of the girls in the co-op, and they pointed out that it doesn't have to be all or nothing. I could just take a break from the Church for a while and see how I feel. If things didn't go well, I could always come back.

November 22

I've stopped going to Church. A few Sundays ago, I was sitting by myself at the big communal table at the co-op after brunch, and I said out loud to myself, "I don't want to go to Church today." And then, for the first time in my life that I can remember, I purposely didn't go to Church, without any excuse other than that I didn't want to go. I haven't been back since. I'm a little shocked, in fact, to find I haven't missed it at all, not even little. People from the ward have been calling and leaving messages on my answering machine. I haven't called them back, and I don't pick up the phone any more when it rings, in case it might be them.

I've been checking out a few other churches. I still believe in God, I think, and wonder if maybe I could feel more comfortable in some other religion. I went to a Catholic Mass and a Friday Shabbat service, and was thinking about trying out some of the local Protestant churches. But so far these other forms of worship feel alien to me, and I suspect the same things that prevent me from believing in Mormonism will make it hard for me to believe in any other church, or in Judaism. It's hard to get very far with any of them when I don't even believe the Bible is divinely inspired.

November 27

A theory: The meaning of life is faith, and faith consists in becoming conscious of what one truly wants and pursuing it.

Leaving religion behind doesn't have to mean leaving faith behind, if I understand faith in this sense; quite the opposite. It's an act of faith for me to leave, the only way I can keep faith with my conscience. It's a risk based in uncertainty, lancing myself forward into being, just like my former commitment to Christianity was.

If I'm right about this, my work on the history of the concept of faith won't have been in vain. But it occurs to me that in these pages, all this time, I've been writing a history of my own concept of faith. And from a spiritual standpoint, this is probably a more worthwhile work than all my Casaubonian endeavors, even if no one but me will ever read it.

February 2

Last night I went out with a bunch of the girls from the co-op and had my first drink ever. I had a sip of someone's beer, and it tasted awful, so one of the girls suggested I try a hard cider. I ordered a Woodchuck Granny Smith and drank the whole thing. It was sweet, fizzy, and good, but it was funny afterward to see the floor swirling a little under me. The girls said you couldn't drink too fast or it would do that, especially with a lightweight like me.

I've been experimenting with drinking black tea, too, but the caffeine sends me into long giggling fits every night at the dinner table, which is embarrassing.

Strange to think that at twenty-four I'm doing all these things for the first time.

I'm even seeing someone now. His name is Liam, and he's a philosophy grad student. One of my classmates introduced me to him in the food court over lunch, and after that I kept running into him after my Greek Prose class. We started to talk more, and finally he asked me out. It turns out it wasn't by accident that we kept running into each other. He knew I had my class then and had been hanging around just so he could see me.

We're still getting to know each other, but I like him. He's good-looking in a philosopher-type way—tall and thin with a reddish beard and funky glasses, beautiful green eyes, and a sensual mouth. He likes Kierkegaard, and his hobbies are reading Irish fairy tales and listening to Celtic music. I was mystified as to how someone as handsome and sweet as him could be interested in me, but he's been so consistent about calling me and wanting to spend time together, I can't doubt his sincerity.

Another first: we're been kissing a lot when he comes over lately. I like kissing him, but sometimes it makes me feel so dizzy. The other day we lay on my bed together and kissed for a long time, and he started touching me under my shirt. Then he started to take it off, but I stopped him and said I wasn't sure if I was ready for that yet. It wasn't that it didn't feel good, it was just that I'd spent twenty-four years of my life never touching or kissing anyone, and so this was all a bit overwhelming for me. He said he wasn't in any rush; he could enjoy just kissing me until I felt ready to do more.

Later we sat at the kitchen table, and I told him I was afraid of getting hurt. He took my hand, looked at me with those beautiful green eyes, and said, "I would never, ever hurt you." As we talked, he traced the outline of my fingers and knuckles one by one and stroked the inside of my palm. When we kissed goodnight, he moved his lips down my neck and kissed me until I thought my knees were going to buckle under me.

It's so different from all the thousands of fantasies I've had. It's reality now—not an *almost*, but an *is*.

So much is changing so quickly now, it's hard to keep up with myself. I'm having to relearn thinking itself, to break my lifelong habit of constantly interjecting pleas and thanks to God into my thoughts. For a while I thought I might still believe in God even if I didn't believe in religion. But the only sort of God I can imagine turns out to be so devoid of content, so indistinguishable from reality itself, that it doesn't make sense for me to call it God. It doesn't make sense to talk to it and thank it and ask it for favors. I figure I might as well just think of it and treat it like what it is, reality.

Besides unlearning the habit of prayer-filled thought, I'm slowly learning the habit of making choices without reference to any law outside of me. It's not the formless abyss I was always so afraid of, but it's not automatic or simple either. I don't want to do things I might end up regretting later when I'm more settled into my own system of values. So I'm proceeding cautiously. In any case, luckily I suppose, I don't have the immediate impulse to run out and get drunk, do drugs, or sleep with everything that has a pulse.

I went to the Student Counseling and Resource Service last week and had an intake appointment. I'm supposed to go back this week for my first real meeting with the counselor they assigned me. I felt like I could use someone to talk to about all this, someone impartial and outside of my regular life, a trained therapist who knows what she's doing. Leaving your religion and having to invent your own system of values is a big deal, after all. Plus, I had another one of my bad spells before Christmas, during finals week. It was scary. Before I snapped out of it, I had set a date for killing myself. But I'll keep fighting this illness in any way I can.

Over Christmas break I saw Mark Tierney, who was visiting from Boston. We had a good talk. I told him all about my decision to leave the Church, and he asked if it made me happier to be free of it finally. I said I didn't necessarily know if it would make me happier. It was all very different, and a lot of things were still hard for me. But even if it didn't make me happier in the end, I still felt it was the right thing to do. I had no regrets.

ACKNOWLEDGEMENTS

Thanks to those who offered critiques and suggestions on drafts of this manuscript, including Terry Weatherstone, Rebecca Gale, David Masad, Patrick McNeil, Shatina Townes, Adam Watson, Dani Lowry, Stephanie S. Kuehn, Kristen Williams, Carol Hanson, Lorran Garrison, and John Wallace. Sadly, I can't blame the book's many remaining flaws on any of these folks.

The excerpt quoted on pages 63–64 is from Thomas Mann's *The Magic Mountain*, translated by John E. Woods and published by Vintage International, New York, 1996, page 195.

On page 64 Marguerite quotes a verse from the *Book of Mormon* slightly inaccurately. The correct wording from 2 Nephi 2:27 reads: "For it must needs be, that there is an opposition in all things."

The book Marguerite refers to on page 167 is Frederick V. Grunfeld's *Prophets Without Honor: Freud, Kafka, Einstein, and Their World*, published by Kodansha America in 1996.

The excerpt quoted on page 189 is from Søren Kierkegaard's *Either/Or: Part I*, translated and edited by Howard V. Hong and Edna H. Hong and published by Princeton University Press in 1987, page 307.

The idea of comparing Socrates and Galateia, as Marguerite does on page 192, derived from a brief mention of the idea in Kenneth Dover's *Greek Homosexuality*, published in 1980 by Vintage Books. The portion of Chapter 21 that follows was also influenced by Martha Nussbaum's discussion of Greek tragedy and philosophy in *The Fragility of Goodness: Luck and Ethics in Greek Tragedy and Philosophy*, published by Cambridge University Press in 1986.

The translation of the lines from Pascal on page 242 is my own.

The "June 3" quotation on page 242 is from Umberto Eco's

Foucault's Pendulum, translated by William Weaver and published by Ballantine Books (First U.S. and International Edition) in 1990.

Other quotations and literary works mentioned should be easily locatable online or through library catalogs.

www.ingramcontent.com/pod-product-compliance
Lightning Source LLC
Chambersburg PA
CBHW050726180626
46814CB00002B/630